THE SOUL MASTER SCROLLS

The
Soul Master Scrolls

Gérard Desjardins

GREY DIAMOND BOOKS

Published by Grey Diamond Ventures Corporation

www.greydiamondventures.com

Printed in the United States of America

First printing July 2006

Second printing January 2008

Third printing September 2009

ISBN 978-0-9864825-0-2

For

Carl and Caroline Desjardins

my two children my two best friends

and their wonderful mother Suzanne

and in memory of

Jessie Rock Desjardins

The lady at the gate

For those who seek knowledge look within your Soul and the answers will come…

AUTHOR'S NOTE

This book was written with hopes of enlightening the reader as to what is really going on in the World at present and the dangers that lurk ahead.

The book also serves as a way of awakening the reader's conscious mind, enabling him or her to seek answers from within. And to begin looking for and seeing events as they really are, and not the way they are projected to be by malicious manipulators.

There is an old Asian legend, where it is said that the Soul lives within one's inner eye. Presently, in modern times, this inner eye is often referred to as one's sub-conscious mind.

When people can learn to view with their inner eye the elements that surround them, only then will they truly understand the reason for their existence.

The writing of this book was made possible by events that took place during the past eighty years and an unlikely circumstance where perfect strangers meet.

Apart from factual - Resemblance of characters in this book to anyone living or dead is coincidental.

ACKNOWLEDGMENTS

My heartfelt thanks to every one who had a part in this book, particularly Magician-Mentalist, Paul Drake, for allowing me full access to his library material and photo archives.

To author, Pauline Edward, thank you for your guidance and continuous support in bringing this final edition to market. Your constructive opinions and suggestions were beneficial and greatly appreciated.

To my Editor, Janice Tomkins, thank you. It has truly been a pleasure working with you.

A special mention and thanks to the ever Great Architect up above, who makes all things possible, and to my special and kind Guardian Angel who takes care of me and my loved ones.

Contents

From a moment in History

'I believe that banking institutions are much more dangerous to our liberties than standing armies. If the American people ever allow private banks to control the issue of their currency, first by inflation, then by deflation, the banks and corporations that will grow up around the banks will deprive the people of all property until their children wake-up homeless on the continent their fathers conquered.'

Thomas Jefferson

The 3rd President

of The United States of America

1802

Preface – Factual

Royal Canadian Air Force Base

Senneterre, Canada.

November 21, 1964

Time 20:00 hours

The curtain was going up. It was show time at the air force base gymnasium. Air Canada was presenting its variety show to military personnel. This variety show toured military bases across the U.S.A. and Canada. This was the cold war era. The Americans feared that nuclear missiles attacks could be launched from Russia over Canadian skies. These missiles could target and hit American cities.

In the audience that evening Peter Walker an airman from England was enjoying the show. He was on leave and visiting friends at this northern air base. The show was nearing its end when the featured act was presented. An astounding young magician by the name of Paul Drake amazed the audience with his mind reading act.

Following the show, all were invited to the officers' mess for drinks allowing the base personnel to mingle with the show's performers. During that cocktail party, Peter Walker and Paul Drake first met and talked together. That lengthy conversation would bring about the writing of this book, forty years later. Had fate not arranged this fortuitous meeting, then possibly this story would never have been told…

Preface – Factual

Even forty years later, Paul Drake, could still clearly remember that evening, when he had met and talked with Peter Walker. It's as if it only happened yesterday…

The show was over. Paul Drake sat at a table in the officers' mess with a comedy duo who had also starred in the show. The show's pianist joined them, and they all had a few drinks and relaxed following another successful show.

A young man came over to their table and introduced himself as Peter Walker. He told Drake that he was impressed with his mind reading act. Peter had a story that he wanted to tell Drake about a discovery that his father had made in Egypt, some thirty odd years ago.

It seemed that Drake reminded Peter of his father's best friend, Charles Bouthillier. A French gentleman who was also involved in that discovery made in 1931. Peter and Drake spoke for a few hours during that evening. The story he told Drake was intriguing, but somewhat hard to believe. However, Drake told Peter that he would certainly like to see his father's old journals referring to the fantastic story.

It ended up that Drake gave Peter his business card, a promotional photo of himself and suggested they write each other when he returned to England. However it would be two years later in the summer of 1966, before a package from Peter arrived in Montreal. In it were copies of the pages from Earl Walker's journals, and a copy of Charles Bouthillier's memoirs.

Now we are the year 2006 and the time as come to tell the entire world this story. For if mankind doesn't change its ways, it's heading towards obliteration!

This book explains why…

Archive Photos

Air Canada Show Cast – Senneterre, Canada – Nov 22nd 1964.

Paul Drake – Mentalist – 1964 ©

- Prologue -

Earl Walker had just concluded his lecture about The Fall of the Roman Empire. This would be his last day as a professor at the prestigious Oxford University in England.

It was raining on that Friday and, as irony would have it, he would end his teaching career on May 22, 1931. Exactly one year ago to the day that his son, Peter, was born.

Before leaving the University grounds, he stopped at The House, which had been founded as Cardinal College in 1525 on the very site of the famous St. Frideswide's Monastery. This was re-founded and renamed Christ Church, in 1546 by King Henry VIII. It was an architectural treasure and Oxford University's largest and most magnificent college.

As he walked through the Picture Gallery, where a superb collection of paintings and drawings from the 14th to the 18th century hung, he stopped to admire a painting by Michelangelo. He remembered the times, both he and his wife stood there admiring that very same painting.

Suddenly, he heard a bell ringing. It was great Tom, a huge bell weighing over seven tons. It hung in the old Tom tower, and it would ring exactly 101 times. He set his pocket watch to exactly five minutes past nine. It was time for him to leave…

Prologue

He would remember 1931 as the year of his awakening. He needed a break he no longer enjoyed teaching history. He longed for a different life, filled with adventure, travel and discovery.

He had arranged with the rector to take a year's sabbatical leave. This would allow him to travel and devote time to his real passion in life, Archeology. He looked forward in anticipation to his planned voyage, where he would search for rare artifacts in the areas surrounding the great Pyramid of Cheop at Giza.

This time Elizabeth had decided not to accompany her husband to Egypt. Their son, Peter, was only one year old. Elizabeth thought the child was too young to endure the hardships that such a voyage would inflict upon them. She also had an uncomfortable feeling 'you could say a premonition', about this journey her husband was about to embark upon.

The voyage had been planned the previous year. He would cross the channel to France and stay several days with Charles Bouthillier a trusted friend of many years. From there he would cross the sea to Egypt, and he would once again enjoy doing what he loved best.

He could not imagine the course fate had set for him. Soon and at a place he never expected to be, he would stumble upon a great discovery. It would change the history and beliefs of Mankind forever. Life, *as he knew it*, would never be the same again.

ONE

The Beginning

Saturday June 6, 1931 was a sunny day, perfect for traveling. Earl Walker arrived at the fishing village where he had arranged with a local fisherman, to be taken across the channel to France. It was a beautiful day to start his voyage. A good Omen, *he thought to himself.* His old friend Charles Bouthillier would be waiting for him.

Most of the time, the waters were rough when crossing the English Channel. Today would be no exception he was bound to get seasick again. He did every time he dared to venture out onto these waters. It was a small price to pay considering the pleasure this adventure would bring him.

The ride across the channel was as rough as expected. Now, all he prayed for was to see the French Coastline appear before him. However, much to his surprise, his stomach behaved quite well. He was as anxious as a child, when there on the horizon, he saw the French coastline.

As the boat pulled into the port of Le Havre, Earl could see his old friend waving at him from the dock. They had not seen each other in over five years. It would feel good to be reunited with Charles again. They would have a lot to talk about.

Charles was considered an expert in numerology. He also collected old *talismans and held a particular interest in the study of ancient books and the **Cabala. A bit of an eccentric, he had a flair for the good life.

He could always be found mingling with the elite of French society. Most of his friends called him by his nickname, *** L'Illuminé.

Charles ran up and put his arms around Earl as he walked down the gangplank to greet him.

"Comme c'est bon de te revoir mon vieil ami."

"Et moi aussi mon cher Charles."

A superb 1931, silver colored Bentley was waiting on the dock. It was Charles' automobile. The chauffeur took care of the luggage. As the two old friends took their place in the back of the Bentley, Charles popped open a bottle of Dom Perignon. Welcome to France, toasted Charles.

There would be more than one hour of driving through the picturesque countryside, before arriving at Charles' mansion near Rouen. This allowed time for them to reminisce.

Earl could not help but notice the talisman that Charles wore around his neck. It was round and had seven triangles inside of a circle. Each one interposed within the other.

A gold ring that Charles was wearing on his right hand also drew on Earl's curiosity. It held a dark opal stone upon which was inscribed a five pointed star inside of a circle.

* A necklace, reflecting the tradition of the Cabala.

** Mystical body of ancient Hebrew wisdom.

*** The Enlighten one.

"I see you noticed my talisman, my good friend" *said Charles.*

"How could I miss it." *replied Earl.* Tell me, what does it mean?"

"It is believed to bring good health and prosperity to those who wear it."

"Come now Charles, you don't seriously believe that. Do you?"

"But I do my good friend. I certainly do. I will tell you about it later."

Finally, the Bentley pulled up to Charles' mansion. The trip had taken its toll. Earl was tired and he now looked forward to a comfortable bed and a good night's sleep. The old friends would talk again in the morning.

Before closing his eyes, Earl could still see the worried and concerned look that was on Elizabeth's face as she kissed him goodbye earlier that morning.

Sunday, June 7th. Earl was sleeping peacefully that morning when Charles' maid came in to draw the curtains. A beautiful woman he thought. Charles always did possess a way about him, and loved to surround himself with beauty and class.

"Bonjour Professor, did you sleep well?" *asked Iris,* with her delightful French accent.

"Yes Iris, I slept very well thank you. How have you been since we last met?"

"I have been fine, thank you," *answered Iris.*

"Monsieur Bouthillier, on the other hand, seems concerned these days. Something is bothering him. It will do him good to be with you again."

"Breakfast will be served on the garden grounds in one hour, Professor." *Iris advised.*

As he approached the garden, Earl saw Charles talking with a man in a dark blue suit. Surely a business associate, judging by the serious allure the grey haired man projected.

"Bonjour Earl, please meet Sam Bernstein." *said Charles* as both men stood up.

"A pleasure to meet you Monsieur." *replied Earl,* as the two shook hands.

"I must leave you now Gentlemen." *said Sam*, thanking Charles for breakfast as he left.

As they ate breakfast together, Earl could see clearly, as Iris had mentioned previously, that something was indeed bothering Charles. He knew his old friend better than anyone else. He could tell, just by looking at him, when things were not going right for him.

He wondered if the visit by Monsieur Bernstein had anything to do with it.

"Sam seems quite impressive. Is he one of your business associates?" *asked Earl.*

"He is one of my financial advisors and he comes highly recommended by the Rothschild people. You may not know Earl, but Europe may be heading towards hell." *answered Charles.*

"What are you telling me my friend? What do you mean by heading towards hell?"

"There is, at present, a racist extremist in Germany who might get control of that Country soon. If he does, all of Europe could be in for troubled times."

"I guess you are talking about Hitler." *suggested Earl.*

"Of course I am… And one thing I can tell you for sure my dear Earl. When the Rothschild people start being concerned about someone taking power in a Country, then everyone better share the same concern."

"I really can't give you an opinion on that situation." *replied Earl.* "As you know, I have no interest whatsoever in politics."

"Enough talking for one breakfast." *said Charles*, with a frown. "This afternoon I will take you to visit Rouen. You will find it has changed for the better during the past five years."

On their way to Rouen, Earl noticed the same talisman on Charles' neck. The one he had seen the day before.

"I see you are still wearing that same talisman, my friend." *stated Earl?*

"Oh yes, these days I am never without its protection," *Charles commented.*

"One of these days, Charles, you must explain what it means to you."

"Tomorrow, my good friend, we will talk about it. Now, let us enjoy our short ride to Rouen. Tell me all about Elizabeth and little Peter. What is she up to while you are away?"

It was quite obvious that Charles was changing the course of the conversation. Earl had no idea what was going on, but surely something was dreadfully wrong here!

Monday June 8th. It was raining that morning, and Earl was looking through Charles' book collection in the library. There were books and rare manuscripts by famous authors and philosophers going back centuries.

Plato, Socrates, Leonardo da Vinci, Thomas More, Shakespeare and Michel de Nostredame, more commonly known by the Latinized form of his name, Nostradamus … *Earl thought to himself.* These must be worth a fortune.

One manuscript in particular, attracted his curiosity. For some reason, the author's name seemed to mean something to him but he could not remember why.

The manuscript was by Sir Thomas More. He would ask Charles about it later in the day.

Iris came to tell him that lunch was being served. He followed her to the dining room. Charles came in at the same time, seemingly in a fine mood.

During lunch, Charles explained the legends surrounding the Talisman that he wore around his neck. He explained how the legends were as old as time.

The Cabala, clearly states that all things in creation are related to one another and this without exception…

By associating special symbols or inscriptions on the talismans, certain powers could be transferred to the person wearing the talisman in question.

Back in the 14th and 15th Centuries, people carried them in pouches and this was believed to attract favorable influences.

In those days, the back of the talismans were always inscribed with numbers. These numbers always related to one of the seven known planets.

Each planet was associated to one of the seven Archangels. The numbers for each planet were written within a square called a kamea, made up of rows of numbers. The sum of any row – vertical, horizontal, or diagonal – equals the same number. This would be the sacred number assigned to its particular planet.

Charles invited Earl to see his collection of talismans.

"My God Charles, where on Earth did you find all these Talismans?" *Inquired Earl?*

"I have accumulated them over the years. They were plentiful in the14th to 16th centuries. Most come from the many friends I have in the antique business."

Earl noticed they were of different metals; gold, silver, bronze, and all inscribed with symbols. There were at least a hundred pieces to his collection. Some were only the size of small coins and others were as big as saucers.

There were two common things about them. All were round in shape and each had the square kamea on the back, just as Charles had explained.

Charles removed the talisman that was around his neck and handed it to Earl.

"Look closely at this one, my friend. As you can see it's not an old talisman."

Earl held the talisman in his left hand and carefully scrutinized it as Charles placed his collection back in the vault.

"You are right, Charles, it looks new and seems much different than the others."

"Correct, my dear friend. Now pay attention to the numbers of the kamea."

"I see six vertical and six horizontal rows of six numbers each, forming a square. The square is inscribed with the numbers from 1 to 36 in a mixed order." concluded Earl.

"Exactly," replied Charles. "And the sum of each row in this kamea equals 111. That number is not the sacred number of a planet. It is in fact, the number of a Star. That Star is our Sun and its kamea leaves me somewhat perplexed."

It had stopped raining and Charles suggested having a brandy in the garden. There they could relax, and continue their conversation.

As Earl walked towards the garden with, Charles' talisman in hand, he kept staring at the kamea wondering and trying to understand what his friend was talking about.

His curiosity was by now fully aroused.

The face side of the talisman showed seven triangles with each one seated within the other and perfectly encircled.

Talisman's face side

The backside of the talisman showed the so-called Sun's kamea with a pre-arranged sequence of numbers set in thirty-six squares also perfectly encircled.

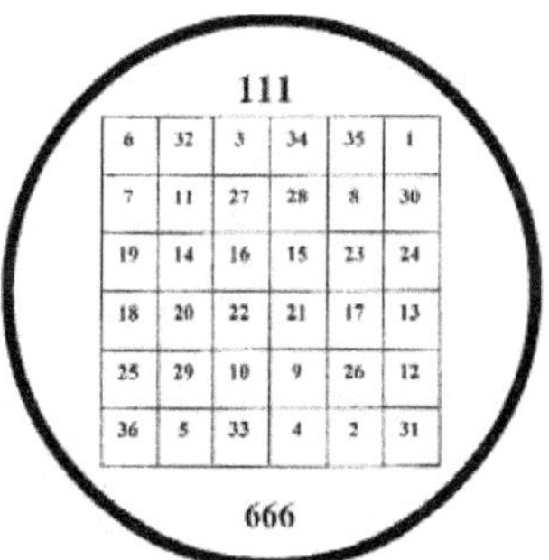

The Sun's Kamea

6	32	3	34	35	1
7	11	27	28	8	30
19	14	16	15	23	24
18	20	22	21	17	13
25	29	10	9	26	12
36	5	33	4	2	31

"Tell me Charles, what is it about the Sun's kamea that puzzles you so?"

"It is the sum of the total numbers in the kamea that worry me my dear Earl. Why don't you add them up and see for yourself." *said Charles as he smiled.*

"Oh my God… They total 666… Now I see what you mean. Surely it's only a coincidence, isn't it?"

"I certainly hope so" *replied Charles.* "If not, we may be in for a time of turmoil."

Charles then explained how he came about having this modern talisman. He had purchased it at a roadside market in Cairo during a holiday two years previously.

The road merchant, that sold it to him, had explained how the talisman in question came to be.

The merchant told him that he made many of these talismans. And that the symbols inscribed were copied from drawings he saw in a cave located some 20 or so kilometers from the market place.

The cave was believed to be an ancient home dug into the mountainside. Not considered a burial site and without the possibility of treasures, it had no apparent value. It has lied virtually untouched for possibly hundreds of years.

"Do you really believe the story the merchant told you?"

"It's true", *replied Charles.* "You see my friend. I visited the cave in question. The drawings were on the wall exactly like the merchant had told me."

"What did the cave look like? Describe it to me." *asked Earl with anticipation.*

"There was a stone stairway leading up to a square door. The inside of the cave appeared to be almost like a cube. It had only three full walls, a ceiling and a floor."

"On the left wall there was a drawing of one vertical line crossing one horizontal line. Both lines seemed to be the same length, crossed at the center, and were set inside of a circle. The center wall had the drawing of seven triangles set within each other and centered inside of a circle. The right wall had the drawing of the kamea with its numbers set in thirty-six squares. The kamea drawing was also centered inside of a circle. That is all I can tell you about the cave. You, my dear Professor would have probably understood a lot more about that cave had you seen it. After all, you're the archeologist."

"You are right Charles. I would have to agree with you on that observation. Now, my friend, I believe that you may have a hidden agenda to this bizarre tale you are telling me."

"I think that you are purposely creating an interest in me to visit this cave during my visit to Egypt. Could my conclusion be right?" *inquired Earl*, "and if so why?"

"You are a wise man, Earl, and you are right of course. I would love for you to visit the cave for me. I, of course, would reward you handsomely for any rare artifacts found." *answered Charles.*

"You see, my friend, if some old talismans were found in Egypt that would be a great discovery. They would be worth a fortune to the finder. Need I say more?" *said Charles with a smile.*

The day had passed quickly and Charles invited Earl for an evening of entertainment. They would visit the Casino in Rouen where both would try their luck at roulette.

As they sat down at the table to play, Charles told Earl to look at the numbers on the roulette wheel. He saw the numbers, they were 1 to 36. They were the same as the talisman. The old friends looked at each other and laughed heartily as they begun playing.

The two friends played at the roulette for a few hours. Earl would win some bets but overall he was losing more times than he won. By the time they were ready to leave, he was losing by several hundred francs.

Charles on the other hand had been winning two or three bets for every five he made. Surely he must be winning thousands of francs. *Earl thought to himself.*

As they left the Casino, Charles confirmed that he had won 8000 francs during that session of play.

The chauffeur was waiting in the Bentley at the Casino entrance. They got in the car and left the casino grounds.

Charles opened another good bottle of Dom Perignon. "Cheers" toasted Charles, as they were driven back to his mansion.

"OK Charles. Now tell me how you manage to win all of those francs? And please don't answer that it was your lucky talisman." *said earl,* with a chuckle.

"Of course not" *answered Charles.* "Roulette is a game of numbers and I am a man of numbers, as you well know. However, I am surprisingly lucky these days."

It had been a long day, and Earl once again looked forward to a comfortable night's sleep. He was about to doze off, when he heard Iris, the maid, crying down the hallway.

He soon realized that he was hearing cries of joy. Charles and Iris were obviously in love with each other. Earl believed that it was time for Charles to take a wife, and have a real family of his own.

Morning came and Earl was suddenly jolted from his deep sleep. Something had bitten his foot. As he looked down at the end of the bed, the something under the blanket was creeping up towards him.

In a panic, he jumped out of bed knocking over a lamp as he pulled off the blankets. There, looking at him was Citrouille, Charles' huge tabby cat.

He was laughing quite heartily, when Charles having heard a commotion came running into the room asking what was wrong.

"Nothing's wrong," *said Earl.* "Your cat just gave me an awakening that I will never forget." Both men were now laughing, as they made their way down to breakfast.

"Is everything all right with you Professor?" *enquired Iris.*

Yes, I am fine, thank you, Iris. Citrouille was just being naughty. No harm done." *Earl replied.*

"How did you gentlemen make out at the casino last night? Or shouldn't I ask?"

"Charles made out quite well. Need I say more," Earl answered with a grin.

Following breakfast, both men enjoyed some brandy in the garden. They talked for what seemed to be hours.

Charles was anxious to know if Earl would, in fact, visit that cave near Cairo. He was overjoyed when Earl told him that he would do it as a favor.

He wondered if he should tell Earl about the warnings he received from Sam Bernstein, the man sent to him by the Rothschild people. It could worry Earl, so he elected not to tell. After all, it could be pure nonsense and either way Earl would only be gone for one year.

That evening Charles would prepare a map for Earl, with instructions for locating the cave. It shouldn't be hard to find and the expedition could prove worthwhile.

Earl would be leaving for Egypt tomorrow and Charles knew that he would miss his friend of many years.

When would they meet again? *Charles wondered.* However they would now go horseback riding together and enjoy the beautiful scenery around the mansion.

They rode their horses side by side, both realizing that their precious time together was coming to an end. Both could feel each other's sadness, as they headed the horses towards the stables.

The sun had begun to set and darkness would soon be upon them. They made their way from the stables to the mansion with few words being spoken. Later they sat by the fireplace, enjoying each other's company and sharing a last brandy together before retiring for the evening.

Before sleeping, Charles prepared a package for Earl which he would give him, just prior to his boarding his ship at the port of Marseille

Charles was sure that Earl would be surprised by its contents. It included several letters with instructions, a book about occult symbols and their meanings. There would even be some cookies, freshly baked by Iris, for him to enjoy during his voyage.

Earl would also find an unexpected surprise in the envelope that would surely please him.

Wednesday June 10th. Five days with his friend had passed so quickly, *thought Earl,* as he finished the packing of his luggage. It was 5.30 a.m. when he made his way to the garden for a final breakfast at the mansion before the long car drive to the port of Marseille…

Iris had greeted him with a kiss to both cheeks that morning. Obviously, she would also miss him.

"Good morning, professor, hope you slept well last night." *said Charles* smiling. .

"Rather well I must admit, and without your cat Citrouille in the room to scare me," *answered Earl.*

"You must enjoy your breakfast this morning Professor. The service on a cargo ship will not be the same as it is here." *said Charles*, as he winked at Iris.

"Maybe I should go with you and take care of you," *said Iris mockingly.*

"Must you rub it in," replied Earl. "You both know that I will miss you dearly."

The chauffeur advised them that the luggage had been loaded into the Bentley and that they could leave for Marseille, whenever they were ready.

On their way to Marseille, the old friends shared some good bottles of Dom Perignon, as they sat comfortably in the back of the Bentley. "We are leaving the same way we arrived" Charles said, as he lifted his glass in a farewell toast. It would be a long tiring drive to Marseille.

The scenery was so beautiful and there were so many places to be visited between Rouen and Marseille, but there would be no time for sightseeing on this trip, *Earl thought.*

It was close to midnight when they arrived at the cargo ship and they talked while the chauffeur carried the luggage aboard.

What a ragged looking ship, *Charles thought to himself.* "This will not be a luxury pleasure cruise" *uttered Earl,* as if he knew what was on his friend's mind.

"The luggage is now aboard ship Professor," *advised the chauffeur.* "I wish you a safe journey."

Moments before boarding, Charles handed Earl the package. Open this later, my friend, when you are settled in your cabin. The two shook hands and Earl boarded the cargo ship. Earl waved to Charles as the Bentley pulled away from the wharf. He went down to his cabin quarters. The luggage was already there.

As he examined his new quarters for the voyage to Egypt, he found himself somewhat disappointed.

There was no porthole, plus the cabin was extremely small and smelled of mould. This sea voyage could certainly prove to be rather unpleasant, but nothing could change the situation now.

It could have been worse *he thought to himself,* what if a drunken sailor had shared his cabin or used the upper bunk!

He sat on the bottom bunk and opened Charles' package. Inside, there was a letter with directions explaining how to locate that mysterious cave. Another letter explaining how to play roulette to win, that is if he should dare to try his luck at a casino in Cairo.

Next Earl found a book relating to occult symbols and their meanings. He was delighted to find homemade cookies, seemingly from Iris, and lastly there was a rather thick envelope.

In that envelope he was astounded to find the 8,000 francs that Charles had won in the Casino at Rouen.

He then remembered an old saying:

The end of one journey is the beginning of another.

TWO

The Voyage

Earl could feel the vibrations as the ships engines revved and the ship pulled away from the dock. The voyage across the Mediterranean Sea had finally begun. He was on his way to Alexandria in Egypt.

When a bell rang from the ship's deck the sound of that bell reminded him of his last day at Oxford. However, *he thought to himself,* this bell would not ring 101 times. He had never in his life felt as alone as he did at that very moment. Solitude, he realized, would now be a part of his daily life.

As he-read Charles' letter, giving instructions for locating the mysterious cave, Earl realized that he recognized the area where it was located. It could be none other than Mokattam Mountain situated on the east side of Cairo.

An area easily accessible by foot, however he also knew that the mountain had many caves. This could make finding the right one somewhat difficult. When he got to Cairo, he would have to find the bazaar where Charles had acquired the talisman. With a bit of luck, maybe that same merchant who sold it to Charles would still be there.

Earl went up on the ship's deck to light up his pipe. Smoking in his quarters could prove rather suffocating.

There is nothing more breathtaking than to view a clear starry night sky from the deck of a ship at sea. Suddenly, he saw a shooting star and made a hopeful wish. At that same moment, someone in uniform came towards him. It was the Captain who had come to speak with him.

"Good evening, Monsieur Walker. Welcome to our ship, I see you are admiring the stars this evening."

"Good evening, Captain. Yes, I am I must admit they are quite awe-inspiring."

"Yes, they certainly are. Quite a wonder this Universe isn't it? Tell me, Monsieur, what is the purpose of your trip to Egypt, *asked the Captain,* business or pleasure?"

"Just pleasure, my dear Captain, a deserved holiday from teaching," *replied Earl with a sigh.*

"The ship will be stopping for one day at Bizerte in Tunisia. I would recommend, you go ashore and visit for the day." *advised the Captain.*

"Yes, I certainly will Captain, thank you." *replied Earl,* as he shook the Captain's hand.

The sea was calm. I should sleep well, *thought Earl* as he made his way back to his cabin.

Before retiring, he read Charles' instructions for winning at roulette. It was all mumbo jumbo to him, *what a character that Charles was.* But, he did win the 8,000 francs apparently with this method. Maybe once in Cairo, he might try his luck.

He was not a gambling man by any means, but one must take a chance now and then. Who knows where it could lead?

As he relaxed in his bunk, Earl thought of his wife Elizabeth, and their son Peter.

The Voyage

God, he missed her and how he hated being away from her warmth. He could still picture her walking up the pathway towards him at their wedding. It had been held outdoors and it was the most memorable day of his life.

He could remember the sparkle in her green-blue eyes as she looked at him that wonderful day. Her long blond hair was blowing gracefully in the wind. She was beautiful and looked magnificent in her flowing white gown. *He closed his eyes and slept contentedly.*

The voyage across the Mediterranean Sea was going rather well, *contemplated Earl,* as the ship was approaching Bizerte. Bizerte, one of the few seaside cities of Tunisia and was established around 1000 years B.C. It is by far the oldest and most European city in Tunisia.

It served as a French military base for five years until the Tunisian independence. The French only left the city after approximately 1000 young Tunisians had died, in attacks towards the French military base. The French had wanted to keep that base in Tunisia.

The ship's captain had advised earl that excellent restaurants were to be found in the old city, and Earl had no objection to enjoying a good meal on land. This would also give him a chance to practice his French, as that language was still currently spoken here.

After docking he visited the central port, Earl marveled at the beauty of this historic city. The houses around the port were painted either grayish white or pale blue.

He enjoyed a tasty lunch in a restaurant by the harbor then visited the double Kasbah that defended the city from attacks coming from the sea.

The visit to the double Kasbah was worth the stop-over in itself. It was in perfect shape despite its turbulent 400 year old history. The original structure, dated back to Byzantine times.

What a feeling to experience, when standing in a city that was founded some 3000 years ago. It's simply astonishing, he thought to himself.

Evening was approaching and it was time to board the cargo ship again. The next and last port of call, during this part on the trip, would be Alexandria in Egypt.

"Did you enjoy your short visit to town?" *the Captain inquired,* as Earl boarded the ship.

"I certainly did, Captain" *replied Earl*, thanking him at the same time for his excellent suggestion.

Night had fallen and the ship once again made its way to the open sea. Earl went up to the ship's deck to smoke his pipe, as he usually did before retiring for the evening.

This was a habit he had to break, *he thought to himself.* The Captain was on deck and Earl went over to speak with him.

"Good evening, Captain, the sea seems rather calm tonight."

"Well, good evening, Monsieur Walker, I see that we will be admiring the stars again this evening."

"Yes Captain and also enjoying smoking my pipe. One of the bad habits, I can't seem to get rid of."

"Some of the crew will be playing cards later on. Is gambling another one of your bad habits?" *asked the Captain laughing.*

"Oh no not me, Captain, I don't believe in games of chance." *replied Earl.*

"Life is a game of chance Monsieur," *replied the Captain*, as he set his watch to the sound of a bell, ringing on the cargo ship's bridge.

"I see you set your watch to the sound of a bell, Captain?" *said Earl,* as he stroked his chin.

"Yes, Monsieur, the bell rings every hour on the hour on this ship when it's out at sea. Sailors set their watches by it. Does this surprise you?"

"Not really Captain. At Oxford University in England, there is a bell that rings 101 times, at exactly five minutes past nine, every night." *replied Earl.*

"Why a 101 times?" *inquired the Captain.*

"It rings one peel for each member of the original college. There were 101 of those original members," *explained Earl.*

"What an interesting tradition! Englishmen never cease to amaze me," *said the Captain,* as he walked away.

"Good luck at the card game Captain." *said Earl,* as he emptied his pipe tobacco into the ocean.

Alone now on the ship's deck Earl suddenly remembered where he had heard the name, Thomas More, the man who wrote the manuscript he had seen in Charles' library.

While talking to the Captain a few moments ago, the mention of the bell ringing 101 times jolted Earl's memory.

Sir Thomas More was one of the original members of Christ Church in Oxford. So, of course, one of the peels that rang every night was in memory of him.

How on Earth did Charles manage to possess a manuscript from this man?" *Earl thought?* He would ask Charles, when they meet again. Time for some sleep now!

As he made his way down to his cabin, Earl passed by the ship's galley where a loud discussion was taking place.

He glanced in and saw some of the rowdy crew engaged in a heated controversy over the card game they were playing.

The Captain was laughing heartily as he waved to Earl, inviting him to join in the activities. "Not tonight, Captain," *replied Earl with a chuckle.*

Unexpectedly, the voyage on this cargo ship was turning into a rather pleasant experience. Earl had developed a certain friendship with the Captain, who turned out to be quite charming in his own way.

Soon they would arrive at Alexandria where sand would replace the sight of water for several months.

There was nothing for him to do for the remaining time on the Mediterranean Sea but relax and enjoy the voyage.

It had been quite an exciting day. He lay back in the cabin's bunk trying to read Charles' letters again but to no avail. His eyes kept closing, and soon he was engulfed in a deep sleep.

Basking in the morning sunshine, and there on the horizon, Earl could see the shores of Alexandria. Alexandria the shining pearl of the Mediterranean, as it was called. Time on this voyage had passed quickly. This historic city was built in 331 B.C. by the Greek architect, Dinocrates, by order of Alexander the Great. It was the second largest city and main port of Egypt. Built on the site of an old village called, Rhakotis, it was the renowned capital of the Ptolemies with its numerous and magnificent monuments.

It was along these very shores that history took many a tragic turn in the time of Cleopatra, Julius Caesar, Mark Antony, and Octavian. How many times had he given classes at Oxford on these great leaders that had forged the past?

Finally the ship pulled into port. As members of the crew carried his luggage on shore, Earl shook hands with the Captain and bid him farewell.

Next, would be the trip by train to Cairo, where he would begin the search for that special cave on Mokattam Mountain.

He would spend the night in Alexandria, and take the first train available the next day. After checking his luggage into a small hotel, he would have dinner at a nearby restaurant. Following which, he would spend the evening visiting parts of the city, as he had done before during previous trips with his wife Elizabeth.

The Captain of the cargo ship had recommended a restaurant to him, so he wasn't surprised to find the Captain there when he entered for his nightly meal.

"May I share this table with you, Captain." *asked Earl*, as the two men shook hands once again. "But of course, Monsieur Walker, it would be my pleasure to dine with you this evening. Let me order some wine."

Both men enjoyed a delicious meal accompanied by an excellent choice of wine. The Captain of the cargo ship was obviously accustomed to fine dining.

Earl found this Captain extremely interesting and did not quite understand how the Captain of a cargo ship in such dismantle could possess all of these qualities.

"Tell me Captain, I noticed that your ship flies the German flag. Is she owned by a German gentleman?"

"Non Monsieur, she is owned by a Jewish gentleman who lives in Germany. She is registered under a German charter and flies the German colors."

"I see answered Earl. Tell me Captain. Do you know anything about German politics and the political climate in that Country these days?"

"I am not much for politics Monsieur, but I do know that the ship's owner, Monsieur Bernstein, wants to move his shipping fleet to another Country. This ship will be flying Greek colors in the very near future." *answered the Captain* as he poured more wine in Earl's empty glass.

Both men were feeling no pain at that point and the wine kept flowing. One problem Earl had if he over-did it when drinking was that he became quite jolly and talked too much.

"Tell me! Are you married Captain?" *inquired Earl.*

"I am a man of the Sea" *replied the Captain.* "And we Seamen have only one wife, and she is the Sea." *He said,* with a note of sadness in his voice. *He then asked* "And you Monsieur Walker. Are you married?"

Well now! That was too much to ask Earl in his condition and the Captain would surely regret having asked that question. Earl went on and on talking about his wife.

He described how they meet, the wedding day, the birth of his son… Good Lord there was no stopping to his babbling now… He explained to the Captain how his wife was a love child. How her elderly lame father, who was confined to a wheel chair, condoned an affair that his wife Elizabeth's mother was having with her German lover. That love affair went on for many years, and my wife was conceived from that relationship.

Her biological father would visit her several times a week and he did that faithfully until he passed away sometime during her late teens.

He went on to explain that Elizabeth even speaks perfect German, and then the Captain said that he must call it a night. They left the restaurant, shook hands and went on their separate ways. Earl made it to his hotel bed and slept like a log that evening.

Earl boarded a train early the next morning. He was now close to his final destination. In a few hours, he would set foot on the sacred soil of Cairo, the Jewel of the Orient, the City of the Thousand Minarets, and the Melting Pot of Ancient and Modern Egyptian Civilization.

It was the capital of Egypt, the cradle of civilization, the largest city in the Middle East and Africa. It lies at the center of all routes leading to, and from the three continents: Asia, Africa and Europe.

Cairo is the city where the past and present meet. On its east side stands the evidence of 2000 years of Islamic, Christian Coptic, and Jewish culture that still flourish to this day. On its west side, lies the Ancient Egyptian city of Memphis (Giza), the renowned capital of the Old Kingdom and the site of the Pyramids.

A journey through Cairo is a journey through time. It is a journey through the history of an immortal civilization.

Just knowing he was approaching Cairo, sent shivers up and down Earl's spine. He lit up his pipe and quietly observed the other passengers on the train.

There were many tourists, many priests and nuns, obviously there on a pilgrimage to the holy sites. Earl was so carried away by the experience that he almost forgot the mission he had promised to fulfill for his friend, Charles.

The Pyramids at Giza would have to wait until he found and explored the mysterious cave at Mokattam Mountain.

Earl could not believe what he was experiencing. Here he was in Cairo, with the great Pyramids within his sight, and yet all he could think of was locating the mysterious cave that Charles had told him about.

For days he would visit the market places in hopes of finding the merchant who sold Charles the talisman. Finally, on the fourth day as he visited one of the markets, there before him was a merchant wearing the same talisman he had seen on Charles' neck.

He had found him! After a short conversation it was clear he had found the right man. The merchant remembered Charles, and inquired about his whereabouts.

Earl explained that he wanted to visit the cave where the drawings, inscribed on the talisman, were copied from.

He asked the merchant if he would guide him to the location of that cave. The merchant accepted to guide him in return for a set fee to which Earl agreed.

They would visit the site the next day. For now he could enjoy a quick visit to the great Pyramid of Cheops.

He had seen it many times in the past, but still marveled at its majestic setting when glanced through the branches of the acacia, eucalyptus and tamarind trees, that line the boulevard leading to the plateau on the edge of the Libyan Desert.

Its grandeur was simply overpowering, with its ground area of 13.1 acres and the 2.3 million limestone blocks, weighing an average of two and a half tons each. The Pyramid's blocks were enough to build a wall, of foot square cubes, two-thirds of the way around the globe, at the equator, a distance of over 16,000 miles.

It was without question, one of the Seven Wonders of the World. Who had really built it, and for what reason? Surely not a burial chamber, *Earl thought to himself,* and when was it really built?

Well that was enough for one day. He would need his rest for tomorrow's expedition to the mountain's cave. He was so excited, that sleep only came late into the night.

The next afternoon, both men arrived at the bottom of Mokattam Mountain. There they met with several of the local people, who told some of the stories and legends surrounding the cave. Most of the local habitants were afraid to go into that cave. They claimed that strange things went on inside that cave. When it was warm, the cave's interior stayed cool, and when it was cold, the interior stayed warm.

Also when the sand was blowing in the area, no sand ever entered the cave. Considering that there was no door in the entrance, the locals believed the place to be inhabited by spirits of people that died there a long time ago.

That kept the cave virtually free of intruders, with the exception of the odd tourist that visited out of curiosity. Legend has it that in the past, some who dared entered the cave never came out and were never seen again. Of course, these were stories told from generation to generation.

No one seemed to recall anyone disappearing in the cave during the past years, but for those who believe in superstitions, that is enough to keep them out.

This is an area that is full of stories and mysteries, and a place where superstitions and tales of old are plentiful. The top of the mountain was rumored to be a place reserved for a Prophet and yet there are cafes set out on the top where you could view Cairo in its splendor. It would seem that modernization and business doesn't take into account any of these tales and superstitions.

The merchant led Earl up the mountain to the location of the cave. He would have no problem finding his way there from now on. The sun was beginning to set, and Earl decided that he would call it a night and only explore the cave the following morning.

THREE

The Search

It was Tuesday morning June 30th. Earl was standing in front of the entrance to the cave on Mokattam Mountain.

Finally, he would set foot in the mysterious cave that Charles had asked him to investigate.

Before going in, he turned his back to the entrance and looked straight before him. There on the horizon, he could see the Great Pyramid of Cheops standing out in its enigmatic majesty from the rocky Giza plateau.

He estimated that the Pyramid stood at a distance of about 20 kilometers towards the west of the Mountain. From within the cave, you would be able to view the Pyramid directly before you. Possibly, that could be one of the reasons why this particular location was used. But there had to be another reason, apart from the breathtaking view, to explain all of the drawings inscribed on the walls of this particular cave.

One thing stood out for sure. The view from within this cave would be spectacular. He couldn't help but wonder who could have stood on this very spot hundreds and even thousands of years before him.

He turned again to face the entrance, took a deep breath as if to gather his composure, and entered the cave.

A strange feeling overtook him as he stood inside the cave facing the wall with the strange drawing of the seven interlocked triangles inside of a circle. As he looked to the wall on his right side, he observed the second drawing of the kamea also in a circle.

On the wall to his left side was the drawing with the crossed lines. This drawing was also inscribed within a circle like the others, but the lines slightly extended past the circle. Possibly the crossed lines were not inscribed at the same time as the circled triangles and the kamea, *he thought to himself.*

The drawings were as Charles had described them to be. Each circle containing the drawings had a diameter of two meters, and those circles were set perfectly in the center of a square wall that measured four meters by four.

Each of the crossed lines measured slightly over two meters. The ceiling and floor measured the same as the walls, thus giving this cave the form of a perfect cube. The open entrance was two meters wide by two meters high, again forming a perfect square.

Someone a long time ago worked extensively in this cave to give it the shape of a perfect cube.

For what purpose was this done? *He asked himself,* and what craftsmen of ancient times could have achieved the mirror like smoothness that the cave's interior walls had?

Earl also noticed that the temperature within the cave was extremely comfortable. He wondered if this was the phenomenon the town people talked about yesterday.

Something overlooked by Charles and the merchant, caught Earl's eye. On two of the circled drawings, there were four small extrusions dividing the circles in four.

Earl reasoned that maybe this could refer to the east, south, west and north.

Also, and puzzling to him, was the fact that on both of the center and right walls where the circles were, the cave walls were without any visible seams. This entire cubic cave seemed to have been made in one piece.

There were also two smooth surfaces in the form of large triangles, resembling the pyramids. These large triangles were slightly recessed into the perfectly smooth walls.

The circles containing the seven inter-locked triangles and the kamea were set perfectly inside of these large, sanded triangles. There was no sanded triangle on the wall with the crossed lines. Once again, questioning the reason or purpose of that particular drawing.

He decided to look around the area close to the cave for possible clues to the mystery. He visited several of the neighboring caves, but couldn't find any with similarities to the cubical shaped cave where the drawings were present.

He would require some excavating equipment and good lanterns to do a proper and precise evaluation of the cave. He would call it a day and would return the following day to continue his investigation.

Upon his return to the hotel, the desk clerk advised that he had found a laborer willing to help him with the carting of the excavation equipment up to the cave site on Mokattam Mountain.

He felt tired now and rested in his bed thinking about the events of the day. What was so special about that mysterious cave and the strange drawings that lined its walls? A lot of questions to be answered, *he thought to himself.*

Wednesday July 1st. Earl and his new assistant arrived at the foot of the mountain with the excavating equipment. They carried the equipment three quarters of the way up the mountain to a ledge close to the cave, and set up a tent to work from during the next few days.

After settling on a fair wage, *Saadi,* the assistant, agreed to stay on the site and assist Earl during the entire length of the expedition. This, of course, providing he was not obliged to enter the forbidden cave, '*la caverne des fantomes' as he called it in French.

Earl would have a chance to practice his French because his new assistant didn't speak English. Fortunately for Earl, many of the people in Cairo spoke the French language, being this was still an influence dating back to the times of French colonization.

As both men sat in the tent having a cup of tea, Earl asked Saadi what he knew of the cave in question. All Saadi could say was that he never entered the cave and that, as a child, his parents warned him to keep away from the mountain and its caves.

Earl was amazed at the effect that plain superstition could have on an adult person. It was time to get some work done.

He picked up some measuring instruments and a few lanterns, and headed into the cave as Saadi fearfully looked on.

He set up the lanterns towards the center wall. He would first examine the drawing with the circled inter-locked triangles. These strange drawing were definitely of fine craftsmanship, seemingly chiseled into the wall some time ago.

*The cave with ghosts.

He carefully measured the circle again and found it to be two meters in diameter, with all of the seven triangles perfectly fitted within it. The circle itself was set in the exact center of the sanded triangular formation recessed in the wall.

The sixteen square meter wall was amazingly accurate, with the sanded Pyramidal form located exactly in the center of the wall.

Why would such accuracy be used in the modification of a cave? *He wondered.* Surely in the past, this cave had served for some important purpose.

He could find no evidence to the possibility of a secret chamber existing behind the wall. Apart from the circle and the sanded form, no other deformities seemed to exist on the perfectly smooth wall.

He could not even find one single crack in the wall. Two things about this wall bothered, and puzzled him.

One being, if the wall was indeed a part of the mountain, then different materials would be noticed in the structure. Yet these walls had a perfectly even surface consisting of the same material.

And the second thing, that was puzzling to him, was that even in these modern times, he knew of no technology that could allow for the construction of such a wall.

It looked as if the wall had been taken from another place, in one piece, and inserted into the cave as it appeared at this very moment. 'Most certainly, an impossible feat!' *he thought.*

This all seemed rather unlikely to Earl, but so was the construction of the Pyramids, which remained a mystery for centuries and perhaps millenniums.

He had an inner feeling that he would be searching for a long time before finding any answers to all the riddles that faced him here in this cave.

He had worked enough for the day and would go back to the tent and enter his observations in his daily journal. He would return to the cave in the morning and examine the other walls, to see if they were exactly the same as the center wall.

He gathered the measuring instruments and the lanterns then made his way back to the tent. Saadi had prepared some tea and was anxiously waiting for Earl's return.

"I am so happy to see you, Professor. What was inside of the cave?" *inquired,* a concerned Saadi.

"You can relax, Saadi. I assure you there are no ghosts in the cave. Only drawings on the walls made a long time ago."

"Who do you think made these drawings Professor?" *asked Saadi.* "That is what I want to find out," *replied Earl!*

Earl and Saadi discussed superstitions from each other's countries. Earl explained, that in England, some also believed in haunted castles and that some feared black cats and again how some would not walk under a ladder. This was all nonsense claimed Earl, just like the superstitions regarding ghosts in the cave.

After some reflection, Saadi expressed that maybe he would go in the cave with him just to see what it looks like. Earl was somewhat pleased that his talk about superstition had an effect on his assistant. Time would tell if the helper would ever enter the cave.

Both enjoyed their tea with some food then prepared the cots for sleeping. Earl wrote notes in his journal and blew out the candles. It was time to rest before the busy day ahead.

The Search

Thursday July 2nd. Both men arrived at the entrance to the cave. Saadi observed curiously as Earl entered the cave.

Earl set up the lanterns towards the right wall, the one with the kamea drawing. The craftsmanship of the drawing was identical to the one on the center wall, but with one astonishing difference.

All of the numbers inscribed in the squares of the kamea did not seem to have been made by the same craftsman. They were of a rough nature and appeared to have been inscribed with no consideration to detail, as was the case of the circle and the 36 squares, nested together making a large square.

Earl concluded that the numbers inside of the squares must have been added at a later date. He also noticed that the numbers resembled a style used by the French during the 17th – 18th centuries. The seven for example had a small line crossing the center at an angle.

He remembered from his history classes, that French troops under the command of General Napoleon Bonaparte were in this area during the summer of 1798. They tried to pierce the secrets of the Pyramids with a corps of French scientist, called Savants.

It was conceivable that some of these soldiers, and possibly Napoleon himself, could have visited this very cave. Earl wondered if any of these men could be responsible for the addition of numbers into the squares of the kamea?

The right wall was of the same making as the center one. A perfectly smooth, sixteen square meter wall. He turned the lanterns to face the left wall with the encircled crossed lines and was beginning to examine it when Saadi called from the entrance advising he had prepared some tea.

Earl waved for him to come inside and join him. To Earl's surprise Saadi came into the cave looking right and left as if he expected something to jump out at him.

"Sit down beside me Saadi and have some tea with me."

"So this is what the ghost's cave looks like, Professor," *replied Saadi,* as he sat down.

"That's what it looks like," *replied Earl.* "However, there is a lot here that cannot be seen as of yet."

Saadi then told Earl of a story that was told to him about the cave. It seemed that, on a dare, one of his cousins slept in this cave one night. Sadddi's cousin reported that during that night he had strange visions and nightmares about people he had never seen before.

Earl asked if he could talk with this cousin to hear about these visions he claimed to have had. Saadi said he would go back to town to see his cousin and ask him.

Saadi left the cave and Earl continued with his examination of the left wall with the encircled crossed lines, the only wall that didn't have a sanded triangle on it.

Once again a perfect sixteen square meter wall with the smooth structure, identical to the other two. Earl carefully scrutinized the crossed lines drawing. The lines both measured slightly over two meters in length. These crossed lines were just a bit longer then the diameters of the circles on all of the walls, and slightly below the crossed lines circle, there seemed to be a thin recessed slot about 20 millimeters wide. 'These discrepancies were puzzling indeed,' *thought Earl.*

The crossed lines could certainly not be evaluated as to craftsmanship, and there was no indication as to when they were carved into the wall.

He called it another day in the cave and made his way back to the tent. He sat on the cot and entered notes for the day in his journal. Saadi had not yet returned from seeing his cousin in town. Earl only hoped that his assistant would convince the cousin to meet with him.

He would certainly love to hear the details of the visions, the cousin claimed to have had in the cave during his overnight stay. He heard two men talking as they made their way up the trail approaching the tent. It was apparent that Saadi had convinced his cousin to meet with the professor and tell his story.

After brief formal introductions, the three men sat and shared a bottle of brandy between them, as the cousin begun telling the story of his unforgettable night spent in the ghost cave, as he called it!

It happened on a Monday night nine years ago, September the 11th, 1922 to be precise. He would never forget that date, explained the cousin, because that night his hair turned from a shinny black to a pale white, caused by the fear he had experienced. In the hope of getting his black hair back, he had returned many times to the cave entrance, *the cousin explained*, but was never able to enter the cave again for lack of courage.

He had arrived at the cave just before sunset and placed some blankets on the floor. He had to stay the entire night.

Two other men camped outside the cave to confirm to the others *'who had wagered against his success'* that he had completed the dare, and did stay in the cave all night.

Darkness came and as he settled upon the blankets, he tried convincing himself that the superstitions about the cave had to be nothing but childish nonsense.

He felt nervous and wondered if indeed he would fall asleep. Then strange things started happening.

Saadi's cousin started to describe the events that took place in the cave that unforgettable night. The sun had set as he lay on the floor of the cave with a single candle for light.

Some time had past and the candle eventually burned out. That is when he noticed that he could see something moving inside the cave even though the cave was in total darkness.

At first, he thought the two men outside came in to scare him out of the cave, but the more he stared at whatever was moving in the cave, the more he could see clearly. It was has if suddenly he possessed the eyesight of a cat. He now saw two men dressed in strange clothing.

They appeared to be talking, yet there was no movement from either of the strange men's lips.

They were seated in chairs facing each other at a table and one of the men seemed to be writing what the other was saying. There also was strange looking furniture in the cave.

Of course he was dreaming, *thought the cousin*, for there was nothing in the cave when he came in earlier.

Then one of the men, who had golden hair and eyes that reflected the color of the sky, stood up and walked towards the center wall, continuing right through it.

That strange man was wearing a silver robe, and he was no longer in the cave. The other man who was still writing at the table was now alone.

This all seemed too real to be a dream. His heart was pounding fiercely and pure fear had taken him over recalled the cousin.

As he lay on the floor, paralyzed with fear, the man writing at the table stood up and inserted a sword into his belt. He looked like a soldier of ancient times with armor and all. The soldier then picked up the book from the table and placed it in an opening within the cave's floor.

The soldier then headed toward the entrance, passing through him, as if he wasn't there. He noticed, as the soldier left the cave, that it was still dark outside and yet the cave seemed filled with a pale bluish light.

Then, he looked upwards in horror. The ceiling of the cave was slowly coming down towards him. He was surely going to be crushed to death if he didn't get out, *he thought to himself.*

He let out a horrid scream as he ran out of the cave and down the mountain with both the watchmen running behind. The three men were now scared stiff and running for their lives, tumbling and stumbling until finally, they found themselves at the bottom of the mountain. They would never forget that night.

Saadi's cousin explained that he and the two other men suffered many cuts and bruises, falling over each other as they ran down the mountain side.

It was only when they brought him home that evening did they notice, that his hair had turned white. It was since that night's incident in the Mountain's cave, that the local villagers called the cave, la caverne des fantomes.

Earl thanked the cousin for the visit and the interesting story about his night in the cave. They had finished the bottle of brandy and Saadi advised that he would walk his cousin back home leaving Earl alone in the tent for the evening.

Earl thought about the story he had just heard. Was the cousin simply dreaming that night? *He asked himself?*

It was time to call it another night. He would get an early start in the morning, scrutinizing the cave for any missed details, and he would also do a basic dig in the cave floor to search for artifacts.

Friday morning July 3rd, was a rather windy day. Saadi came into the tent with fresh fruits for breakfast much to Earl's delight. They had a hasty breakfast and made their way to the cave, bringing along some apples to eat later on.

Earl did some scrutinizing of the walls as Saadi dug at different spots in the cave floor in hopes of finding some artifacts. Earl couldn't find anything new worth consideration on the three walls of the cave.

He was somewhat discouraged when he started to contemplate, that possibly he was on a wild goose chase here.

Earl thought of how his good friend, Charles, would take it when finding out the talisman he believed in so much was nothing but a fake. Nothing more than a hoax built on beliefs that were nourished by stupid superstitions.

In hopes of saving the situation, he would make another effort and gaze at those drawings one more time before giving up. He owed that to both Charles, and himself.

As he paid attention to the encircled crossed lines again, he realized that the lengths of the lines, which were longer than the diameters of the circles, matched precisely with the lengths of the four extrusions he discovered earlier on the other circles. Could this be of any significance, *he now wondered.*

He concluded that, if those crossed lines were placed between the two other circled drawings on the walls, they would fit perfectly within the four extrusions, thought to represent the east, south, west and north. What could this mean? *Earl thought,* as he tried to solve that puzzle.

It could mean those crossed lines were a hidden part of the talisman drawings, and that possibly the drawings in question had absolutely nothing to do with any talisman whatsoever.

Also, there were a few abnormal elements present that defied any logical explanation. For instance, Earl noticed the complete absence of sand and bugs within the cave.

More questions to be answered, *he thought.* He would enjoy his apple first, then, he would concentrate on the dig in the cave floor with Saadi, hoping to find some signs of ancient artifacts. Outside of the cave, the sand had begun blowing everywhere. Surely a sand storm was brewing below.

He now seriously believed that there were no talismans to be found here. He wondered if he should abandon this search and move on to the original plan he had when he first organized this entire voyage.

After several hours of excavating Earl decided to dismantle the tent for the time being, and return to the hotel in town to rest and reflect on this futile search for artifacts.

As he lay in bed, Earl kept thinking about the crossed lines circle. He couldn't help feeling he had missed something important, but couldn't put a finger on what it was. That drawing on the left wall just didn't fit in with the other two.

The cave certainly concealed a secret. However it was not what his friend Charles had believed…

Saturday morning July 4th. Following a pathetic breakfast, Earl returned to his room and looked over his notes of the past days describing the exploration of the cave.

Deep inside, he always suspected there would be no artifacts, resembling European talismans, to be found in Egypt. But he did wonder about the abnormal phenomenon present at times in this mysterious cave.

- The constant comfortable temperature inside of the cave regardless of the outside weather conditions, did indeed remain unexplained.
- Yesterday, with sand blowing everywhere, none seemed to enter into the cave's interior. Another unexplained phenomenon that defies all logic.
- Last but not lease, was the total absence of insects or bugs within the cave's walls, even though they were in abundance outside of the cave's open entrance.
- The story told by Saadi's cousin could be written off to delusion, were it not for the fact that his hair had turned white. This confirmed by many villagers.
- Finally, the many strange stories about the cave passed on from generation to generation, perhaps for hundreds of years. Some credibility must be considered here.

In Earls' opinion there simply had to be, at one time or another, a reason for the existence of this cave. Surely, some sort of message must lay hidden in the cave. Would he eventually discover what it was? *He now wondered.*

He started to read the book Charles had left him about symbols and their meanings. Hopefully he could find some information that would help him understand the messages and drawings on the cave walls. Perhaps even solve the mystery that existed for so long a time about this cave on Mokattam Mountain.

He read what the book said about the symbol of the circle. It consisted of one curved line where, eventually, the beginning joins the end to form a line with no beginning and no end… Eternity! It is said to be the most powerful of all occult symbols, representing the sun, heaven, the universe, infinity and perfection.

The crossed lines was said to be perhaps the oldest talismanic symbol in the world. The cross is an emblem of life, prosperity and divine protection against evil forces.

It was said to represent the four quarters of heaven and can therefore invoke heavenly powers. Christians associate it with eternal life and resurrection.

The triangle was described as the embodiment of the number three. The triangle relates to body, soul and spirit; father, mother and child; past, present and future; wisdom, love and truth.

In Christian doctrine, the triangle represents the Holy Trinity of the Father, Son and Holy Ghost.

There was one symbol in the book that got Earl's attention. This symbol was not present in the cave. It was a hexagram formed by two interlocking triangles.

This symbol was thought to protect against fire, deadly weapons and the perils of traveling. It was utilized as far back as 900 years before Christ.

The symbol was best known for its use as the Jewish Star of David. Earl noticed that the six points of the star appeared as six identical triangles, when the two larger triangles were interlocked.

Six small triangles plus two larger interlocked ones giving a total of eight triangles. The same total as appeared on the center wall of the cave, when you consider the seven triangles within the circle placed inside of the larger sanded triangle. Strange coincidence indeed, *Earl thought to himself.*

As this symbol referred to King David, the second King of Israel, then obviously the symbol was being used in 962 B.C. Earl was now more convinced then ever that the drawings on the cave walls had nothing to do with talismans. They had to serve another purpose, a message of a sort. But for whom and for what reason?

He had enough reflection for the day. He would spend the rest of the afternoon with Saadi, who had offered to show him around old Cairo for a set fee of course.

Saadi guided him through the old part of the city, where they visited places that he would have never seen without a local to guide him. They both had dinner in a small restaurant where Saadi's cousin worked, and the three men ended the evening talking once more about the night spent in the cave.

Earl decided to call it a night. He thanked Saadi for the tour and bid him and his cousin good night and made his way to the hotel for a good night's sleep.

He would return once more to the cave in the morning to make sure he had not missed anything of importance, before moving on to his original reason for being here.

FOUR

The Discovery

Sunday July 5th. It was very warm that morning as Earl arrived at the cave entrance. When he entered the cave, he felt at once the cool interior temperature. It was as if the cave was trying to test his sanity. The more he noticed strange things, the more he would try to find some logical explanation for the phenomenon.

During last night's discussion with Saadi's cousin, he had learned which wall it was that the strange man in the vision had seemed to walk through. It was the center wall with the circled triangles. The cousin thought the man walked into the center of the wall directly where the drawing was.

Earl carefully examined that part of the wall. He was now wondering about that large, seemingly sanded, pyramidal shape. Could it be some sort of secret door?

He examined it minutely going over inch by inch, trying to see if there could be a slight separation between the pyramidal shape and the wall itself but none could be found.

He then considered that maybe this pyramidal shape was not sanded at all, maybe it could possibly be of a different material, one closely resembling the structure of the sixteen square meter wall.

As he stepped back from the wall he noticed the apple cores on the floor which must have been from two days ago. Saadi had forgotten to pick them up before leaving the cave on Friday, so he bent down to pick them up. To his surprise and disbelief the cores in his hand still felt fresh. They looked as though the apples had just been eaten. The cores were not dry; nor had they changed color.

He walked outside the cave looking at the apple cores. He always left the stalk in the core when he ate apples, and he had only eaten three quarters of the apple that day. There was no other explanation possible. The apple core in his hand was the same one he had left on the cave floor two days ago.

Now he had solid evidence before him confirming that there was something to all the stories about this strange place.

He started wondering that possibly it was not the cave, but the three walls that caused unexplained things to happen here. It was as if another dimension, of a sort, existed within these unexplained walls.

Could this possibly be a passage way to another place or world, or even some sort of time warp? Now one thing was for sure; he had to find out more about this place, its mysteries and its purpose for being here.

He would go back to town, contact Saadi and re-engage him to bring equipment back to the mountain and to set up camp again outside the cave. When he arrived at the bottom of the mountain, he noticed the apple cores had turned a brownish color and were starting to dry. They were now deteriorating in a normal way.

If only everything else was back to normality, *he thought to himself*, as he hurriedly made his way to town.

He must get back to the cave site this evening, and spend the night in the cave. This way he might know once and for all, what goes on during the night, in this mysterious cave.

If he did see things in the cave that night, they could only be visions or pictures of the past captured within the walls by some unexplainable force. Images simply cannot hurt you.

Saadi's cousin had got out of the cave alive and he would too, *Earl convinced himself.* We are not in ancient times. This is 1931 and there is always a logical explanation to anything you see. The important thing is not to panic and keep control of your mind.

When he arrived at Saadi's home he advised him to load up the truck. They must set up the tent near the cave this evening, before dark. He decided against telling his assistant what his intentions were for the evening, fearing that he would refuse to follow him due to all those false fears founded on superstitions.

They left the truck at the bottom of the mountain and carted the equipment up to the cave site. The tent was errected with a good half hour left before sunset.

Saadi had a look of concern on his face. He didn't understand why the Professor was so intent on being here before sunset. I hope he doesn't plan to spend the night in the cave, *Saadi thought to himself.*

"Tell me, Professor, why were you in such a hurry to get here before sunset?" *asked Saadi.*

"To tell you the truth, I think the only way to find out about this mysterious cave is to sleep there tonight."

"Oh no Professor, remember what happened to my cousin when he stayed in the cave that night!"

"Saadi, your cousin panicked that night. There is the possibility that there was absolutely no danger for him and no need for him to run down the mountain like a scared rabbit."

"What will you do Professor if it's true about the strange men and you see them too?"

"I would calmly observe the vision knowing they were not real and that they couldn't hurt me. I assure you that I would not run out of the cave and scare you."

Earl then took his cot, water canteen, one lantern and two blankets and made his way into the cave as Saadi looked on in total disbelief at what the Professor was going to do.

Remembering the conversation he had with Saadi's cousin last Friday evening, Earl set the cot down. He was going to sleep between the drawings of the left and right wall. His feet would point to the crossed lines and his head towards the circled kamea.

This would be the same position that the cousin had seemingly taken, the night he stayed in the cave nine years ago. As he lay on the cot with the lantern on, he carefully observed the cave from this new aspect.

When he turned his head to the left, he could see outside the cave, and when he looked right, he saw the wall with the drawing of the circled triangles. The ceiling from this position seemed very much higher than when he was standing.

Darkness was starting to set in and he braced himself for the unexpected. He was quite comfortable on the cot and he had difficulty keeping awake. At least one hour had passed with nothing happening.

He had difficulty keeping awake. He decided to shut off the lantern to try the experience in complete darkness.

One, maybe even two hours had passed and still, nothing had happened. He started wondering what he was doing there. Had he gone crazy? What would Charles say if he saw him? The thought of that scenario made him smile.

Would any strange visions occur, *he thought to himself*, as his eyes started to close. Without wanting to, he was falling asleep.

It seemed to be dawn as Earl opened his eyes. The overnight sleep, in the calm of the cave, left him feeling more rested than ever before. Nothing had happened, he thought as he turned his head to look outside.

"Oh my God," *he whispered.* It was still dark outside and yet he was able to see inside the cave. The story the cousin had told him seemed to be true. Keeping as calm as he could, he glanced around the cave. There was nothing to be seen but the walls with their drawings. No visions of any sort, an empty cave was all he could see around him. He did however feel a sense of well being hard to explain. He felt as if his body was weightless, as if he was floating on water. He sensed an energy running throughout his being.

He now understood what had happened, when the cousin thought the ceiling was going to crush him. Earl was beginning to experience that same phenomenon at that very moment. The ceiling of the cave was slowly approaching him but it was not the roof of the cave that was moving; it was him. He was rising upwards, floating towards the ceiling. Of course, *he told himself*, he was only dreaming.

He kept rising higher and higher until he was but a few centimeters from the ceiling. Instinctively, he put his hand up so as if to prevent himself from hitting the roof when, to his amazement, his hand passed right through the solid stone.

Even if this is only a dream, *he thought*, he was beginning to feel very uncomfortable, for this all seemed so real. He then rolled over and looked down, towards the floor of the cave.

Suddenly he felt fear, such as he hadn't felt since being a child. There below him on the cave's floor, he could see himself there, still sleeping on the cot. Had he died in the cave that night? *he wondered.*

He now saw himself as a spirit form with no apparent substance. Although he did feel exalted; he still wished this dream would end. He wished he could go back into his body down on the cot below.

The very moment that he thought that wish, he felt himself fall downwards, towards the cot, at an incredible speed. Suddenly, he was awake and sitting-up on the cot. His Soul had returned to his body, much to his great relief.

Beads of sweat were rolling down his forehead and his heart was pounding rapidly. Had he simply dreamed or was this experience real? *he thought.* Slowly he got his composure back and he once again felt calmness about him. His heartbeat returned to normal. He wiped the sweat from his forehead and as he drank some water, as he tried to understand what had happened to him a short time ago.

He remembered reading a particular essay back at Oxford written by Helena Petrovna Blavatsky. This lady, of strange beliefs, founded the Theosophical Society in 1875. She was a student of Eastern religion and interested in astral travel. What she described in the essay closely resembled the experience he had just had. Had his Soul momentarily left his body? *He wondered.* One thing was certain. He had never in his entire life experienced anything close to what had just occurred in the mysterious cave that evening.

It was dawn as he made his way out of the cave then back to the tent. Knowing that Saadi would be asking a lot of questions, *Earl wondered*, should he tell him everything?

Monday morning. July 6th. Earl would never look at the world the same way again. What he experienced, within the cave the previous night, completely changed his outlook on life.

He elected not to tell Saadi what happened. He needed to reflect on all of this. There were so many questions going back and forth in his mind.

As he entered the tent, Saadi woke up and as expected, started asking questions. Earl simply replied that nothing had happened and proceeded to heat the water, for some good old English tea.

In the vision that Saadi's cousin had had, he saw the soldier place a book in an opening within the cave's floor. Earl now believing in the cousin's story decided to investigate the cave further, so they both made their way to the cave with lanterns and hammer-chisels.

They would try digging into the 16 square meter floor, in hopes of finding some hidden cavities. This mountain had been formed by a volcanic eruption that had happened, perhaps, millions of years ago. Digging into its iron hard crust of the floor proved to be extremely difficult.

Both men dug until late afternoon with very little results. It was now apparent they would not succeed in penetrating this floor's hardened surface. They needed bigger tools. He would send Saadi back into town to obtain some heavy pointed sledge hammers.

They would continue trying to excavate the floor the next morning. Both men headed to the tent, it was time for a very late lunch, after which Saadi headed to town to find the necessary tools, and would return in the morning. Later as Earl ate his dinner alone, he reflected on what course of action he should now take.

Earl reasoned that the cave's floor hardness was caused by erosion from salt water a very long time ago. This mountain in the past would have been surrounded by seawater. There would have been no desert, vegetation or animal life then. This mountain would be older than mankind itself.

He thought of his experience the previous night. When he had willed his Soul back to his body, it had returned immediately. This meant that he could control, by willpower, what his Soul did when it left his body.

He thought of an idea that he would try that evening in the cave, providing of course that the same phenomenon would happen again. He no longer feared the phenomenon. He believed if he stayed calm, no harm would come to him.

He remembered from the essay, by Madam Blavatsky, that as long as the Soul didn't travel far from the body, it could find its way back.

He took his cot and lantern back into the cave and set them up for his night's stay. He then stepped outside the cave, and lighting up his pipe, he admired the splendor of Cairo when viewed from this mountain campsite.

As he waited for darkness to set in, he visualized how he would conduct himself, should he be fortunate enough to relive the previous night's adventure. He would try to examine the walls with his spirit instead of his body.

The Discovery

The sun was setting as he entered the cave. He lay on the cot waiting and hoping for the out of body experience to manifest itself again. Darkness had set in as he put out the lantern, trying his best to relax.

Although he did feel a certain anxiety within himself, he was confident that he would be able to control the events, should the strange phenomenon reproduce itself.

Slowly he was beginning to be able to see in the dark. The cave was starting to glow with that pale bluish light. Now he was feeling the weightlessness; that same exalted feeling throughout his being. He felt strong and powerful in this state of mind. Normality was nothing compared to this.

As soon as he felt the levitation begin, he suddenly turned and sat on the side of the cot to observe the cave walls. He stood up and walked towards the center wall, looking over his shoulder as he did. Sure enough there he was, still stretched out on the cot. It worked as he had planned. Now it was his spirit walking around the cave and not his body.

He was amazed at how clearly his eyes could perceive details. He looked at the circled kamea and stared in disbelief as he noticed that there were strange looking symbol inside of the 36 squares in place of the numbers he had previously seen.

Somehow, the symbols would have been replaced by numbers at a later date. Who calculated and inscribed them in the squares? *He wondered.* And where did the symbols go?

When he looked at the encircled cross lines, the circle's interior seemed to change into what resembled a mirror.

Then suddenly, before his eyes, numbers, letters and pictures were flashing at incredible speed across the now transformed mirror surface within the circled cross lines.

When he looked at the drawing of the circled triangles, he could now see six different levels of depth within those triangles. Each triangle drawing now appeared to be part of a six step stairway leading to a triangularly shaped door.

As he tried to touch the circled triangles' drawing, his hand simply went through the wall. *He wondered*, what would happen if he pushed his face through the wall. He decided to try this and he found that he was now looking back at the other side of the wall.

It was a complete different world on the other side, a breathtaking view to behold. So beautiful, that there were no words to describe it adequately. He thought of crossing the wall to explore what lay before him. For some unknown reason, he felt as if he belonged to this other world.

Suddenly, an unexplainable force pulled him back towards his body. He was awake again, sitting on the edge of the cot. These were not dreams, he fearfully realized. Had he walked through the wall, he sensed, he would not have been able to return to this period in time.

He now believed the stories and legends about people never coming back from the cave. They had probably crossed to the other side of the wall and could not find their way back.

He now believed more than ever, that the visions the cousin had in the cave, nine years ago, were events that must have happened in the past.

He left the cave and made his way back to the tent. He promised himself, that he wouldn't try experimenting with the strange phenomenon that occurs in this cave again. He had a family waiting for him to return home, and he would not gamble with their future.

The Discovery

When Saadi arrives with the proper tools, earl decided that they would continue digging in different sections of the cave's floor hoping to find something beneath the surface. They would keep searching until they had explored every square meters of the floor and if nothing were found, they would leave this place and never return to this mountain again.

It was Tuesday noon when Saadi finally arrived with the proper tools needed to continue the excavation of the cave's floor. Both men went about digging in the floor's hard crust. They each dug in separate areas, and didn't stop until it was close to sunset. The dig was hard and tiring, and both were exhausted and very glad to stop for the day.

They ate dinner and enjoyed a brandy before retiring for the night. Another day of hard digging lay ahead, and they would need a good night's sleep.

Thursday July 9th. After two days of digging, late afternoon when suddenly an exited Saadi called out. "Professor, I've found something!" When hitting the floor directly in front of the pyramidal drawing, the sledgehammer had bounced back upwards. The sound coming from the cave's floor had sounded hollow signifying a weakness under this location.

This meant that they had found a cavity in the cave's floor. It was unbelievably exiting. They would now have to carefully chip at this section using lighter tools. Once they had slowly chipped away at the softer crust they discovered what seemed to be a metal door, octagonal in shape.

Using small crowbars they were able to lift the cover off the opening in the floor. It was a rather small opening about a meter and a half in diameter. Using the lantern to see inside, Earl estimated the cavity dept was equal to half of its diameter.

It was a strange looking cavity, and was certainly not formed by natural erosion. Saadi, being the smallest one of the two, stepped into the hole to see what lay on the bottom, Earl watched on with excited anticipation tinged with impatience.

"There are articles down here, Professor. What should I do?" *inquired Saadi.* "Don't touch anything, *replied Earl,* climb out of the hole and let me get in to examine what is there."

He was as excited as a child receiving a new toy as he stepped into the hole with dusting broom and lantern. As he shined the lantern towards the sides and bottom of the cavity, he noticed at once the smooth texture of the cavity's walls and floor. The cavity seemed to be made in one piece and of the same metal as its cover. His excitement was mounting as he examined what lay there on the cavity's floor and this could possibly have been for centuries!

There were three metal swords, six strange looking objects that could not be identified and two wooden chests sitting on the bottom. All of the items seemed to be in incredibly good condition. *Strange indeed thought Earl.*

There was no visible rust on the sword, and the wooden chest didn't show any sign of deterioration. Could these items have been here for such a long period of time? *he wondered.* Then he remembered the incident with the apple cores.

Possibly the atmosphere in the cave had prevented the newly found items from aging. Not logical, *he thought,* but possible. He passed the items up to Saadi and after verifying that nothing else was left at the bottom of the hidden cavity he climbed out.

Charles will be pleased with the artifacts that had been discovered, *thought Earl.*

The two men were jubilant; finally their persistence and hard labor had paid off. They had found artifacts and this made the entire journey worthwhile to Earl.

Before carrying the two chests, the swords and the six unidentified objects to the tent for proper examination, they replaced the metal cover over the cavity's opening.

Then, they re-placed the floor scales over the opening, making the secret cavity in the cave's floor invisible, once more, to anyone who would enter this cave by chance. This discovery was one thing that must be kept secret for the time being…

Earl impressed upon Saadi that they must keep their discovery a secret, and that meant he was not to talk about this to anyone at all, not even his family. After Earl had promised him a substantial bonus Saadi agreed to keep the secret. They carried the precious items carefully to the tent.

Once there, Earl examined the chests. He concluded that even though they were in perfect condition, they were extremely old. They were locked with a primitive locking mechanism that was used centuries before. It would be easy to open these locks in question. A penknife would do the trick.

Earl closely examined the three swords. He recognized them as being Roman. He had seen identical swords in a museum in Rome. One sword stood out in particular for it had three letters engraved on its cross handles. – G J C –

- (GAIUS) JULIUS CAESAR (c.101- 44 B.C.) -

This sword would have belonged to an officer of the Roman army in the times of Cleopatra. If it proved to be an original, it would be 2,000 years old.

The ones he had viewed before, in a Roman museum, were not in as good a condition as those now facing him. These were immaculate. They seemed as new as the day they were made centuries ago, and would surely be worth a fortune.

His heart was pounding when with a penknife he was able to pick open the lock on the first chest. Inside it he found two leather pouches.

The largest pouch contained gold and silver Roman coins that were in almost mint condition. As Earl tipped out the last item in the pouch he was astonished to find it was a giant faceted Ruby, so huge that his heart skipped a beat at the sight of it.

The second pouch contained a selection of carefully wrapped precious stones.

There were also several rolled parchments in the chest which when examined appeared to be dispatches from Rome to military commanders in Egypt.

Some of the documents even had the Royal Seal of Caesar. Collectors would surely pay handsomely for these extraordinary artifacts.

The six objects that he couldn't identify would probably be recognized by Charles.

He carefully opened the second chest. In it, he found many handwritten papers and a leather bound book. The book appeared to be an old codex or possibly a journal of a sort that probably belonged to a Roman military officer.

All the writings were in Latin. Fortunately, Latin was one of the subjects he studied in college. He would have no trouble reading the book in question.

His excitement mounted as he started to read the book; he could not believe what he was reading. Seemingly written by a Roman soldier 2,000 years ago, it talked about several of his encounters with the Soul Master in that very cave.

This Soul Master would have told the soldier that he had been present here on Earth for the past 360,000 years.

If this leather bound journal proved to be authentic, it could well be classified as the oldest codex ever discovered and the first written in Latin.

The more Earl read from the soldier's journal, the more he realized the great danger he and Saadi were in. Some people would kill to prevent what was said in this book from being exposed to the world. He had stumbled onto more than he had bargained for.

If news of this discovery ever got out, *Earl felt that he would never leave Egypt alive.*

FIVE

The Scrolls

The more Earl read from the soldier's journal, the more he realized the great danger he and Saadi could be in. Some people would kill to prevent what was said in this book from being exposed to the world. He had stumbled onto something that was far more than he had bargained for.

There were terrible secrets, which were exposed in these writings from the past. This could change what mankind had believed for thousands of years. It was vital that he immediately return to England with the artifacts.

He explained to his assistant what danger they were in and that their lives depended on keeping secret what they had discovered. When they return to town in the morning, there must be no evidence in the truck to show that they had found anything. The two empty wooden chests could not be hidden from sight in the truck so they would have to be left behind, buried in the hidden cavity within the cave's floor. This must be done first thing in the morning.

Both men had difficulty sleeping. A lot of tea was consumed that night as Earl continued reading the papers that were with the Journal in the second chest.

As daylight came they returned the two chests to the cave's floor cavity. The heavy sledge hammers were also left behind in the cavity making room for the artifacts to fit into the small crate that had been utilized for the excavation tools.

The metal door-cover was replaced and covered with the loose floor scales once again making the floor cavity invisible to intruders. They then carried the remaining equipment down the mountain and loaded it into the truck.

These precious artifacts must not be left alone at any time, and Earl wondered if Saadi would consider going to Alexandria with him.

As they drove back towards the hotel, Earl broached the subject and extended the invitation for Saadi to accompany him to Alexandria, which he accepted.

Time was of the essence, and it was imperative that they leave Cairo as soon as possible. So as soon as they arrived at the hotel, they brought the crate and luggage up into their room.

"Stay in the room with the crate, Saadi, until I return. And do not engage in needless conversation with anyone." *instructed Earl.*

"I understand, Professor, and don't worry I will do exactly as you tell me," *replied Saadi.*

Earl left the hotel and made his way to the train station to find out the schedule, for trains to Alexandria.

The next train was leaving for Alexandria at noon the following day. He returned to the hotel and advised Saadi that they would be leaving the next day.

"What will you do with the artifacts you found Professor?"

"They actually don't belong to me, Saadi. They belong to my friend in France. He sent me here to search the cave and he will decide what is to be done with them. Look out of the window. Do you see the dinning room across the street?"

"That is where we will take turns eating dinner this evening, and remember not to talk with anyone."

"Understood, Professor, you go first and enjoy your meal. I will watch over the crate until you get back."

Following his delicious meal, Earl returned to the room and while Saadi took his turn for dinner he continued with his reading of the pages found in the chest.

Both men had slept very little the previous evening and they were both very tired and so, following their dinners, they decided that they would try to get some much needed sleep before taking the train the next morning.

Earl was sleeping profoundly when he began dreaming that he was in a strange house, encircled by seven men wearing black hoods. He awoke from the dream, but exhaustion soon overtook him and he fell into fitful sleep once again.

It was now Saturday July 11th. Both men took breakfast in the room, as they prepared for the train ride to Alexandria. Earl instructed Saadi to return the truck to his cousin at the restaurant where he worked.

"Only tell your cousin that you are coming with me to Alexandria, and that you will be back in a few days. Tell him nothing else. Only after I have boarded the ship, booked to take me to France can you return to Cairo."

"Understood Professor I will do as you say."

After Saadi dropped Earl and the luggage at the station, he returned the truck to his cousin's work place. He then made his way back to the train station, with a good hour to spare before the train left.

There was nothing to do now but wait. Earl thought about writing to Charles, but that would serve no purpose as he would most probably arrive in France before the letter got there.

To assure their complete privacy, Earl had booked a private compartment on the train. Finally, it was departure time. They carried the luggage and the crate onto the train.

They would be alone now until they arrived at Alexandria, and Earl let out a sigh of relief as the train started moving.

"You can relax now, Saadi. You have done well."

"Thank you Professor. I was very nervous you know. I was worried after your warning of possible danger."

"We are all right now Saadi, and we are safe as long as no one knows what we discovered in the cave,"

"Tell me Professor, what could be so dangerous about those artifacts that we found?"

"I will explain it all to you, once we are in Alexandria."

As Saadi slept peacefully in the train, Earl went about reading more of the soldier's papers.

The first thing they did, after they stepped off the train in Alexandria, was to find a hotel as close to the Sea port as possible.

Once installed in their hotel room, Earl explained to Saadi the reasons why secrecy was vital.

"You see Saadi, there are many religious fanatics in the World, who would not want the contents of what was found in that cave made public. These papers written by the Roman soldier, so long ago, changes the very basis of most religions' beliefs and teachings."

"I don't think you would understand the complexity of what I am talking about, but the information found in these papers could prove to be extremely dangerous for all who know about it. You have to take my word for it and not disclose to anyone what was found in that cave."

"Absolutely, I take your word for it Professor, and promise that I will tell no one about what we found."

Earl lay in bed that night and could not help thinking about that cave's construction. All dimensions seemed perfectly, symmetrically proportioned. An architect's work!

Monday July 13th. After two days in Alexandria, Earl had found a cargo ship that would take him to Marseille, France. The ship would be leaving that evening.

Saadi had proved to be a loyal and trusted friend, especially during the last three days spent together.

Once settled in his cabin on the ship, Earl gave Saadi 5,000 francs and assured him that his friend Charles would send him a lot more, to thank him for his loyal and devoted assistance.

Saadi would return to Cairo the next day and Earl would be on the open sea heading home, via France. Earl knew he would never see his assistant again. Even after such a short time he had become a friend and would be missed.

As the ship pulled away from the dock Earl felt a sense of great relief come over him. He no longer had that fear caused by the discovery made in the cave.

No one on this ship knew anything about the secrets that had been discovered. He felt safer at last.

He had purchased several new journals in Alexandria. He would now have plenty of time on this return trip to begin to translate the Latin scriptures he had found, into English.

The occurrences of the past several days had taken its toll. He would go up on deck, light up his pipe and view the open sky. Then hope to have his first good night's restful sleep in days.

Waking, after sleeping soundly for a full twelve hours Earl made his way to the ship's galley for a quick bite then returned to his cabin.

He took out a new journal from his luggage and begun translating the found scriptures into English. The soldier's journal would be the first to be translated. It appeared to talk about the beginning of life on Earth.

It seemed, in essence, to explain the differences between the Soul and Man and disclosed the different levels of the Souls and how they were assigned to every living thing on Earth. The Roman claimed these were the words that were told to him by the Soul Master as he, or it, was called by the Roman soldier. Earl would name these translations, The Soul Master Scrolls.

Translation of the Latin writings:

(c.101 - 44 B.C.)

1… The first living creatures of this land were so small that they could not be seen. These creatures still exist this very day and still cannot be seen. They are hosts to Souls from the first house, the lowest level of Souls.

2... Then there came the second living creatures of this land. They were miniscule and came at the same time as the forest. They live from this forest and you call them insects. These still exist this very day. Both the insects and the forest, with all that grows within it, are hosts to Souls from the second house.

3... Following, came the third living creatures of this land. They could fly across the sky, live beneath the seas and crawl upon the land. You call these birds, fish and reptiles and most of these still exist this very day. They are all hosts to Souls from the third house.

4... Then there came the fourth living creatures of this land. They walked across the land on two and four legs. You call these animals. Many of their kind still exist this very day. They all are hosts to Souls from the fourth house.

5... All of these living creatures are mortals and were fathered by the Star you call your Sun, and all were mothered by the land you call the Earth.

6... All of their Souls are immortal and do not belong to the land for they are part of the Master Soul of the eight house.

7... All living creatures that are host to Souls of the first four houses possess a limited intelligence. They know not the difference between good and bad, and cannot bear malice against any other living creatures of this land.

8... All Souls from the first four houses can never evolve to attain a higher house. They will forever throughout their existence change from host to host within the living creatures originally from this land.

9… The Souls will multiply the same as the living creatures of this land. These Souls will evolve within the living creatures of all the lands from the first house through the fourth house, and then to return to the eight house from where they came and this for time after time.

10… This was the beginning of life on this land since the first day and for thousands of cycles multiplied by thousands of thousands. You call these cycles years and they are too numerous to be counted.

11… Then 360,000 cycles ago came three great ships from three distant lands. These ships brought thousands upon thousands of intelligent beings to this land.

12… These beings were hosts to Souls from the fifth and sixth houses. They could tell the difference between good and bad and were able make their own choices freely. They were brought here to colonize this new land.

13… They have made the world what it is this present day. You descend from one of these.

Translating the Latin writings into understandable and readable English proved to be quite a difficult task. He was starting to feel somewhat sluggish Before he was totally wiped out he thought it better to go up to the ship's deck, and enjoy the Sun and the smell of the salty air from the Sea.

He only spent a short time on the ship's deck. Just enough time to smoke his pipe. Revived, he made his way back to his cabin, for he wasn't happy leaving his belongings unattended. On his way down, he stopped at the galley to collect some food to take with him.

Once back in the cabin and having eaten, he found that the sight of the bunk bed had suddenly become very appealing. He lay down intending to rest briefly, however, he couldn't keep his eyes open. Further translations can wait until tomorrow, *he thought,* as he slowly fell into a coma-like deep sleep.

Morning came, and it was back to the translating of the Latin.

14… Here on this land you call yourselves humans, yet you are the same as when you first appeared on this land. The three great ships came from three different far away lands, each bigger than the other. The beings brought here were different in size and color. The ones from the bigger land were larger beings and those from the smaller land were smaller beings.

15… The three different beings in appearance were placed at different corners of your world, and each of the three brought with them the seeds needed to produce the food to assure their survival in the newfound land. All three were of the same blood, as are all intelligent beings wherever be situated their land.

16… *All were, and are, of the same intelligence for this intelligence comes from the Soul and not the mortal being itself. All have the same capacity for deciding their destiny. All have an inner knowledge to be discovered allowing them to make themselves as immortal as their Souls.*

17… They know fear and joy, also love, hate and greed. In past times all over the lands, some have prospered while others destroyed themselves into oblivion.

18… The Star called your Sun is the host to a Master Soul of the seventh house. All that surrounds it your Earth, your Moon and every living creature becomes a part of it. If your Sun ceases to exist, so does everything around it.

19… I also am a Master Soul from the seventh house, and I have been here since the beginning overlooking the progress of your mankind with no power to change the events and destiny your kind has created.

20… The humans here are all hosts to Souls of the fourth, fifth and sixth houses. Man himself is incapable of emotions. It is the Soul that has that capacity.

21… Therefore mankind in its own self is incapable of knowing the difference between good and evil.

22… The Souls on the other hand can be good or evil. That is a part of the balance that exists in the Universe.

23… Souls from the fifth house are kind, gentle and loving. They are the peaceful ones who search to find and create immortality.

24… The Souls from the sixth house in contrast can prove to be evil and destructive. They are always in endless wars against all the hosts of Souls from all other houses.

25… Souls from the sixth house create the greedy and heartless hosts that care for nothing but their own fulfillment at the expense of all others, never caring of the consequences of their actions.

26… In the place where we meet there are three walls. One of these walls is a doorway to the land from where the three great ships came. These walls follow me from mountain to mountain wherever I dwell. Only Souls can cross this wall back and forth. For a mortal to do so would mean never returning to this land again.

27… As the overseer of this land I can tell you that unless mankind changes the path it has embarked upon it will be destroyed. I will tell you what lies in store for your kind if your ways are not changed

28… I cannot alter the course of the events taking place. It must be mankind itself that corrects the directions taken in the future.

29… Let your kind take heed at what I will now tell you.

Earl sat on the bunk in his cabin reviewing the translations that he had just completed. He found them difficult to understand, and he did not know what to make of these writings. Were it not for the fact they were scribed on papers resembling parchment, the texture of which he had never come across before and that the artifacts were so intriguing, he would have simply would put these writings off as being nonsense.

This story seemed impossible. Maybe a brilliant man with a tremendous imagination had conceived and fabricated this entire scenario. Earl found himself questioning the originality of the found artifacts. Maybe the gold coins and swords were fakes. But why? What could be the reason or purpose?

Either way he had enough of these translations for the moment. Evening was approaching and he realized that he had forgotten to have dinner. He made his way to the ship's galley and considering his surroundings, enjoyed some surprisingly good food. After his meal he made his way onto the ship's deck, where he indulged in his bad habit of smoking his pipe as he gazed over the beautiful Mediterranean Sea.

There would be several ports of calls scheduled on this return voyage to France. However, he had decided not to leave the ship at any time during this trip.

He stayed a good hour up on deck, and again found himself pondering upon what he had just finished translating from the soldier's journal. He descended to his cabin and started reading the pages that were found alongside the soldier's journal. Some of the pages seemed to contain Prophecies.

None of which made any sense to him. Thirteen of these pages each outlined a single different Prophecy. He was unable to associate many of these Prophecies with anything he recollected as having happened.

Then he wondered; when were these Prophecies to take place? Was this Roman soldier another Nostradamus?

The more he thought of this, the more the entire story seemed to border on the implausible. This was until he read the last two pages of the journal, where the Roman soldier claimed to have buried the very artifacts that they had found.

From what the Roman soldier wrote. The artifacts were buried just before he crossed through one of the cave walls, to be where he rightfully belonged, at another place and time the Soul Master had told him about.

It would seem that the soldier had decided to leave this world for a better place, this, after the Soul Master had told him of happenings that occurred once the three great ships arrived on this land.

30… When the three great ships came, they carried to this land thousands upon thousands of intelligent beings. With them, came powerful weapons to protect against some of the existing animals that roamed the land.

31… These animals were of great strength, and without the weapons, the newly arrived beings would not have been able to survive. These weapons were to be utilized only against dangerous predators that roamed the land.

32… The three great ships resembled the stone structure that stands before this very cave. But the ships were 10 times greater in size. They were cities within themselves.

33… All that came with them lived within their walls. As your kind grew in strength over the cycles, more places were built surrounding the great ships creating larger and larger cities.

34… And this until there was across this land, three great Empires where all lived in peace and all was plentiful.

35… Your kind grew and prospered within these three great Empires for more than 100,000 cycles.

36… But then, the hosts to Souls of the sixth house became greedy. They grew jealous of the abundance equally shared by the multitudes that hosted the Souls of the fifth house.

37… The hosts from the sixth house decided that they should have more than the others, and construed a way to take it.

38…Then there came the first great war of this land. It went on between the hosts to the Souls of the fifth and sixth houses. It lasted longer than 100,000 cycles until most of mankind had been destroyed.

39… This war pitted empire against empire, brother against brother and father against son. It was a bloody and merciless war that left none untouched. The only survivors were the hosts of both houses that had fled into hiding in different parts of the land.

40… In the following 100,000 cycles Mankind once again, had grown in strength and numbers and began the rebuilding of cities. But his time without the knowledge and the weapons brought with them, when the three great ships arrived. The Earth had consumed all traces of that passed existence.

41… Without the knowledge from the past, senseless wars went on throughout the land. Man's longevity became shorter and shorter with each passing cycle.

42… Unknown sicknesses and plagues followed mankind wherever it wandered, and Mankind suffered as never before. The suffering would be a long time standing.

43… Since then, man has continued on to this day with the land's people of both houses, still at war against each other, seemingly unable to achieve the peace and harmony that reigns in the great lands from whence they came.

44… During the last 6,000 cycles, I have spoken with many of your kind, in the same way as I am speaking to you and this all over these lands.

45… The time of this land is soon to be counted, for none seem to take heed at the words I say…

The more Earl would re-read these writings, the more he asked himself questions. What kind of a mind could have contemplated such a story and for what reason?

These writings challenge the very essence of the Bible and Genesis. Everything we were taught for centuries was being put into question here.

All of this had taken its toll on his energy. He would continue with the translations in the morning. Now he would try to relax by going up to the ship's deck to smoke his pipe. Then he would attempt to get more of the needed sleep that had eluded him recently.

Another morning came and Earl had enjoyed a long, refreshing and peaceful night's sleep. He made his way to the ship's galley and shared breakfast with some of the crew before returning to his cabin below.

He thought of that Roman soldier and of how he described the Soul Master he had encountered. The soldier had written, that the Soul Master moved about without walking, and that he appeared to float and glide above the ground. He seemingly had no hands or feet, and resembled a shadow that would change in form and blend in with the backgrounds.

He resembled a human, unrecognizable as either a man or a woman. The soldier wrote that the strange person seemed to have no face, but in place possessed only a form of a face.

He had what appeared to be long golden hair that reflected the likes of fire and where the eyes should be, the soldier could only see a reflection as of the color of the sky above.

The soldier understood what the Soul Master was trying to convey even though he never spoke out loud. He answered the soldier's questions without the questions being asked. It was as if this strange person knew every thought the soldier had.

Yet as strange as the man appeared to be, he projected such warmth and gentleness that the soldier felt no fear whatsoever in this person's presence.

The soldier's journal ended with the following words:

"The time of this land is soon to be counted,
for none seem to take heed at the words I say…"

Earl concluded from all these readings, that the soldier must have been hallucinating, or suffering from a fever causing delirium. Fever causing delirium was a common occurrence those days, especially, in that part of the world.

Nonetheless, he took another journal from the luggage and would get on with translating, the thirteen Prophecies that were on the papers found with the Roman soldier's journal.

Prophecy

- I -

Helpless are some that are the hosts to the Souls of the fifth house. For they possess knowledge from within, thus making them creators of beauty and achievers of wisdom. They will find themselves rejected, feared, and at times put to death, by hosts to Souls of the sixth house.

Having translated the first Prophecy, Earl concluded that this Prophecy would relate to our past, (or the future of when it was written by the Roman Soldier).

If we are to look at this first Prophecy, It obviously applies to recorded history of the years, when the beliefs of the Church and Kings, caused many to be executed as heretics or people possessed by the devil. And yet these victims were just brilliant people ahead of their time.

A perfect example of this would be the gifted astronomer and mathematician Galileo (1564-1642).

Galileo's bold advocacy of the Copernican theory brought severe ecclesiastical censure. He was forced to retract before the inquisition, and was sentenced to indefinite imprisonment for his beliefs, even though they were ultimately proved to be right.

Eventually, his sentence was commuted by the pope at the request of the Duke of Tuscany. Under house arrest in Florence, he continued his research even after becoming blind.

This great man discovered the law of uniformly accelerated motion towards the Earth, the parabolic path of projectiles, and the law that all bodies have weight.

Galileo improved the refracting telescope and was the first man to apply it to astronomy. Yet still to this day, the validity of his scientific work has never been recognized by the Roman Catholic Church.

During 1692 and 1693 Salem, in America, young women were hanged as witches by the puritans of Massachusetts.

Most of these innocent victims were unjustly put to death by religious hypocrites and this mostly because; these young women refused to submit themselves to sexual demands made onto them by these so-called righteous ones.

Prophecy

- II -

Pity for the numerous who are the hosts to the Souls of the fifth house. For they are the innocent ones, and they will be lied to, plundered and robbed of their labor, by the greedy hosts to Souls of the sixth house.

Here again, the second Prophecy could not only relate to the Kings and Lords of Ancient times but also to modern times. Kings, Governments, politicians, dictators, greedy landlords, businessmen, thieves and many more would fit into the descriptions in this second Prophecy.

If one was to compare the first Prophecy to the second, one could conclude that, there could be a difference of a few centuries between them.

The first Prophecy could easily be applied to the era leading up to and including the seventeenth century, while the second Prophecy, would definitely apply to the nineteenth century and thereafter.

Prophecy

- III -

All of these wicked deeds, it will be said, must be done in then name of prosperity and for the betterment of the collectivity. Thus skillfully hiding, their real ploy, for personal greed and the lust for power. This always sought across countless lands, by scheming hosts to the Souls of the sixth house.

Once again, the third Prophecy could obviously relate to both to Ancient times and modern times. Although by the way it was written, it would seem to bring it closer to the present time, 1931, when the almighty dollar is placed above everything.

Prophecy

- IV -

When men like birds in the sky will fly and men like fish in the sea will dive. Then pictures in a box will seem alive. Shortly thereafter in leaps and bounds, unseen knowledge will be found. This will be the sign for all to see, that the end is coming and for all to flee.

Except for that last sentence, the fourth Prophecy brings us right up to the present time. It refers to planes, submarines and movie projections. Surprising it doesn't indicate or expressly spell out as being 1931. *Earl thought to himself mockingly.*

When reading Prophecies 5 through 13 Earl could not associate those with any present events. Therefore, it had to be concluded that those Prophecies referred to the future.

Earl observed that as the Prophecies went on, the events mentioned became more and more worrisome. He felt a certain discomfort at what was written on the next nine pages which described the Prophecies five to thirteen.

As well as the remaining nine pages of Prophecies, there were six other separate pages. They eventually proved to contain a paradoxical text that could possibly be a 14th Prophecy.

He found these last six pages hard to understand. They seemed to refer to the end of the World and describe a horrific apocalypse of a sort. What awaits us? *He wondered.*

Could this be Armageddon? He would require help from colleagues back at Oxford to correctly translate those complex writings.

Earl reflected on his attempted translations that he had just completed. This was the best he could do. When translating from Latin to English, it is easy for some meanings to be miss-interpreted or miss-construed.

Some of the written words by the soldier resembled nothing short of poetry. Could a roman soldier, 2,000 years ago have had the intellectual capacity to compose such writings. Not probable, *he thought,* but then who wrote them?

Regardless of what he thought. This bizarre story does have certain credibility and should be looked into and thoroughly investigated.

As he had had no way of advising Charles that he was already on his way back. He could only imagine the surprise that it would cause when he suddenly appears at the door of the mansion near Rouen.

Once in France, he would write to Elizabeth explaining the reason for such a drastic change of plans. Possibly both Elizabeth and Peter could cross the channel from England and join him at Charles' mansion.

Earl was sure that Charles and he would be spending considerable time together.

The trip back to France was going rather well. He would enjoy the rest of the time left, relaxing on the ship as it made its way across the Mediterranean Sea.

SIX

The Surprise

Sunday July 26th. The cargo ship was one hour away from the port of Marseille. Earl was overjoyed at the thought of eating in a French restaurant again. He would spend the night at *l'Auberge des Trois Canards.

This was one of the good hotels that his friend Charles stayed at when in Marseille. Earl would have someone from the hotel arrange for his transportation to Charles' mansion in Rouen.

He was ready and eager to go ashore. The ship docked and he was the first to walk down the gangplank. How it felt good to stand on French soil, *he thought to himself.*

A short cab ride and he would be at the hotel. The timing could not have been better. He arrived at the hotel at 5.30 in the afternoon, just in time to enjoy the reputable cuisine in that hotel's fine dining room.

All was arranged. The hotel would have someone available to drive him to Rouen anytime the next day. As he made his way to the dining room, he decided he would have some ***Canard a l'Orange* for diner. This was one of the hotel dining room's specialties.

* The Three Ducks' Inn.

* Orange Duck.

Later after a hot bath, the first in quite some time, Earl lay in bed reflecting on the last six pages written by the Roman soldier. These were complicated and hard to translate.

The terrible catastrophic events that were cited on those pages were unimaginable. Surely, he was misinterpreting these Latin wordings. Such things could never happen on Earth, *he thought*, as he fell asleep.

Earl woke up at dawn that Monday morning. He was exhausted. The responsibilities he was now liable for had caused the stress he had suffered with since leaving Cairo; and had taken its toll upon him.

He had not spoken of this discovery with anyone yet, and he couldn't wait to share this with Charles.

Following an enjoyable but hasty breakfast, he was finally on his way to Rouen. He would arrive at Charles' mansion later in the evening.

During the trip, the hotel's chauffeur and he talked quite a bit. This made the long drive seem much shorter.

Midway, the car had mechanical problems and needed some repairs. This is just what I needed, *thought Earl.*

He decided that he might as well do some sightseeing and grab some lunch while he was stuck in this village.

One hour later, when Earl returned to the garage the mechanic advised that he would have to go to the next town for some parts.

"When will the car be ready to drive?" *inquired Earl.*

"Not until this evening." *replied the mechanic.*

The Surprise

This is certainly not Charles' Bentley, *thought Earl*, as he looked at the broken automobile. And to make matters worse, the weather was turning to rain. They would only be on their way to Rouen the next morning.

There was a small hotel in the village and two rooms were available that evening for Earl and the driver. They would continue on to Rouen first thing in the morning.

They were making good time, and should arrive at Charles' mansion late afternoon. The last few hours of the trip seemed like an eternity to Earl.

At last he could see the mansion in front of him. He had made it back to his friend's place, safe and sound. At times, since leaving Cairo, he feared that bad fortune would befall him. He was truly happy and relieved when the car finally pulled up to Charles' mansion.

Iris, Charles' maid, came out and greeted him. "What a surprise to see you so soon Professor. Is everything all right?" *inquired Iris*, "What happened?"

"Everything is fine Iris. Is Charles at home?"

"No, Professor, Monsieur is at the *Rose-Croix Lodge this evening. It's initiation night and as you know, he is the grand master of the lodge."

"I see Iris, thank you. Charles will have a surprise waiting for him when he gets back, won't he?"

"He certainly will, Professor, he certainly will. Please come in. Your usual room is waiting for you. I will prepare some tea for you." "Thank you Iris, do you expect Charles to be back soon?"

* The Rosicrucian.

"I don't think so Professor. I only expect him back late this evening. These initiations sometimes drag on until morning."

"Fine then, I guess I will see him in the morning. Could you please bring the tea up to my room?"

As Earl made his way towards the bedroom, he couldn't help but notice a new painting hanging in the hallway. He hadn't seen that one before. It was surely a new addition to Charles' collection. It was by Rembrandt.

"Here is your tea Professor. You must be tired now. I will see you in the morning at breakfast."

"Thank you Iris. Good night," *Earl said yawning.*

As he sat in the comfortable chair beside his bed, he relaxed and sipped his tea. So Charles was the grand master of the Rose-Croix in Rouen. Earl knew of Charles' involvement with this occult movement, but he never knew the high rank Charles held within this organization.

The Rose-Croix, or Rosicrucian, as they are called back in England, is an old institution going back centuries. Christian Rosenkreuz, a mythical knight of the 15th century, is said to have launched the movement in 1614.

The society flourished in the 17th and 18th centuries and was devoted to metaphysical and mystical lore of life, and power over the elements. Its world headquarter is situated at an ancient *Chateau here in France.

Earl went about placing all of the artifacts in the commode, then once in bed, he decided to read the Roman soldier's journal once more before sleeping. He could no longer keep his eyes open and slowly drifted into a deep sleep.

* Castle.

The Surprise

His peaceful sleep was disturbed by a horrific nightmare. He dreamed he was looking down at the Earth, as if he was watching from the clouds in the sky.

From this position he saw thousands of men, women and children spread all over the ground below. They apparently were all dead. Their flesh was being picked at by millions of birds, the same way vultures pick at dead animals' carcasses.

He also saw in his dream, a huge fireball come down upon a city destroying it and all within it. Some of the people's flesh was melting clean off their bones. He heard loud horrible screaming and saw skeletons of bodies lying everywhere.

He knew he was dreaming of course, but the sight of such tragedy even in a dream, left him trembling with fear.

Suddenly, he was jolted from his sleep and awake. He wondered if this nightmare had anything to do with those last six pages written by the Roman soldier in the cave.

He looked at his pocket watch and saw it was ten o'clock in the morning. Surely Charles was back, and had decided to let him sleep in that morning. Earl got up and made his way to the garden. Charles was already there, having a late breakfast. Charles signaled for Earl to join him at the table. They would have a lot to talk about this morning.

"Good morning, Earl. I was concerned when I learned of your early return. Is there anything wrong? Did you find that cave in Cairo." *asked Charles apprehensively.*

"Yes I did Charles. I found the cave and all went well. I made an incredible discovery there. But it had nothing to do with talismans."

During breakfast Earl told Charles about the incredible expedition that had taken place, since his leaving for Egypt.

Charles sat totally mesmerized, as he listened to Earl's detailed account of the discovery made in Cairo.

It seemed both men had been talking for hours when Iris brought them some fresh tea. "You men can talk longer than any woman I know." *said Iris mockingly*, as she set the tea on the table.

"That is enough talking for now my friend. Come to my room and see the incredible artifacts that were found in the cave." *said Earl,* brandishing a great smile.

Charles stared in disbelief, as Earl opened the crate and displayed the three Roman swords he had found.

As Charles examined the swords, Earl laid the precious gems on the bed. For a brief moment, it seemed like Charles' eyes were going to come out of their sockets. "I can't believe this," said Charles "These gems must be worth a King's ransom."

There was a giant ruby worthy of belonging to a Royal Family's Crown Jewels. This ruby alone was worth a fortune. There was also a raw blue diamond that surely weighed at least twenty carats. There were some beautiful green emeralds, several smaller rubies and a fair quantity of diamonds.

"My dear Earl, you are now a wealthy man. Do you have any idea what these precious stones are worth?" *said Charles,* as he carefully examined each gem.

"We will share the money these gems can be sold for." *replied Earl.* "You are entitled to half of what was found. Without you insisting I visit the cave in Cairo, I would have never come across these precious stones."

"Now Charles, take a look at this exceptional old Roman journal and these old documents."

"Now take a look at these old Roman gold coins. Do you think they are authentic?" *inquired Earl.* "We will have them looked at by competent people. Then, we will know for sure." *replied Charles*, obviously overwhelmed by the chain of events.

Charles was also well versed in Latin. He started reading the Roman soldier's journal. As he read, he would glance from time to time in Earl's direction.

Earl decided to leave Charles alone in the room, and headed out to the garden to relax and smoke his pipe. A good hour later, Charles finally joined Earl in the garden with two glasses of brandy.

"Well my friend you certainly have had the ultimate experience of your life, haven't you?" *said Charles.*

"Yes, Charles, you are right of course. This story is hard to believe. Isn't it?" *replied Earl*, as he looked into his friend's eyes.

Earl then told Charles of the strange events that took place in the cave on Mokattam Mountain. He described the phenomenon he had experienced, where his Soul seemed to have left his body. Surprisingly, Charles seemed to know and understand a lot about this phenomenon.

"My friend what you experienced is completely normal for those who practice the use of this method of astral meditation. It has been utilized for centuries."

Charles went on to explain exactly what had happened to Earl in the cave. The Rose-Croix, are practitioners of this very phenomenon. It's called an astral voyage!

Charles told of a story he had heard about Caroline Larsen an American lady who, one autumn evening back in 1910, experienced one of these astral voyages.

As she lay in her bed one evening, she was seized by a weird feeling of apprehension as though she were about to faint. She felt this overpowering oppression deepening and soon every muscle in her body seemed paralyzed.

The next thing she recalled was that she was standing on the floor beside her bed looking down at her own physical body lying there on the bed.

She then went about walking around the house, and it was when she entered the bathroom and looked into the mirror that she noticed a strong whitish light emanating from he face and body that illuminated the entire room.

"You must admit my friend that this incident seems to be the same phenomenon that you described a few moments ago, *explained Charles,* we often discuss this at the lodge."

They had talked so much that they had not noticed the time fly by. Iris approached and advised that dinner would be served in one hour.

Earl returned to his room to freshen up before dinner. It would feel good to dine with his friend again, *he thought,* as he made his way back to the dining room.

He arrived at the table, as Iris was opening a bottle of champagne, Dom Perignon, of course. Charles sure knew how to enjoy the good life. Maybe now he too would start enjoying the good life, *thought Earl to himself.*

"Good evening Professor, we are having roast beef for dinner. If my memory is right, that is one of your favorite meals."

"You are right as usual Charles. It's always been my preferred meal next to fish and chips, of course."

"Tonight my friend, we relax. We have done enough talking for one day. After dinner I challenge you to a game of chess. Think you can win a game?" *said Charles.*

"You won the last game we played. But maybe this time, chance will favor my style of play." *replied Earl.*

As they enjoyed their meal, Earl mentioned that he would like to have Elizabeth and Peter join them here at the mansion. Possibly they could stay for several weeks.

Charles thought that was an excellent idea. He had not seen Elizabeth in quite some time and never baby Peter. Why not have them fly here from England. Planes are quite safe now, and there is a small airport near Rouen. There is also a suitable landing strip that could be used right next to the mansion.

After dinner, both men made their way to the library for their game of chess. One hour into the game, Charles moved his Pawn from B-2 to B-3 leaving his Tower on A-1 exposed to attack from Earl's Bishop on G-7 should his Pawn on F-6 be moved forward to attack Charles' Queen on G-4. Had Charles made a mistake, or was this a trap?

Earl studied this move for 5 minutes. He concluded that Charles had made a fatal mistake that would cost him a Tower and the game. He moved his Pawn from F-6 to F-5 attacking both Charles' Tower and Queen. Of course Charles had to save his Queen on G-4 by moving it away.

He moved his attacked Queen from G-4 to F-4 leaving the Tower on A-1 free for the taking by Earl's Bishop.

Earl immediately took the Tower by moving his Bishop from G-7 to A-1. Charles looked at Earl with the devilish look he often had during chess games.

Charles moved his second Tower from B-4 to B-8 check to Earl's King on E-8. With a Pawn on D-7 and E-7 a Bishop on F-7 and his Tower on A-8, Earl's King could not be moved and was trapped behind its own lines.

He had fallen into Charles' trap. His only possible move was to eat the checking Tower on B-8 with his Tower on A-8. But when Charles had moved his Queen to F-4 he also covered the B-8 square. If Earl ate the tower, Charles would be one move away from a checkmate. Earl had no choice but to abandon, and knocked over his King. Darn that Charles, he had won again.

"We should call it a night, my friend. We are both tired this evening. It has been a long day."

"I completely agree with you on that Charles. I will write a letter to Elizabeth before going to sleep."

Earl returned to his room and proceeded to write a letter to his lovely wife asking her and Peter to join him here at Charles' mansion in Rouen.

Charles in turn was writing invitations to some of his friends. He wrote to the antique dealers and jewelers that he knew in Rouen, inviting them to the mansion.

He told them that he urgently required their expertise to evaluate items that he had recently acquired. He would have the chauffeur deliver these letters first thing in the morning. The next day they would decide on what would be done with the jewels and artifacts.

Wednesday July 29th 1931. Following breakfast that morning, both men went about deciding the fate of the items brought back from Egypt.

Charles would look after the selling of the jewels and the gold coins. Proceeds would be split 75% for Earl and 25% for Charles. Earl objected, calling this split unfair.

Charles insisted being he would keep the three swords and the letters from Rome to military commanders in Egypt. These would not be sold and would be added to Charles private collection of rare artifacts.

Earl would keep the journal and papers written by the Roman soldier for himself. Those also, would not be sold.

Earl believed a lot of study would be required on these ancient writings before the true meaning of the Scrolls and Prophecies could be fully understood.

Both agreed, that for the time being, it would be wise and prudent for both of them, not to disclose anything about the Scrolls and Prophecies found at the cave in Cairo.

Even the discovery of the Roman soldier's journal and papers should be kept a secret. Either way, because of the mint condition of these artifacts, no one would believe the story or the discovery that was made.

That was enough work for the day and they decided to go horseback riding in the countryside before dinner.

Once the horses were returned to the stable, following an enjoyable ride, both men made their way to the dining room.

Their talk was centered on the Roman soldier. Both agreed that the story seemed far fetched and hard to believe.

Charles wondered why the soldier would have buried such valuable gems in the cave, instead of taking them with him. Being a history professor, Earl came up with a plausible explanation.

In the days of Caesar, when a Roman officer was sent abroad, he would have family living in Rome. This assured the Emperor of the soldier's loyalty. In those days, if a Roman officer was killed as he served abroad, his family in Rome would be taken care of by the Emperor himself.

Should that Roman soldier abandon the Emperor's service for whatever reason imaginable, it would be considered as an act of treason and would result in the slaughter of his entire family back home in Rome. Our soldier would have known this and had to conjure a plan to save his family.

When his Soul would have left for another world, his body would have died in the cave. Now, with both his sword gone along with the valuable gems he had possessed, and upon discovery of his body, his death would have been considered a murder committed during a robbery.

This way, he would have died serving the Emperor and his family back in Rome would be spared.

Charles admitted this made a certain sense, providing this entire story was true. They would leave it at that for the time being. Earl stepped out to the garden to smoke his pipe, and Charles joined him with some brandy a short time later.

They talked for a while and Charles decided it was time to call it an evening, leaving Earl alone in the garden.

Earl stayed a few moments longer observing the starry night sky. We wondered when Elizabeth and Peter would get here. God, he missed them and couldn't wait to be reunited with them again.

That evening during his sleep, Earl had a strange dream where he floated upwards through the mansion's roof and was riding the wind currents alongside a magnificent golden eagle.

The Surprise

Several days had past. Charles and Earl were looking over the writings in the soldier's journal, when Iris came in the library announcing a visitor.

"Monsieur De Bellefeuille is here to see you Monsieur."

"Show him in Iris" *replied Charles,* as he quickly hid the journal they were looking at. "Bonjour Bernard, please meet my friend, Earl Walker from England" *said Charles,* as they shook hands.

"A pleasure to meet you, monsieur Walker" "The pleasure is mine, monsieur De Bellefeuille" *replied Earl,* as the two shook hands.

"Well Charles, I understand you have some gems to be evaluated" *said the old jeweler.*

"I certainly do, my friend. Here, let me show you".

Charles took out the precious stones, as the jeweler looked on. The jeweler gasped in astonishment when Charles handed him the large ruby.

"Good Lord Charles… Where on earth did you find such a gem?" *asked the jeweler*, as he held the large ruby in his trembling hands.

The jeweler claimed he had never in his life seen such a marvelous ruby. He estimated the weight of the large ruby at 200 carats or more. It was priceless, the jeweler claimed! The large uncut blue diamond was also worth a small fortune.

"Too much money for my means" *said the jeweler*, as he shook his head. The Roman gold coins were rare items indeed. It would take an expert to say if the coins are authentic. Seeing the incredible mint condition of the Roman coins, most collectors would say they are fakes.

The jeweler advised them of an auction, taking place in Paris that September.

"It's the biggest event of the year in Paris. Rare, expensive items owned by society's elite from England, Italy and France are offered for bidding" *advised the jeweler.*

"These items should be offered at this auction," *said the jeweler.* "There, they would fetch what they are worth."

"Bernard, I would like to ask you a favor," *said Charles.* "I would appreciate if you could look after the inscribing of these items for sale at the Paris auction."

"But of course my good friend, with pleasure," *confirmed the jeweler,* as he shook Charles' hand.

"It was a pleasure to meet you, monsieur Walker," *said the jeweler,* as he bid goodbye to Earl by shaking hands.

As Charles walked Bernard to the door, Earl noticed him slip one of the gold coins into the jeweler's hand.

"Good news for you, my dear Earl. The currency used in that Paris auction will be in English pounds-sterling."

"The jeweler is a reliable, trusted friend of many years. I have full confidence in his advice," *confided Charles.* "Trust me we will do very well at that Paris auction."

All that was left now was to have the artifacts looked at by an antiquity expert, to prove whether the items were authentic. There was one such expert coming to the mansion within the next few days.

They would soon have an idea if the swords, coins and military dispatches from Caesar to Roman officers in Egypt were ancient and genuine.

The Surprise

The soldier's old journal and papers would be kept secret for the time being as previously agreed.

Both men spent the rest of the day talking about the writings by the Roman soldier. They questioned the possibility of an advance civilization having been here on earth such a long time ago.

Earl told Charles the story about a British explorer who gave a lecture at Oxford University several years ago. The explorer said that he had been trying for years to find evidence of the lost city of Atlantis.

He claimed that in 1924, during an expedition to British Honduras, a strange crystal skull was unearthed in an old temple near ancient Mayan ruins.

He showed the skull that was carved out of a solid piece of crystal. The jaw was separate and fitted perfectly onto the head part of the skull. It was a marvel to see.

One of the college Doctors, a metallurgist, examined this skull and concluded it was impossible for men to have carved this skull from a solid crystal.

There was no logical way to comprehend where such an artifact could possibly come from. The skull, in the Doctor's opinion, simply could not exist. Yet there it was!

The college staff often talked about this incredible skull. It bewildered all who saw and touched it.

Charles then told Earl of a legend that was included in a manuscript written by Sir Thomas More. Sir Thomas was a past Grand Supreme Master of the *Societas Mentis Secretum in the year 1529.

* Secret Mentis Society.

The legend spoke of a German King who was visited on the battlefield by three Archangels. They ordered the King to stop waging wars. The King paying no attention to this demand was killed by a bolt of lightning, right before the eyes of his army.

Two hundred years later it was said that Frederick the Great, King of Germany, following the seven year war (1756-1763) that helped make Prussia great, had a vision during a dream.

During this dream, those same Archangels in turn, ordered him to stop waging wars. This King had waged more wars than any other King in history. But he knew of and feared that old legend. He never waged war again.

It is believed that In 776, the King ordered the building of a monastery dedicated to these three Archangels. Its construction was completed in 777 on a site chosen by the King himself.

The Monastery was built at Beuron in the Swabian Alps. Why this specific location was chosen by the King remained a mystery.

It was however rumored that the location would have been requested by the Archangels themselves.

The King died nine years later without having waged another war.

"You know Charles there must be thousands of these stories and legends going back to the beginning of recorded history. They must all have some significance of a sort."

Well that was enough for the two men's imaginations for the day. They would call it a night.

The Surprise

During breakfast, Earl discussed the legends that Charles had related the previous night. He had thought about it before falling asleep. He found it a strange coincidence, that three Archangels are mentioned in the legends.

Furthermore, the King had a monastery erected in their memory in the year 777. Religion claims there are seven Archangels. The Soul Master, referred to by the Roman soldier, claimed to be from the seventh house.

"Do you know my friend, the more I look into this the more I am starting to believe the writings of that Roman soldier. I now really believe he existed 2000 years ago and that he did write the journal and papers that I have found. There are simply too many coincidences present here."

"My dear Earl, who knows what to believe, I for one never believed the legend about Frederick the Great, until I visited the monastery built in 777. I saw it with my own eyes. It's sitting there at Beuron in the Swabian alps."

"Please Charles. Don't ask me to visit that monastery."

"Certainly not, my friend" replied Charles, *laughing.*

"I have some business to attend in Rouen. Why don't you come along with me," *suggested Charles.*

"If you don't mind Charles, I will not go with you to town today. I would rather read more of your books."

"By all means my friend, please feel free to do as you wish. I will be back for dinner later this evening." *replied Charles.*

Earl walked Charles to the Bentley. He then made his way to the library. He wanted to read the manuscript by Sir Thomas More, one of the original members of the House at Oxford University in England.

He started reading Sir Thomas' manuscript. Well, the manuscript spoke of past members of the Societas Mentis Secretum. If one was to believe what was in this manuscript, it meant that Plato, Socrates, and many other great philosophers belonged to that same secret society.

As he read on and much to his surprise he discovered in the manuscript's contents, that Sir Thomas knew of that hillside location in the Swabian Alps and that he and other members of the secret society often visited that very place.

It seemed that the secret society of which he was the Grand Master often meet at this location for ritual purposes.

To hold such rituals in England would mean certain death for all members, as they would be declared heretics.

Sir Thomas described the great beauty of this valley bordered by steep hillsides, over which stood a majestic forest, overlooked by a small mountain. Sir Thomas claimed that in this valley, one could feel the presence of the Higher Powers. He had gone there to seek guidance.

Henry, King of England, wanted Sir Thomas to accept him as head of the English Church. Sir Thomas knew that refusal to obey the King's will could mean imprisonment and could lead to his beheading.

Earl stepped out in the garden to smoke his pipe when a police car pulled up to the mansion. Three *gendarmes, wearing side arms, stepped out and made their way to the entrance. They spoke with Iris and entered the mansion.

Earl wondered what was going on and decided to go inside to find out. I hope nothing has happened to Charles, *Earl thought to himself*, as he approached Iris.

* French Police.

"What is going on? Is anything wrong?" *Inquired Earl* obviously concerned.

"No Professor, everything is fine. Monsieur Bouthillier has hired round the clock security for the mansion. Surely this has something to do with your discovery in Egypt."

"Yes Iris, it must surely have to do with the discovery in Egypt." *replied Earl,* absent mindedly stroking his chin, as he considered this development.

It was nearing dinner time and Charles should be arriving from town, soon. Earl headed to his room to freshen-up for dinner.

Charles arrived and dinner was served. Earl made his way to the dining room greeting his friend as he sat down.

"Did you have a successful day in town, Charles?"

"Yes I did Earl, and did you do some reading."

"I certainly did but I was somewhat distracted by the arrival of the French police."

"Just a precaution, my friend," *replied Charles.*

Both men enjoyed a delicious meal that evening. There was a surprise for Earl. A good old fashioned fish and chips dinner was served that evening. Following dinner, both men made their way to the library for some brandy.

"I read Sir Thomas' manuscript today. What was his decision regarding the King's wish?" *asked Earl.*

"All Englishman should know what happened," *replied Charles.* Sir Thomas was jailed, and beheaded."

"Goodness, it means he died for a religious conviction."

"Many have done that over the years," *replied Charles.*

"Tell me Charles, do you think this security is really needed here at the mansion?" *inquired Earl.*

"Better to be safe than sorry as you Englishmen say. From what Bernard has told us. We may be sitting on a fortune here. No chances to be taken." *replied Charles.*

They discussed the other six objects found in the cave's cavity, the ones that Earl couldn't identify.

Charles could not explain what they were either. The items were certainly not artifacts and didn't seem to have any value whatsoever.

Charles had commented that those six items looked like some kind of rulers for measuring. Earl didn't agree because there were no numbers or scales showing on the items, but did agree that they looked like rulers.

Charles pointed out that there appeared to be a series of small dots forming several lines on the surface of the strange looking items. At a glance it looked like there could be hundreds of these dots and they all seemed to be nested evenly apart.

The items seemed to be made of glass or perhaps a crystal like substance and were not transparent. They had a bluish-black color and were very light in weight. They were about 2 cm wide by 15 cm long and the thickness was estimated at between 2 and 3 mm. All six of these items looked identical. They decided to put those items aside for the time being.

Following several brandies and long discussions, they agreed on calling it another day. Tomorrow, the antiquity expert would be here to examine the swords, coins and papers.

Tomorrow, they would finally know if the items found in the cave were authentic and ancient.

The next afternoon Monsieur St-Pierre arrived to inspect the artifacts. Charles thought it better not to disclose the origin of the items to be examined.

Following a formal introduction, Charles escorted Monsieur St-Pierre to the library, with Earl following close by.

Charles removed the items from the library vault, and placed them on a desk for examination by the antiquity expert. After a short period of examination, monsieur St-Pierre gave Charles a bewildered look.

"Well Charles, if I didn't know you better, I would have to say these items were probably stolen from the Vatican vaults in Rome. They seem quite authentic. The condition they are in would mean they would have been conserved in a safe place for many centuries.

The only place I could think of, capable of having such treasures in this condition, would be the Vatican. May I ask where all of these artifacts come from?" *The antiquity expert inquired suspiciously.*

"They have been in our family for many generations, Gilbert. I assure you that they are rightfully mine." *replied Charles*, seemingly insulted.

"Look at this Roman gold coin. Notice, it's slightly scratched. This means it's soft and probably has a pure gold content. These days, you could not find gold of that purity.

If we add to that, the likeness of Caesar on the face of the coin, then, we must conclude that it could possibly be 2000 years old."

"I see," *said Charles*, smiling at Earl. "And what about the swords and the military dispatches?"

"The papers are most probably clever forgeries. The condition of these papers, make it hard to believe that they could be authentic. They look new and it's improbable that they could be 2,000 years old. As to the swords, like I said previously, if I were looking at them in a Vatican vault, I could believe them to be authentic.

However here in your mansion, I really don't know what to say. You must admit, they look like they were made yesterday. I noticed the gendarmes when I arrived. A lot of security for a few gold coins"

"Thank you Gilbert, for your expertise and time," *said Charles.* "My chauffeur will drive you back."

"I don't trust this man one bit." *said Earl,* fearfully.

"Not to worry, my friend. He may seem a little strange, but rest assured, he is completely trustworthy. I have complete confidence in him." *answered Charles.*

"The Paris auction is a good month away, my friend. I suggest you take a few weeks holiday and relax here at the mansion. You certainly deserve a break after what you have just been through."

"You know Charles. I will take you up on that offer. You are right as usual. The expedition to find the cave in Cairo has been draining and a rest will do me good." *answered Earl with a sigh.*

"Excellent my friend, take two weeks off. I have a funny feeling we might have more to do than we anticipate in the coming weeks." *replied Charles.*

SEVEN

The Auction

Following dinner that evening, Charles, left for town to attend a meeting at the Rose-Croix lodge. Earl decided to return to his room to translate more of the prophecies.

As he started reviewing the papers that held the fifth prophecy, an intense headache manifested itself. His head was splitting with crucifying pain as he lay down to rest. After a short time he slipped into a deep sleep and began dreaming.

Meanwhile, Charles had arrived at the lodge for a secret meeting with three of the lodge elders. Charles went about explaining to the elders, the events that took place in the cave at Cairo.

Lodge brother, Picard, a man of profound religious beliefs suggested that this story should be brought to the attention of Monsignor Bellini, a high ranking Bishop at the Vatican.

Charles became furious as a heated exchange took place between the lodge brothers. Charles insisted that what was said during their conversation was private and should be kept a secret as to the tradition of the lodge.

"What is said and heard at the lodge remains in the lodge." *cried out Charles*, as his temper slowly slipped out of control.

Picard kept insisting that Monsignor Bellini should be told the story. "This was much too important not to involve the Vatican." *cried Picard.* Charles realized he had made a mistake disclosing that information to other lodge brothers.

Picard could not be trusted to keep secret what he had heard. As Picard was leaving the lodge, Charles, followed him trying to convince him not to repeat the story he had heard to anyone. It became more and more obvious that Picard would tell the Bishop.

As they left the building, Charles, removed a battle-axe from the old armor of a knight that stood at the lodge entrance. Once outside Charles delivered a crushing blow with the battle-axe to Picard's head splitting it in two.

*Mon Dieu, what have I done, thought Charles, as he looked around to see if anyone had witnessed what had just happened. There was no one around concluded Charles and being Picard did not cry out, no one would have heard anything.

The other two lodge brothers were still inside. They would know what happened, thought Charles. He had no other choice but to go back inside the lodge and dispose of the only two people who could incriminate him.

He really had no choice he convinced himself. He certainly didn't cherish a rendezvous with the guillotine.

As Charles walked back into the room, the two other lodge brothers were still engaged in conversation.

They gasped in horror when they saw the battle-axe in Charles' hand for it was covered with blood.

* My God.

"***No, Charles, please.***" They pleaded for their lives as he swung the battle-axe at first one and then at the other. It was a bloody carnage as the helpless men put up their hands in futile attempts to protect themselves and stave off the wild attack.

Many blows had been delivered before both men lay dead on the floor. Blood was spattered everywhere as well as all over Charles' body and face. He dropped the battle-axe to the floor and left the building without looking back as if this would erase from his consciousness what had just occurred.

It was a good thing that he had decided to drive himself in the Bentley that evening, *he thought.* He removed his blooded clothing, using them to wipe his hands before bundling them into a small car rug and driving back to the mansion.

All were asleep when he arrived at the mansion. He washed himself then dressed in fresh clothes. His next action was to place the blood covered clothes into the fireplace and start a fire to destroy the incriminating evidence.

Making his way to Earl's room, he had to tell him what had happened. "Wake up Earl, Wake up" *he shouted*, as he entered the room and shook Earl out of his deep sleep.

Earl woke up and clutched Charles by the shoulders, *and whispered in a trembling voice.* "Heaven help us my friend. How could you have done such a thing?"

Earl was shaking, and his grip on Charles was tightening. Charles was taken aback by Earl's comment. He stood back freeing himself from Earl's grip.

"What are you talking about my friend you were just having another one of your nightmares, you were sobbing and crying. I came in to wake you up." *replied Charles.*

Earl collapsed onto the bed holding his head in both hands. He felt he was losing control of his mind and was obviously frightened.

"My God Charles, I have had another one of those horrible dreams, and you were a part of it this time." *exclaimed Earl.*

"You must come down to the library and tell me about this nightmare." *said Charles*, as he helped Earl put on his bathrobe. "Some brandy will do you good."

Charles served Earl a large brandy which he gulped down, and asking for another. Earl was not his usual self, thought Charles. Could the events he experienced in that cave at Cairo have an effect on his brain, *Charles wondered.*

"Now tell me about that dream," *insisted Charles.*

Earl could remember the nightmare in detail. It was as if he had witnessed a real live event taking place. He went about describing the dream to his good friend Charles.

Charles paid serious attention to every details of the dream. It was as if he tried to analyze his fried's mind. By the time the dream was completely revealed, Earl had drunk four brandies, in quick succession and was now obviously in a calmer state of mind. He should sleep well now, thought Charles.

After helping his friend back to his room and putting him to bed, Charles returned to the library and noted the accounts of the dream in his daily journal. This would be the third of Earl's dreams that were recorded since his return from Cairo.

Charles observed that all of the dreams had a mixture of horror and distress. I will send for my Doctor, *thought Charles*, and will have Earl examined by him.

Charles knew that his friend had never visited the Rose-Croix lodge and yet in his strange dream Earl clearly described the knight's armor (battle-axe and all) that stood inside the lodge next to the entrance.

How on Earth could he know about this armor without having visited the lodge? *Charles wondered.* Could his friend, have possibly inherited some psychic powers, when he was exposed to those strange elements in the cave on Mokattam, mountain.

The next morning, Charles was having breakfast when Iris hurried into the dining room advising that the Professor was not well and seemed to be running a fever.

"Have the chauffeur drive to town and get the Doctor right away." *instructed Charles.* "We must have the Professor examined at once."

Iris hurried out to send the chauffeur to town for the Doctor as Charles made his way upstairs to Earl's room where he found him delirious and burning with fever.

"Bring some ice and cold water," *shouted Charles*, as Iris entered the room. "Right away Monsieur," replied the maid as she ran back down the stairs.

They both washed Earl down with cold water and placed ice over his forehead. Slowly his temperature returned to normal and he was now sleeping comfortably. It seemed like an Eternity, before the Doctor finally arrived.

"Bonjour Charles, what is wrong?" *asked the Doctor.*

"It's my friend from England, Doctor. He his not well Iris will show you to his room," *advised Charles.*

Iris quickly escorted the Doctor up the stairway to Earl's room. "This is Professor Walker, Doctor. He had quite a high temperature this morning." *advised Iris*, showing concern. "Fine, Iris. Please leave us alone now that I may examine the patient." "Of course Doctor," she replied, as she left the room and made her way downstairs to join Charles below.

An hour passed and the Doctor had not come down yet. Charles was pacing back and forth in the library obviously concerned about his old friend. At last the Doctor came down to talk with Charles.

"You have a sick friend up there Charles," *explained the Doctor.* "He seems to be suffering from some sort of delusions. Physically, there doesn't seem to be anything wrong with him. Is there anything I should know about him?" *inquired the physician.*

Charles reflected on what the Doctor had just said. He knew that both Earl and he had agreed to keep the discovery a secret. But here, Earl's mental health seemed to be at stake. The Doctor was a good and trusted friend.

He was also a lodge brother and was taken an Oath as a doctor to keep secret anything relating to a doctor-patient relationship. Charles had no choice but to tell the Doctor the entire story from beginning to end.

"You might as well sit down Doctor. It is a long story. I will have some tea brought in, unless, you prefer a brandy?" *said Charles*, taking in a deep breath. "Brandy would seem to be in order." *replied the Doctor.* Charles poured out two brandies and went about telling the Doctor the entire story from beginning to end. He also told the Doctor about the dreams or nightmares that Earl was having.

It was the Doctor's opinion that Earl was totally exhausted and had suffered a severe psychological trauma.

He suggested that for the time being, earl should stop reading and trying to translate those Latin documents from Egypt. A few weeks of rest and a change of activities should have his friend back to normal again.

"I must agree with your recommendation Doctor. My friend's wife will be arriving from England in three days. I am sure that being reunited with his family will do him good." *said Charles*, expressing concern.

"It certainly won't hurt him Charles," *replied the Doctor.* "When your chauffeur takes me back, I will give him some special medicine to bring to you. Place two or three drops of the medicine in his daily tea. This will calm his mind. He will feel tired, and he will sleep a lot."

"Rest is the best medicine, Charles, believe me." "Of course Doctor, the chauffeur will take you back."

Charles walked the Doctor to the door shaking hands with him as he left then made his way to the garden. He sat quietly in the garden contemplating on what had happened to Earl. 'Have I sent him to hell' *he wondered.*

He remembered reading about an Asian cult that practiced a form of mental projection called *Ki-Do or Chi-Do. They would draw a rectangular door on a solid wall using white chalk. One of the members would sit in front of the chalk door holding a handful of sticks in one hand.

Each one of the sticks represented an emotion or a life event such as love, hate, fear, pain, death etc…

* The way of the Soul.

The cult member would then pick the sticks from his hand one at a time and drop them to the floor. This until there remained only one stick in his hand.

The eyes remained closed during the entire ritual assuring the cult member didn't know which stick remained in his hand. Once the last stick was held, the practitioner would '*with closed eyes*' mentally visualize the chalked door until it would open. Then he would mentally walk through the door to face whatever lay on the other side.

It was said that many of the cult practitioners, who succeeded and penetrated the chalked door, went insane or committed suicide.

Charles wondered if Earl could have experienced Ki-Do, when he pushed his face through the wall of the cave and saw the other side.

Later that afternoon, Iris, prepared a tray with some home made soup, bread, cookies and tea. She brought them up to the Professor's room to serve him some dinner in bed.

As per the Doctor's instructions, three drops of medicine had been added to the tea.

"I have some food for you Professor. And how is our patient feeling this afternoon." *inquired Iris*, as she set the tray down on the bed.

"I am feeling fine Iris. Just a bit tired, that's all."

"Glad to hear that Professor, Monsieur Bouthillier, insists that you to stay in bed today. He will be up shortly."

This was the best borsch soup he had ever tasted, thought earl, as he finished his meal and drank his tea. He was feeling quite relaxed when Charles entered the room.

"You gave us quite a scare my English friend. The doctor believes that you have suffered a psychological trauma caused by your experience in Cairo. He advises that you should refrain from reading or translating the Scrolls you found and this for at least a few weeks."

"Nonsense, Charles. I feel fine. Just a bit tired that is all. I don't see how translating the Scroll Prophecies can hurt me in any way." *protested Earl.*

"I am sorry my friend but I completely agree with the doctor. I'm afraid I must insist on your obeying the Doctor's instructions to the letter. I have placed all the Scroll documents in the vault for the time being."

"Very well Charles. I trust your judgment on this matter and I will do as you and the Doctor say. For a few weeks anyway," *answered Earl reluctantly.*

"Good then! It's settled. Either way, Elizabeth and Peter will be arriving here in a few days and we will have a lot to do in preparations for the auction that is coming up in September. If you want me to, I will work on some of the Scroll translations for you."

"Yes Charles, I would appreciate it if you did that for me. The sooner the translations are finished, the sooner we will understand what it all means."

"Excellent my friend, you must get some rest now."

Charles then made his way to the dinning room for dinner. He had important visitors to the mansion this evening.

Sam Bernstein from the Rothschild group was here with an associate. They would be discussing world events and expected changes in world monetary policies.

It was beautiful outside that evening so Charles would propose holding that meeting with his guest in the garden following dinner.

Sam Bernstein was in the library having a drink with his associate Manuel Goldenberg. Both stood up and shook hands with Charles as he walked in. Following a brief chat, all three made their way to the dining room.

"We noticed you have armed security men on your estate, Charles… Having problems?" *inquired Sam.*

"No problems gentlemen, just precautions. Let us enjoy our dinner gentlemen." *replied Charles.*

"Our reliable sources tell us that Japan is planning to invade and occupy China. If Japan took control of China and its population, it could well create the largest and strongest army the world has ever seen." *said Manuel.*

"On that point, I would certainly have to agree with you," *replied Charles.* "However how would that affect us in Europe and in the rest of the world?"

"This would force each of the European countries to invoke the Kellogg Pact and would place all of Europe on a collision course with a possible war." *answered Manuel.* "Maybe even a world war."

"There is something else Charles," *interjected Sam.* "Our sources also tell us that possibly England and India are both on the verge of going off of the gold standard. If they do so, most of all the Countries will follow suite and suspend the exportation of gold."

"Well gentlemen, if what you are saying happens, gold will become a rare commodity indeed," *commented Charles*, unconsciously lifting both eyebrows as he spoke.

"Its value will shoot skywards and in contrast all hard currencies such as the Pound, the Franc, the Mark, the Dollar, the Yen etc…Would take a drastic plunge value wise." *Added Charles*, brandishing a serious allure.

"That's exactly the point we are making Charles. Fortunes will be lost by some and made by others. That is why we are advising our friends to begin converting their hard currency to gold before it's to late," *said Sam*, as he lit up a cigar.

"You know my friends, what we have discussed this evening brings to my mind a political report I read a few months ago by Joseph Stalin, a man I'm sure you have all heard of." *said Charles.*

"Let me tell you about this report. It was written last August when Stalin, was addressing the USSR central committee. In that report, Stalin claimed: 'That the world was facing a turning point and this not only for the USSR, but also for all the capitalist countries. We in the USSR are turning in the upward direction with a new and bigger economic upswing, while all of the capitalist countries on the other hand are turning downwards and are experiencing an economic decline.' Stalin claimed that last year. By God he was right, wasn't he?" *said Charles*, with a frown.

"We have to admit that Europe and the Americas are in financial and economical turmoil." *replied Sam.*

"Yes and what do countries do when this situation arises?" *exclaimed Charles.* "They wage bloody wars. History always seems to find a way to repeat itself.

"Well gentlemen, thank you for your insight and information. I know that you have a meeting scheduled tomorrow morning in Rouen with other associates."

"My chauffeur will drive you back to your hotel. Let us hope and pray that your information is wrong and that what we have discussed this evening never materializes."

Charles walked the two men to the Bentley, shook hands and bid them goodnight as the car drove off. He went to the garden, sat on a comfortable chair and pondered on what was said during dinner that evening.

If in fact governments do go off the gold standards '*Charles thought*' he would make a fortune as the bulk of his wealth is already secure in gold bullion and safely deposited in Swiss banks.

He just remembered that he had completely forgotten about having the meeting in the garden as previously planned. The discussions were so intense that it slipped his mind.

Charles found that the songs of the crickets were rather loud that evening. Tomorrow it will be warmer, *he thought.* After tomorrow, who knows?

Saturday August 9th. Charles had arranged with a close friend who owned a Bristol aircraft, to fly over the channel to England that morning. Earl's wife and son would board the plane and fly back to Rouen that afternoon. They would land on a small landing strip, situated close to the mansion on the south side of Charles' estate.

This would be the first time flying for Elizabeth and Peter. It was a clear sunny day. Perfect for flying over the channel that separates England from France. Earl was exited and anxious to be reunited with his love ones.

It was mid-afternoon, when Elizabeth could see Charles' estate from the plane. "Attach your safety belt," *cried the pilot.*

The pilot circled the estate prior to attempting a landing approach as if to give the passengers a last view of the estate's mansion from the sky.

This spectacular view from the sunny French sky left Elizabeth breathless. This was the first time in her life that she looked down on the Earth from above. She would always remember that moment, when the plane descended and made its landing. It would be burned in her mind forever. Here they were safe and sound on Charles' estate.

Earl and Charles were standing by the landing strip as the Bristol plane came in for a perfect landing. Earl had tears in his eyes as he saw the plane's door open and there appeared Elizabeth holding Peter in her arms. My God she is magnificent, *Earl thought to himself.*

He ran to her and holding her by the waist and with Peter in the other arm, walked back towards Charles.

"Welcome to France Elizabeth and son," *said Charles.*

"I'm so happy to be here my dear Charles." *she replied.*

"Did you enjoy flying my darling." *inquired Earl.*

"A fantastic experience," she answered. "You must try it yourself as I'm sure you would enjoy it."

Charles led his friends towards the mansion as the pilot passed the luggage to the chauffeur who loaded it unto the Bentley. Iris came running and took young Peter in her arms as they all walked together towards the mansion.

"I have prepared a folding crib for young Peter in your room." *advised Iris*, as she stroked Peter's hair.

"Thank you Iris for your care and concern." *replied Elizabeth*, firmly holding onto her husband's arm.

As they approached the mansion's entrance, Elizabeth noticed the armed guard at the door. She turned her head towards Charles, then back towards Earl. "What is going on here dear." *she asked.* "What's with this armed guard?"

"Nothing to be concerned about." *replied Charles*, "Earl will explain it to you when you once you are settled."

"Why don't you all go to your room and relax until dinner is served." *suggested Charles.* "We will have a lot to talk about during dinner this evening."

During dinner that evening the old friends reminisced about past times they spent together. Charles had a surprise for Elizabeth. Earl looked puzzled as Charles handed her a small box and told her to open it.

"What a beautiful ring Charles. Thank you so much." *said Elizabeth*, showing the ring her husband.

Earl looked in total amazement at the gold ring bearing the resemblance of Julius Caesar. It was magnificent. Charles must have had it made from one of the Roman coins he had brought back from Cairo.

Now he understood why Charles had slipped one of the old Roman coins to Bernard, the jeweler, after he had examined the gems, and was leaving the mansion's library the other day. "How can I ever thank you enough Charles, for your kindness." *said Earl*, as they vigorously shook hands.

"That is what friends are for," *said Charles*, as he slipped the gold ring on Elizabeth's finger.

"So Charles…Earl, tells me that we may be wealthy come the auction in September?" *said Elizabeth*, as she glanced at her new gold ring.

"He is absolutely right my dear. Come let us go to the library where you can see the gems and judge for yourself."

Charles removed the gems from the vault and set them on the table in front of Elizabeth. She seemed totally mesmerized by the large ruby.

"Surely this gem is priceless. What will it fetch at the auction?" *she inquired*, obviously exited.

"We can't be sure." *replied Charles.* "But the jeweler advised us that it is worthy of a King's ransom."

"I have more good news for both of you. My cook, Annett, as offered to act as a nanny for young Peter if you wish to go out alone together," *advised Charles.*

"I think we had better call it a night." *advised Earl.* "We can talk more during breakfast in the morning".

"Excellent idea," *said Charles.* "Following breakfast both of you should take the Bentley and visit Rouen."

"Thank you Charles, we will take you up on that offer." *replied Earl*, as the couple headed up the stairway.

"Perfect my friends and while you are visiting Rouen tomorrow, I will do some work here translating more of the Latin scriptures," *advised Charles.*

Elizabeth wanted to go to Sunday mass so they had an early breakfast the next morning before leaving for Rouen.

Charles had slept in late that morning, leaving his two friends enjoy breakfast be themselves.

They had a lot of catching up to do and it would do Earl a great deal of good to spend some time alone with Elizabeth

Following a late breakfast, Charles went directly to the library to start working on some translations of the Scrolls. He would start by translating the fifth Prophecy and with time permitting, he would also work on the sixth Prophecy.

Prophecy

- V -

Then by hosts to the Souls of the fifth house, the Father's power will be found. Then Mankind will have close at hand, abundance and peace throughout the land.

Charles could not decipher that Prophecy nor could he attribute it to any past or present event. It probably referred to a discovery that would be forthcoming in times ahead.

Prophecy

- VI -

Pity to humanity across this land, should this power fall upon wrongful hands. Soon after man will venture and stand far away on a newfound land. These will be signs that will show mankind a new era of a different kind.

The intrigue was now growing in Charles' mind. He would translate the seventh Prophecy to know more and possibly understand the meanings of the fifth and sixth Prophecies.

Prophecy

- VII -

Man will not know peace on Earth, but will be plagued by famine, sickness, war and destruction for as long as there are Demons on Earth governing Mankind. They will be called wicked and evil men, but they are in reality none other than the greedy hosts to the Souls of the sixth house.

Charles reflected on the three translations he had finished. He wondered if the power referred to in the fifth Prophecy could be gunpowder. 'Apart from laying railway tracks, how could gunpowder benefit mankind?' *He asked himself.*

One thing he knew for certain was that gunpowder had been used for war ever since its discovery in China in the 10th century. By the 14th century its military uses were well established all over Europe.

It has been the foremost military explosives for five centuries now and has had a profound effect on weapons and warfare. It could well be the power referred to in that 5th Prophecy. He would discuss this with Earl another time.

Enough of these scriptures for today, *thought Charles.*

The next two weeks went by quickly. Elizabeth did a lot of sightseeing with her husband. In the evenings Earl and Charles worked on translating the last six Prophecies.

Each was more complex than the other and harder to understand. Much study and discussion would be required to fully understand the meaning of what the Roman soldier wrote on those Scrolls 2,000 years ago.

Both men agreed that the last six pages containing the paradoxical text could indeed refer to the end of the World, and could well be a fourteenth Prophecy. Earl knew one man at Oxford who could possibly help in translating those pages.

"Well my friend we have no more time to devote to the Scrolls for now, as we will be leaving for Paris in a few days, *said Charles,* as he rubbed his hands together.

During the next few days, preparations were made for the Paris auction. All items were carefully wrapped and bundled for the short car ride to Paris. Four suites, next to each other, were reserved at the hotel Du Cadran facing the famous Eiffel tower. All rooms would be on the same floor. For security reasons two of the armed guards would watch over the artifacts at all times.

Friday August 28th. All were jubilant as they left the estate for Paris in the chauffeur driven Bentley closely followed by three security guards in a marked police car.

Charles lifted a glass and toasted, * "*La Bella Vita.*"

*The nice life.

EIGHT

The Reward

It was late afternoon when they arrived at the hotel Du Cadran in Paris. The sight of the Eiffel tower standing majestically overlooking the Champ de Mars never ceased to amaze Elizabeth. Paris was by far the most beautiful city in the world.

It was said that every time you return to Paris, you rediscover its beauty as if you had never seen the city before. It was an architectural marvel. Charles would always say: 'That, to live and not have walked in the streets of Paris, was to never have lived at all'. How right he was.

All of the four adjacent rooms were located on the third floor of the hotel. At least one of the gendarmes would stand guard outside the rooms at all times. The gems would remain in Charles' room until the auction was held at the Rodin museum on September 2nd.

Once installed in their room, the Walkers joined Charles in the dinning room. Following dinner, they went for a stroll along the Champ de Mars to enjoy the view of the Eiffel tower at night. Elizabeth commented about the huge illuminated sign for Citroen that adorned the Eiffel tower.

"What a shame to disfigure such a beautiful monument with an ugly advertisement for a French automobile."

"I must agree with you." *said Charles.* "It's been there for five years now. It is by far the largest billboard in the world. Many are trying to have the mayor remove it."

"The mayor should listen and have it removed from the tower." *she replied.* "It belittles the French Savoir Faire."

Did you know Elizabeth, that five years ago, a con artist by the name of Victor Lustig sold the tower for scrap, and this not only once but twice." *said Charles,* laughing heartily, as they made their way back to the hotel.

They would all call it a night and get some rest. There would be a lot to do here in Paris for the next few days.

The next morning, Charles was up early and having breakfast in the hotel dinning room, when a stranger sitting at the next table started a conversation with him.

"Are you here for the auction monsieur?" *he said.*

"Yes I am," *replied Charles*, "And you monsieur?"

"Yes monsieur, so am I." *replied the stranger.* "That is an interesting medallion you wear around your neck…May I inquire where it comes from?" *the stranger then asked.*

"It's a gift from a friend and I don't really know where its from." *replied Charles.* "And tell me monsieur, where do you come from?" *asked Charles,* suspiciously.

"I am Egyptian monsieur, and the reason the medallion attracted my interest, is that I saw a similar one in Cairo. Please accept my apology if my questions have upset you." *said the stranger*, as he stood up and left.

That's all I needed this morning, *thought Charles.* A nosy Egyptian, staying at the same hotel, who possibly knew something about the talisman and the cave in Cairo.

Charles left the dinning room and headed towards the front desk to talk with the hotel's concierge,

"That gentleman who is leaving the lobby, what is his name and what is he doing here?" *asked Charles*, as he slipped some folded francs in the concierge's hand.

"I will see what I can find out monsieur," *replied the concierge*, as he slipped the francs in his pocket.

Later that day, there would be a meeting at the museum with Bernard the jeweler. Preparations must be made for the advance showing that will be held the day before the auction. They must decide on the best way to present items for auction.

Charles' chauffeur picked up Bernard in Rouen and drove him to Paris for the meeting. Earl and Charles were waiting in the lobby as the Bentley pulled up to the hotel's entrance.

They got in the Bentley and made their way to the Rodin museum. Charles looked back and noticed a grey Citroen following behind. Could it be that curious Egyptian *he wondered.*

"Francois, there is a Citroen following behind. Take a different route before going to the museum that we may see if the car is following us." *instructed Charles.*

"Very good monsieur," *replied the chauffeur.*

"Is there a problem Charles?" *inquired Earl.*

"I had a curious encounter with an Egyptian earlier at breakfast." *answered Charles*, "Just being careful."

Earl looked back to see what Charles was talking about. Sure enough there was a car following close behind.

After several useless turns while driving, the chauffeur advised that the grey Citroen was indeed following them, and was certainly not trying to hide that fact either.

"Very well Francois, at least, now we know. You can head towards the museum now." *instructed Charles.*

As the Bentley arrived at the museum, the Citroen stopped for a brief moment then drove away. Charles had a good look at the driver. As suspected, it was the Egyptian.

As the three men made their way to the museum, Earl stopped for a brief moment and stood before one of his favorite sculpture by Rodin, 'Eve' it stood some distance in front of the museum. Then, a short walk later in the garden he admired 'the Gates of Hell' a real masterpiece.

Charles' favorite sculpture was of course. *Le Penseur de Rodin,' he even had a copy at his mansion in Rouen.

Once inside, they made their way to the exhibition hall where the auction would be held. Bernard had made a cabinet with a glass cover in which the artifacts offered for auction could be viewed. Charles and Earl approved of the location where the cabinet would stand. It will certainly look impressive with the two gendarmes standing by.

Bernard had spread the word about the large ruby and the rare Roman coins that would be on display. He also advised that there should be a lot of interest generated about these items at the pre-auction showing. A lot of questions would be asked about the origin of these artifacts. Therefore, answers should be well prepared in advance.

All that remained to be done now was the polishing of the uncut gems and coins. Bernard would stay at the hotel until the auction to take care of those tasks.

All was done there, so the three men made their way back to the Bentley.

Once back at the hotel, Charles had the chauffeur take Elizabeth on a quick tour of some of the sights in Paris before taking her back to the mansion in Rouen.

Charles and Earl had a lot to discuss so they found a quiet sidewalk café where they could relax as they talked.

"The assistant you had in Cairo. Any chance he could have talked about what you found?" *inquired Charles.*

"I don't think so, but you can never be sure can you?" *replied Earl.* "Are you worried about that Egyptian?"

"To be honest with you Earl, I am somewhat concerned about this morning's incident with that Egyptian."

"You are probably over reacting Charles." *replied Earl.*

"I certainly hope so. Either way, I have asked the hotel concierge to check him out for me," *advised Charles.*

As they returned to the hotel, the concierge signaled to Charles. They spoke for a few moments then Charles made his way upstairs to the rooms. Once there he instructed one of the guards to accompany Elizabeth and the chauffeur back to the mansion in Rouen. The guard was instructed to keep watch over the mansion until the auction was over.

Earl accompanied his wife to the waiting Bentley for the short ride back to Rouen. The gendarme opened the rear door for Elizabeth then he got into the front seat next to the chauffeur. Earl kissed his wife and helped her into the Bentley. "Do drive carefully Francois," *instructed Earl,* as he closed the car door. He stood there and watched until the Bentley drove out of sight. Then he went to his room.

He had brought with him from the mansion one of the unexplained artifacts found in the cave and carefully examined the increments of dots that Charles had noticed previously. But, he still could make no sense as to their arrangement. This had been an exhausting day for him and he suddenly felt very tired. Once in bed, sleep overtook him within minutes.

Earl was tossing and turning in his bed. His eyes were blinking in rapid succession. He was having another one of his nightmares... It was as if he was by himself in a strange cinema, watching a movie screen, while sitting in a chair that was floating well above the viewing room's floor.

There was a large Roman number showing on the very top of the screen and below that number, events were being observed by the dreamer. The Roman number was MMXXV.

The events observed seemed so real and lifelike yet Earl knew it was only a dream. He was so used to these nightmares by now that his subconscious accepted these dreams without causing him any discomfort or fears.

There was chaos and turmoil in that dream. There was fire everywhere, and earthquakes. Cities seemed to be sinking into the sea. Instead of beautiful clear sunny skies, it seemed to be hazy. A reddish color filled the sky and the sun seemed to be hidden by grayish clouds.

There were birds by the millions and they were feeding on human remains wherever the land was dry. It seemed as if there were no more humans or animals left alive. Those feeding black birds were huge and had red eyes.

Earl woke up wondering what was happening to him. Why was he having all of these nightmares and what do those dreams mean? He slowly drifted back into a peaceful sleep.

Morning soon came when he was awakened by a loud knock on the door. "Time to get up my friend." *cried out Charles.* "Meet me for breakfast in the dinning room."

"Will be down in ten minutes." *shouted back Earl.*

"Had another one of those nightmares." *grunted Earl*, as he sat down to breakfast.

After listening to the detailed recollection of Earl's dream. Charles mentioned the fact that, the birds eating at the flesh of corpses was once more present in his latest dream. It was obvious *'claimed Charles'* that those dreams or nightmares, would seem to relate to those last six paradoxical pages of the scrolls still left for translation.

"Either way," Said Charles, "We must put off discussing the subject for now. There will be plenty of time for that once the auction is over." "Agreed." *uttered Earl.*

Charles then told his friend what the hotel concierge had found out about the Egyptian. The man was asking a lot of questions about them and the items they would be offering at the auction. He was asking if anyone knew were the artifacts to be auctioned originated from.

It was now clear to Charles. Saadi, the assistant who had helped Earl excavate that cave in Cairo, had talked to others about what was found there. The secret was out. The question now was whether that Egyptian was interested in the gems or was the interest directed towards the Scrolls?

"I don't like this at all," *exclaimed Charles.* "That dam Egyptian really has me worried now. It's not much of a concern if he is after the gems or money. If however he is after the scrolls. Then, he could be a religious fanatic and that my dear Earl, could prove to be quite dangerous for all of us.

"There is only one thing that puzzles me." *Said Charles*, as he stroked his chin. "If in fact the Egyptian does know about the discovery. Then, how on Earth did he find us here in France?" *Charles now wondered.*

"I think I can answer that." *replied Earl.* "You see, I told Saadi about you and the mansion in Rouen.

"Well now, that certainly explains the Egyptian doesn't it. Now we have to wait and see what he is up to." *said Charles*, quite concerned with the turn of events.

Following breakfast both returned to Charles' room, were they found Bernard polishing the gems and coins. It was decided that all three men would keep together at all times while in Paris. Any displacements would always be made accompanied by one of the armed gendarmes.

Finally, it was the pre-auction showing day. Everyone, including the two gendarmes, left for the museum in a marked police car. Earl noticed that there was no Citroen following this time. Possibly, Charles had worried himself for nothing, *thought Earl.* They arrived at the museum at noon and had two hours to prepare for the exhibition that would be open to the public, from 2 to 6 in the afternoon.

Earl looked on as Bernard carefully set the items in the cabinet for viewing. The cabinet was lined with a black velvet cloth which created the proper atmosphere for the gems. Bernard had purposely set the cabinet beneath a fairly strong light, causing the gems to shine brilliantly.

The large red Ruby stood out and even seemed much larger as it lay on the black velvet lining surrounded by the smaller emeralds and diamonds.

The gold and silver Roman coins were marvelous to look at. There would surely be a lot of interest generated by the visitors today.

Charles had decided to show off his Roman sword by including it in the cabinet. However it would not be for sale, it was there for the sole purpose of giving the Roman coins authenticity.

Charles thanked Bernard for a job well done in setting up for the exhibition. The display was a real eye catcher. Specially, with the two uniformed and armed gendarmes posted at each end of the cabinet. All was ready for the visitors as they begun entering the exhibition hall.

Charles noticed the Chinese exhibition that was set up next to their booth. Fine artifacts from China were exposed for the visitors. Beautiful ancient pottery was being displayed along with some golden dragons offered for auction. He might bid on one of those dragons himself.

The Chinese lady at the booth caught Charles' eye. She was wearing a short, emerald green, dress that was split on each side showing off her great looking legs. She was by all means the most beautiful women he had ever seen.

She seemed so elegant and graceful that his heart pounded at the very thought of her. She of course had the attention of every man who passed by her booth.

He had to meet and talk with her. It was as if she already possessed his Soul. He slowly made his way towards the booth and much to his surprise, she spoke a fair but broken English.

Her name was Moon Zhang, and she was staying close by at the hotel des Saints Pères. Perhaps later, they could meet and share some French wine together, he suggested.

She didn't reply but smiled, keeping her eyes on him, until he had returned to his booth.

"All work and no play, makes for a dull, dull day." right Charles, *said Earl mockingly.*

"No comment my good friend" *replied Charles.* "Now where are all those interested visitors?" *he inquired*, giving Bernard a concerned look.

"Not to worry monsieur, they will come." *replied the jeweler,* as he proudly looked over his display.

Within minutes of the opening, the exhibition hall was half full with visitors. A good Omen, *thought Charles.*

Earl nudged Charles, as he saw a Roman Catholic Bishop walking close by. "His name better not be Bellini." *said Earl*, as both, he and Charles, chuckled inwardly.

Two elderly Englishmen approached the booth. Their attention focused on the silver coins bearing images of Marc Antony and Cleopatra. These two men were evidently experts and collectors of antique coins, thought Earl. They were from the 'Antiquaries of Newcastle' a society engaged in the preservation of historical artifacts.

"May we examine one of the silver coins," *asked one of the men.* "The coin bears the caption 'Antoni Armeni' on one side and 'Cleopatra regum filiorumque regum' on the other side," *said one gentleman to the other*, as both closely examined the silver coin. "This silver denarius would have been issued by the mint of Marc Antony somewhere around 30 B.C." *replied the second man confidently.*

"Thank you gentlemen for letting us examine this fine coin." *expressed one of the visitors.* "Your collection of Roman coins is in exceptionally good condition."

"I would even say mint condition." "Truly amazing!" *said the second man*, as they left the booth.

"Well Earl, this is good news indeed," said Charles, "if we were to judge by the figure of Cleopatra on the face of the coin. We would have to conclude that she obviously was not a beautiful woman. But these silver coins bearing her image are certainly beautiful to us. Aren't they?" *said Charles*, as he vigorously rubbed both hands together.

By 4 o'clock in the afternoon, the exhibition hall at the museum was swarming with visitors. The pre-auction showing was a big success and there were half dozen people standing around the cabinet looking at the artifacts.

One of the gentlemen, a grey haired man wearing a dark blue suit and sporting a monocle over his right eye, was conversing with Bernard, the jeweler. Charles was nowhere to be found. Where on Earth is he, *wondered Earl.*

As soon as the gentleman with the monocle left, Charles appeared out of nowhere. Bernard told him that he had just missed the man who was at the service of the Royals. That man was always present at these annual auctions and he showed a particular interest in the large ruby. "We should see some interesting bidding tomorrow," *said Bernard*, as he lit up a cigar.

Two men approached the booth and were looking at the artifacts to be auctioned. They were dark skinned and were speaking to each other in an Arabic dialect. Charles was scrutinizing them like a hawk. Surely friends of that nosy Egyptian, *Charles thought to himself.*

The pre-auction showing was only a half hour away of closing, when two unexpected visitors showed up.

That Bishop they saw earlier came over to the booth accompanied by a Cardinal. The Cardinal bent over the cabinet to have a closer look at the Roman sword that Charles had placed in the cabinet. He then whispered something in the Bishop's ear and came over to Charles.

"Tell me monsieur, where did you get that old Roman sword." *asked the Cardinal*, "and at what price will the auction bid start for that particular sword?"

"The sword has been in the family for generations, Eminence. It is only here for display purposes and will not be offered for auction tomorrow." *replied Charles.*

"I have seen many old Roman swords at the Vatican." *said the Cardinal.* "But only one that has the same three engraved letters on the cross-handle, as present on your sword. Have you ever had the sword authenticated by an antiquity expert?" *inquired the Cardinal.*

"No your Eminence, being the sword had been in the family for hundreds of years, it was always believed to be genuine." *answered Charles,* trying his best to hide the lie.

"It was believed that there was only one sword with those markings left in existence. Should yours prove to be genuine and if it could be traced to its first original owner, then monsieur, it would be priceless and would command a King's ransom. Should you ever wish to have the sword authenticated by our experts at the Vatican, feel free to contact us." *said the Cardinal*, as he gave Charles his card.

It was 6 o'clock and the visitors started leaving the exhibition hall as the closing of the pre-auction viewing was announced. Moon Zhang, that nice Chinese lady from the neighboring booth, came over for a quick look at the artifacts.

.

Charles accompanied Moon Zhang back to her booth as Earl and Bernard carefully wrapped the gems and coins. "Charles does seem infatuated with that lady doesn't he." *said Bernard.* "He sure does Bernard." *replied Earl.* "He sure does."

All were ready to leave as Charles returned to the booth. He asked Earl and Bernard to return to the hotel with the gendarmes. He would join then later on in the evening.

On their way back to the hotel Earl noticed the grey Citroen was following them again. "Charles should not have stayed at the museum alone," *commented Earl.* "There was not much you do about that monsieur. We both know that Charles is a bon-vivant. I would not worry about him." *answered Bernard reassuringly.*

When Earl entered his room, he noticed that the room was not as tidy as he had expected. When looking through the commode's drawers, he found that his clothing was not set the way he had placed them before leaving earlier. A quick verification of both Charles and Bernard's rooms showed the same messiness in all of the commodes. 'Someone had indeed searched the rooms' *he concluded.*

Earl was talking with Bernard when he heard the door in Charles' room open and close. Charles was back and not as late as expected, *thought Earl,* as he glanced at his pocket watch. It was only 20 minutes past 9. He walked over the see Charles to tell him of the un-invited visitors they had.

"Glad your back early my friend. We had some visitors that searched our rooms while we were at the museum." *advised Earl.* "I kind of expected that would happen." *replied Charles.* "Our Egyptian friends were looking for the documents you found in the cave. Good thing we left them in the vault back at the mansion."

"That grey Citroen also followed us back here when we left the museum." *Earl continued.* "That's no surprise either." *said Charles.* "Let us go downstairs for a brandy."

They left the room and invited Bernard to join them for a brandy in the hotel bar. The gendarmes would keep watch until they returned. Comfortably seated in the bar and sipping their brandy, they discussed the up-coming auction in the morning. After a few brandies they called it a night.

It was a bright sunny day that September 2nd when the Bentley pulled up to the entrance of the hotel Du Cadran. The chauffeur got out and opened the rear door for Elizabeth who was there for the auction.

"Merci beaucoup Francois." *said Elizabeth*, as she stepped out of the Bentley and made her way to the hotel lobby where the men were waiting for her. "You look ravishing darling." *said Earl*, as he kissed his wife.

"Well my friends. This is an important day for all of us." *said Charles.* "Today my dear Earl you will be a rich man."

The Bentley made its way to the museum with all aboard except Bernard who followed behind with the gendarmes in the police car. They arrived at the auction hall one hour before the auction was to take place. There would be a small reception for societies' Elite, where champagne would be served as the guests mingled prior to the auction.

Bernard was busy talking with the auction master while Charles was enjoying some fine champagne with the Cardinal and the Bishop he had spoken with the day before. Earl and Elizabeth were exchanging words with the gentleman who was at the service of the Royals.

Bernard had arranged for the artifacts to be auctioned off in five lots. The first lot would be the emeralds and sapphires. The diamonds would be the second lot offered. Third would be the 20 silver denarius followed by the 12 gold coins and finally the fifth lot would be the giant ruby.

The bell finally sounded announcing that the auction was to begin and inviting all guests to take their places. Upon hearing the bell, Earl couldn't help but think of Great Tom in the Tom Tower. "This auction bell won't ring 101 times." *he said to his wife,* as he took her hand and escorted her into the auction hall.

The prospective bidders were registered and assigned a numbered pallet to be utilized when a bid was offered. Earl was extremely nervous as he sat beside his wife who was as cool as one could be. "Relax darling. It's only an auction." *she said*, trying to calm her husband as Charles looked on.

The auction master stepped up to the podium and struck the mallet plate three times with his auction mallet and declared the auction open for bidding.

First off for bidding was a collection of fine oils paintings dating as far back as the 16th century. The next items for auction were some gold and silver dinnerware offered by an Italian Madame. Later on, when one of the solid gold dragons from China was offered, Charles successfully won that item with a bid of 350 pounds sterling.

Next up for bid was a magnificent unicorn sculpture that stood one meter in height and was made out of bronze. It was offered by Madame Berezowsky, a young and upcoming Polish sculptor. Earl had looked at the unicorn during the pre-auction viewing and thought of bidding on that item for his wife.

The bronze unicorn sculpture would look great beside their fireplace back home and he was sure that Elizabeth would love it. He won the bid at 150 pounds. The unicorn was now theirs. Finally! Earl's artifacts came up for auction…

With each bid closed by the third strike of the auction mallet, Earl's wealth was increasing along with his blood pressure. Elizabeth had now lost some of her previous coolness and was just as excited as her husband, who by now was close to fainting from the stress brought on by the auction. Charles on the other hand was quite calm as he and Bernard looked on with great satisfaction, at the events that were taking place on the museum's auction floor.

Bernard tried unsuccessfully to win the bid on the twenty caret blue diamond but was beaten by another French jeweler on that item. The bids on some of the gold and silver coins were won by the Cardinal from Rome. It was now time for auctioning of the large giant ruby.

The starting bid was set at 2,500 pounds sterling and had now reached 5,000 pounds. The English gentleman with the monocle on his right eye was into a bidding war, against a gentleman who was at the service of a rich Italian family.

"I have 12,500 pounds. Going once, going twice…sold to that gentleman with pallet number 8 for 12,500 pounds." *cried out the auction master.* The English gentleman had won the large Ruby for the Royals. The auction was over…

Earl and Elizabeth were now richer by fifty-three thousand pounds. "Congratulations my friend, you are now a rich man." *said Charles*, as he shook Earl's hand. Earl was somewhat in a state of shock. Elizabeth on the other hand was jubilant and was hugging Charles and thanking him for what had just taken place here in the museum's auction hall.

Charles decided that they should all leave Paris at once and return to the mansion in Rouen. Bernard would stay on in Paris with one of the gendarmes to take care of the arrangements, for shipping the bronze unicorn to England and to collect the promissory notes, payable to Earl for the sale of all artifacts. Once these tasks accomplished Bernard and the gendarme would return to the mansion in Rouen to join in on the celebration party that would be taking place later on in the evening.

With the three old friends sharing some Dom Perignon in the back seat, the Bentley made its way back to Rouen. The gendarme was sitting in front with the chauffeur keeping watch on the road behind. Much to everyone's relief, the guard reported that no one was following them.

NINE

The Aftermath

Upon arrival at the Rouen mansion, they disbursed to their respective rooms to freshen up before the evening's celebration party. Charles locked his Roman sword and his newly acquired Chinese gold dragon into his vault alongside the soldier's journal and papers which were already kept there for safekeeping.

The staff was busy in the mansion's impeccable garden, where a gourmet buffet table was being set up and preparations were underway for the celebration party that would take place a short time later.

A selection of fine cheeses and cold cuts would be served with some of the best wines from the mansion's wine cellar.

Annett, the mansion's Polish cook, had made a large quantity of Polish perogies and potato pancakes. These dishes were two of Charles' favorite entrées, especially when served along with strong red horseradish.

Several of Charles' Lodge brothers had been invited to the festivities along with their wives, thus assuring that Elizabeth would have many women to converse with during the evening. In all, over two dozen people were expected to attend the evening's festivities.

The party was in full swing, and the guests mingled with each other. However, they tried their best to take the opportunity to converse with the 'attraction of the evening', which was of course Earl the now rich archaeologist from England.

Many questions were being asked of Elizabeth by the women, being the curious nature of the ladies. These questions were mainly because they admired the ring that she wore, and which had been made from a 2000 year old Roman gold coin.

Two hours into the party, Bernard the jeweler and the gendarme returned from the museum. Then, after having all the promissory notes payable to Earl placed in the vault, Bernard and the gendarme joined the ongoing celebrations.

Charles was talking with Bernard who was busy helping himself to some Polish perogies from a dish on the table. Earl inquired about what was an unfamiliar food to him, *asking* "what is this dish that everyone seems to be so crazy about?"

"These are the most delicious treats you could ever eat," *replied Bernard enthusiastically.* "Try them with some red horseradish."

Well now! Earl had never seen perogies and certainly didn't know how potent the Polish horseradish could be to an unsuspecting person. So he boldly took a teaspoon full of the Red horseradish and placed it in his mouth as Charles looked on with amazement, and with a huge grin breaking out on his face.

"Ho Mother of God… I have been poisoned," *cried out Earl,* clutching his throat as his eyes filled with tears. Both Charles and Bernard were by now laughing heartily.

Elizabeth, concerned, came over to see what was wrong with her husband, who by now seemed to be gasping for air.

"What is wrong my dear," *she asked*, looking puzzled at seeing Charles laughing so much at her husband's discomfort.

"Your husband has fallen victim to Polish, horseradish," *replied Charles*, still unable to control is growing laughter.

Bernard and some of the lodge brothers were laughing so hard now that it became contagious and all joined in the fun.

Once Earl had finally regained his composure, Charles explained how this horseradish must be eaten in very small portions. (Which Earl had realized by now). And even when in small amounts, this should be eaten only at the same time as other food such as ham, cold cuts or perogies. Just like the potent English Mustard he was familiar with. Eaten alone it could easily be considered a remedy for clearing congested sinuses.

Elizabeth tried some of the Polish perogies with just a touch of the red horseradish and claimed that she had never tasted such a delicious dish before. She would ask the cook for the recipe so she could make some herself back home.

The hour was late when the evening festivities were drawing to an end. The guests were preparing to leave, and were busy shaking hands while bidding each other "goodnight".

Once all the guests had left, Charles gave instructions to the gendarmes regarding security for the night. Two guards would stand watch while the other one slept. They would rotate and replace each other every two hours.

With all the champagne and the wine consumed that evening, Earl and Elizabeth were ready for bed. Bernard the jeweler would stay over until the next day. Charles bid his friends goodnight and made his way to the bedroom.

Charles couldn't sleep well that evening. He had an uncomfortable feeling about the situation caused by that nosy Egyptian in Paris. It could prove disastrous indeed for all concerned if that Egyptian turned out to be a religious fanatic. Something told him that Earl should return to England with his family as soon as possible.

The cooler season was approaching, and this was just about the time of the year when he usually left for his summer cottage in Tuscany. He always spent the cold season in Italy. Maybe it would also be wise for him to leave for his winter retreat a bit sooner than he had expected.

Thursday September 3rd turned out to be a beautiful warm sunny day. At Charles' request, Earl and Elizabeth accompanied by Bernard and a guard went to meet with a banker at Rouen. All of the promissory notes from the auction that were made payable to Earl were handed to the banker, who in turn assured Earl that the Bank would collect all of these notes for him. They would then wire the money to his bank in England.

Meanwhile, back at the mansion Charles was copying all the Latin wording from the Roman soldier's journal and papers. This was so that he would have an exact copy of all of the Latin writings. He decided that he also needed to copy extracts from Earl's personal journal, in the hope of finding in them answers as to why his friend kept having those bad dreams.

The Bentley arrived back at the mansion with Earl, Elizabeth and the gendarme. Bernard had stayed on in Rouen.

"Did all go well with the banker," *asked Charles*, as he greeted his two friends. "Like clockwork," *replied Earl.*

The Aftermath

"Tell me Charles, why were you in such a hurry for us to do the bank transactions today?" *inquired Earl.*

"To be honest with you my friends, I fear that you could possibly be in danger, if you stayed any longer than necessary, here at the mansion. I have been informed by the security guards that the mansion was being watched for over a week now. This surely has something to do with the Scrolls discovery and the Egyptians. We shall discuss the situation following dinner this evening." *replied Charles.*

Later that evening, following dinner, Charles explained what he believed should be done and why it had to be done quickly. The Egyptians, without any doubt, knew about the discovery and they probably have a good idea of what was found in that cave. We must remember that there was a Legend about this cave and that this legend could also go back for centuries.

We must also conclude that possibly other's apart from Saadi's cousin, could have ventured into the cave and have experienced the bizarre happenings that went on there. Who knows how many before you could have tried to solve the mystery surrounding that cave.

During the auction's pre-showing, that Cardinal's eyes lit up when he saw the sword with the cross-handle markings. It wouldn't surprise me at all to find out that the Vatican knew something about that cave and its legends.

Unfortunately for us, you my dear Earl discovered what was hidden in the cave and it has made you a rich man. However, this could also prove to be a two edged sword. We have maybe not only one, but two religious fractions that are interested in what was found. Religion my friends, has caused the downfall of many a fine people over time.

I suggest that you both return to England by plane, and then they could not follow you. It would be next to impossible for these people to find you once you were settled in England. That is why I think you should leave here as soon as possible. As for me, I would go to my winter retreat in Italy until spring. There I would also be quite safe and hard to find.

With time this entire matter will blow over and we can go on enjoying life without any fear about our safety.

Earl and his wife agreed with Charles and would leave as soon as an arrangement could be made to fly them back to England. It was getting late and Elizabeth decided to go up to their room and spend some time with their son Peter before retiring for the evening.

Charles and Earl enjoyed brandies in the library while they discussed translating the rest of the prophecies. They would both work independently agreeing to exchange their findings and to keep in touch by mail.

It was decided that next April, Charles would leave Italy and go to England to stay with the Walkers for a month or two. With these decisions having been made, another tiring day was brought to an end. It was now time for rest…

Friday September 4th. It was raining that morning, as Charles' chauffeur drove over to Rouen's small airport to talk with the owner of the Bristol aircraft. He arranged for an urgent flight to England for the Walker family. The chauffeur upon his return advised Charles that all arrangements had been agreed upon. The Walkers would leave for England the next day at 14:00 hours.

All was now set for the Walkers departure for England.

Charles and Earl went to the library to sort out the artifacts that would be taken back to England by Earl. These included the Roman soldier's journal and all of the original papers written by the soldier. Earl would take three of the six items found in the cave that could not be identified. Hoping that maybe, his colleagues at Oxford could identify those unusual items.

Copies of the soldier's Journal and all the Latin writings found in the cave would be kept by Charles.. He would continue to work at completing the translations of the six remaining prophecies, and the paradoxical text that could possibly turn out to be a 14th prophecy.

Following dinner that evening Charles explained to the Walkers a plan he had made to mislead the Egyptians who were watching the mansion. The plane was to arrive at the small landing strip beside the mansion at precisely 14:00 hours the following day.

As a decoy, at 13:45 hours, Iris with her black hair covered by a foulard, accompanied by a gendarme, dressed as Earl, would get into the Bentley. With this done in full view of the Egyptian who would be watching from a distance, they hopefully, will think that it's you seated in the Bentley.

The chauffeur will then drive into town followed by a second gendarme driving the marked police car. We expect our Egyptian friends to follow the two cars into town.

If all goes right with our plan, you will then board the plane and be on your way to England without our Egyptian friends having any idea that you have already left the Country.

In town, the chauffeur will then do a couple of errands, leaving the fake 'Walkers' inside the car.

Meaning that when the Bentley returns to the mansion with the passengers still inside, the Egyptians will assume that both of you are still staying here at the mansion.

There was nothing left for the old friends to do now but relax as best they could, and enjoy each other's company for the short time they had left together. With few words being spoken, they sat in front of a roaring fire, sharing yet another bottle of vintage French brandy.

It was getting late so Earl and his wife decided to retire to their room. Charles remained seated in front of the fireplace until sleep overtook him.

Saturday morning had come, and Charles was still asleep on the chair facing the fireplace, when his tabby cat, Citrouille, jumped up on to his lap waking him up with a start. He glanced at his pocket watch and saw that it was eight o'clock.

He could hear muted conversation coming from the kitchen. Curious, he made his way there and saw that it was Elizabeth and Iris chatting away over coffee and crêpes. However, not wanting to disturb them, he quietly made his way upstairs to freshen up.

A short time later Elizabeth went upstairs to pack their belongings for the flight back to England. Earl had just woken up and was getting ready for their last lunch with Charles at the mansion. It would not be until the following spring before the old friends would find each other together again.

Earl was in no way keen on flying. 'It's amazing how fast time goes by when you don't want it to' *he thought to himself*, as they finished lunch and it was almost time to go.

The plan was set in motion. Iris 'wearing the foulard' and holding the gendarme's arm, walked to the Bentley.

The Aftermath

The chauffeur was waiting with the rear door open covering them from full view, as the couple stepped into the automobile. The chauffeur closed the door and walked around to the other side, got in and drove away with the marked police car following close behind. With great relief they watched as the Egyptians followed the two cars as they left the mansion and they were fully expected to continue their pursuit into town.

Ten minutes later the Bristol aircraft made a pass over the mansion and prepared for a landing approach. Earl was trembling as he saw the aircraft turning in the sky and then come in for a perfectly smooth landing.

Elizabeth hurried to the aircraft carrying young Peter as Charles and Earl followed with the couple's luggage. Earl helped his wife and son onto the aircraft as Charles passed the luggage up to the pilot.

The two old friends exchanged brotherly hugs and then Earl turned and climbed up and into the aircraft. Elizabeth blew a kiss to Charles as the aircraft lifted off from the mansion grounds.

Charles stood watching the aircraft fly away, until he could no longer see it in the French sky. He had arranged for the pilot to circle Paris a few times before heading towards the English Channel. He wanted his friends to see how magnificent Paris was when seen from the sky.

When the aircraft reached Paris and was preparing to circle the area surrounding the Eiffel Tower Earl sat quietly watching every move the pilot made. As the craft tilted into a circling pattern Earl got extremely nervous and gripped his wife's arm. Elizabeth gently patted his hand to comfort him as she held back showing her own anxiety.

The pilot advised the couple, that if they looked out the left side of the aircraft, they could see a bird's eye view of the Champ De Mars located below. Encouraged to do so by his wife, Earl looked down and marveled at the sight the Eiffel Tower when viewed from the sky.

Suddenly the fear he had of flying dissipated and a peaceful calmness set in for the rest of the flight back to England. The couple's excitement grew as the English Channel came into view.

Meanwhile back in Rouen, Charles was being informed by the gendarme, who followed the Bentley earlier, that the grey Citroen, containing the Egyptians, had indeed followed them. They had followed them at a short distance, from the time that they left the mansion until their return. 'That was excellent,' *thought Charles.* It was assumed that the Egyptians still believe the Walkers are here, when in fact they are no longer on French soil.

Later on that evening, Iris confided to Charles, part of the conversation she had with Elizabeth in the kitchen earlier that morning. It seemed that Earl was not acting like himself any more and this worried her. During all the time here together at the mansion, her husband never came to her once and that was not like him at all. Elizabeth also mentioned that Earl was now talking a lot in his sleep and that it sounded like he would be talking in Latin.

Meanwhile, the Bristol aircraft was into its final approach to the landing strip at the Oxford airport. The Walkers clapped and cheered as the pilot executed a perfect landing. They were home at last. They disembarked, thanked the pilot and took their luggage to a waiting taxi. 'It's good to be back in England,' *thought Earl*, as they headed home…

Later, Charles sat in the library with his brandy, which was the only comfort he had for the moment. He thought about the extraordinary events that had recently occurred, especially things that had been revealed since his friend had returned from Egypt. He thought about what Iris had recalled to him earlier and of the strange dreams his friend was having. He would end that evening in Iris' arms…

Charles woke up and looked at Iris who was still sleeping peacefully by his side. She looked so beautiful lying there naked before his eyes. She was intelligent, beautiful and sexually appealing, but she had one troubling problem. She was a chronic alcoholic.

This tiny, exciting and passionate woman could easily drink any man under the table. To make things worse, once enough alcohol was ingested, she would keep on talking and repeating the same things over and over again.

This idiosyncrasy drove him crazy. He had tolerated her behavior for some time now. It wasn't her fault, *he would say to himself.*

She came from a family of alcoholics and this problem was part of her genetic inheritance. Her Father and two brothers were even worse than she was. Iris had told him the story about her family, so many times before, as if to justify her irrational conduct when under the influence of alcohol. At times she even had to be helped to her room.

He really cared about this woman but realized that he should consider ending this relationship and sending her away. With each passing day is patience was wearing thin.

He gently climbed out of bed and walked to the window overlooking the garden.

Birds were chirping and several of them were having their morning bath in a water fountain situated close to a flower bed in the very center of the beautifully manicured garden.

His tabby cat Citrouille was well hidden in the flower bed stalking the unsuspecting birds. The cat was over ten years old now making him to be over sixty years old in human terms.

However, he no longer had the required energy to chase the birds. So now, he simply contented himself by watching them from a distance, and dreaming of the days gone by when he could catch them.

Charles loved nature, he could often be found observing all of the living creatures created by the Great Architect up above.

Following a hearty breakfast he had a horse saddled and he went riding in the country side. He enjoyed the peace and quiet experienced when riding one of his beloved horses. Many important decisions in his life were taken while he rode along the country side bordering his mansion.

He started thinking of Moon Zhang, the Chinese woman he met at the auction. He wondered what it would feel like to be in her arms. Simply thinking of her again made his heart pound once more.

When they last spoke, Moon had told him that she would be staying in Paris for another week.

This could have been an invitation, *he thought*. He would go to Paris in two days and find out.

As he rode back towards the stables he thought of his cat watching the birds earlier that morning, and he remembered what the Roman soldier had written about the animals having Souls of their own. He wondered if this could be possible.

He decided that as soon as he got back to the mansion, he would read the soldiers writings again and work on translating the last six Prophecies.

Charles left his horse with John, the groom, and made his way to the mansion passing by Francois who was occupied washing and waxing the Bentley. Once in his library, he read his copies of the Roman soldier's writings.

The Soul Master had told the soldier that animals were the fourth living creatures to appear on this land and that they were host to the Souls of the fourth house.

From what was written, they would seem to have immortal Souls and would reincarnate here on Earth time after time. Charles had also always believed that animals possessed a Soul. He would now go about translating more of the Prophecies.

Prophecy
- VIII -

The day will come when the old and the weak will be cast aside by the young and strong. For the young, in great numbers, will have seen through false promises made across these lands by governing powers that lie and deceit. For they know and fear that the end of their reign is soon to be near. These false Kings let it be known, are none other then host to the evil Souls of the sixth house.

Much reflection would be needed in order to begin understanding that confusing Prophecy. Charles certainly couldn't make any sense as to its possible meaning. As he read through the Latin wording of the next Prophecy, he found that this particular one made no sense at all.

Prophecy

- IX -

Then the day will come when the big powers of the World with all of their might, will fall helpless to small numbers of men. For these men of small numbers will have with time, become the most evil and dangerous of hosts to the Souls of the sixth house.

How could the big powers of the World be overcome by a small number of men, this seemed absurd and totally illogical, *to Charles.* Then when reading the next Prophecy to be translated, he couldn't believe what he was reading. That tenth Prophecy not only made sense, but could be a revelation that would astound all who understood it.

Prophecy

- X -

There can only be peace on this land when none could be found to host a Soul from the sixth house, and that mankind no longer be burdened by the mark of its number of six for each of the three far away lands from whence they came 360,000 cycles past.

This tenth Prophecy could be interpreted as a passage from the Bible, and as far has he knew, there was no record of any Biblical writings 2,000 years ago. If the date of these writings by the Roman soldier could be authenticated, they would change the very concept of all existing religions.

This Prophecy could disrupt and even destroy beliefs that had been engrained in the philosophy of mankind for centuries. It could cause turmoil amongst religions. It would also indicate that this so-called Soul Master would have been in contact with many others, before and after, the encounter with the Roman soldier in that cave 2,000 years ago.

In his journal, the Roman soldier wrote how the Soul Master would meet with mortals on mountain summits. In most of religious folklore, their respective prophets met their Gods on mountains. The Christians believe that Christ addressed his disciples, for the last time, on a mountain side before ascending to his Father's house. To confirm this text Charles took an old Bible from his library, opened it to Revelations and compared the tenth Prophecy to the following passages.

– *REVELATION 13* –

13:16 – And it puts under compulsion all persons, the small and the greats, and the rich and the poor, and the free and the slaves, that they should give these a mark in their right hand or upon their forehead, 17: And that nobody might be able to buy or to sell except a person having the mark, the name of the wild beast or the number of its name. 18: Here is where wisdom comes in: Let the one that has intelligence calculate the number of the wild beast, for it is a man's number; and its number is six hundred and sixty-six...

There was no longer any doubt in his mind. The three numbers of six was present in both the Prophecy and the passage from Revelations. Now he knew that his friend had indeed been exposed to an unexplained force that possibly altered his mind causing him to have those weird visions.

He felt a cold shiver creep up and down his spine when he realized the full extent and the consequences that could emanate from these findings. The discovery made in Cairo was without a without doubt so significant, that it placed in peril all persons that would become aware of its content.

He would write to Earl in England warning him of the dangers that could be encountered by his family, if he exposed those findings to other parties. In that same letter Charles would also include all the translations he had just completed.

Suddenly he was disturbed by Francois, his chauffeur, who came running into the library announcing bad news. Iris had over consumed again and had passed out in the garden.

"That's the last straw!" *shouted Charles.* He had warned her enough times. Now, she would have to go. He went to the garden and picked her up. He then gently carried her to her room and put her into bed, she being totally oblivious to what was happening to her. He covered her with a blanket and then returned to the library. Iris' behavior had upset him once more.

He recalled of how he came to know Iris and of how they first met. It happened several years ago in a posh casino in Marseille. He was playing at the roulette table and Iris who was seated next to him, was using an irrational method of play which was causing her to lose consistently. He struck up a conversation with her and suggested that she change her method of play.

Following their session, they ended up at the bar where a serious discussion was undertaken to improve her method of playing at the roulette wheel.

They started playing roulette together as a team and shared the profits equally. They played several times a week for three consecutive months and had acquired a substantial amount of playing capital. One day Charles invited Iris to accompany him for a long week end at l'Auberge des Trois Canards, in Marseille. She accepted and from that week end on, they became a couple.

It was during that week end that he became aware of her drinking problem. She would drink two or three Brazilian coffees before he had even finished drinking one glass of red wine. Their first night together, he had consumed so much wine trying to keep up with her, that any attempt at love making on his part proved to be futile.

He had considered ending this liason on the spot, but Iris did have a certain exotic charm and he succumbed to her obvious passion. Her passion did reward his patience over time, and they enjoyed a relationship as a couple for a full year.

During a winter holiday on a secluded Caribbean Island, they mutually agreed to end their relationship as a couple and from that moment on they would only consider themselves as friends and nothing more.

Because of the harsh economic situation facing everyone across Europe during that period of time, Charles agreed to keep her on as a maid at his mansion in Rouen until she could find another source of revenue. On occasions he would weaken and would find himself in her room and in her arms, but he now realized that it would be better all around if he sent her away…

There would be no more work done on the translations for that day. He placed all the copies of the soldier's writings back into the vault and he poured himself a brandy. He needed to get away from the mansion for a few days and decided that he would leave for Paris in the morning.

The next morning the chauffer had prepared the Bentley for another trip to Paris. Ten short minutes after leaving the mansion grounds, the chauffeur advised Charles that the grey Citroen was not following them. This confirmed what Charles had suspected that the Egyptians were only interested in the Walkers.

"Where do you wish to go in Paris?" *asked the chauffeur.*

"Take me to the hotel des Saints Pères," *instructed Charles.*

"Very good Monsieur." *replied Francois*, as he drove on…

Monday September 7th. It was mid-afternoon when the Bentley pulled up to the hotel, des Saints Pères, in Paris.

"Francois, go into the hotel and inquire if Madame Moon Zhang is still a registered guest. If she is, then book us two rooms for this evening," *instructed Charles.*

"Very good Monsieur," *replied the chauffeur.*

Several minutes later, the chauffeur returned to the Bentley advising that Madame Zhang was still at the hotel and that the two rooms requested were booked for that evening.

The hotel concierge took the luggage and brought it up to their rooms. Charles made his way to the front desk and asked for Madame Zhang's room number. She was staying on the second floor but had gone to the museum that morning and hadn't yet returned to her room.

Charles took a comfortable chair facing the entrance in the hotel's lobby and waited for her return. Half an hour had passed when she finally arrived at the hotel.

Her face lit up at the sight of Charles standing there waiting for her. He kissed her hand and invited her to join him for a walk in the Champ de Mars. She accepted and they both left the hotel lobby talking and smiling at each other. It was now obvious to Charles that the chemistry and attraction he felt towards Moon was reciprocal.

They shared dinner at a nearby terrace and talked together until late that evening. They agreed to meet for breakfast the next morning as they still had a lot to talk about. He walked her back to the hotel and escorted her upstairs to her room.

He kissed her hand once more and gave her a warm hug then headed to his room. He had a feeling of exaltation as he never felt before. 'Had he finally found true love,' *he wondered.*

Charles woke up feeling exceptionally fine the next morning and quite anxious to see Moon at breakfast. They had set a time of 9 a.m. to meet in the hotel's restaurant. He arrived there 15 minutes early to make sure that she would not be left alone waiting for him.

When Moon came in to the lunch room she was wearing a long dress that molded her body from neck to ankle. The dress was of a sea blue color with red and yellow flowers and had a gold Chinese collar that fitted tightly around her tiny neck.

Most of the gentlemen having breakfast that morning turned their eyes in her direction to have a second look at this oriental beauty. The sight of her standing there was breathtaking.

Charles moved towards her and kissed her hand, causing a slight blush on both of Moon's cheeks. She told him that no man had ever kissed her hand before and that she had never met such a polite and distinguished gentleman in all of her life. Following breakfast they left the hotel to do some sight-seeing. Charles had given the chauffeur the day off and would drive the Bentley himself. He took Moon on a long drive showing her some of Paris' historical sites

After driving the Bentley back to the hotel's parking, both walked together once more on the Champ de Mars grounds. But this time Moon tenderly held onto Charles' arm as if she didn't want to lose this newly found male friend.

During the long and interesting conversations exchanged between them that day, they had gained a lot of information about each other. Both were starting to feel a lot closer to one another. They shared another dinner at a secluded, romantic terrace and then returned to the hotel and enjoyed some fine wine from the hotel's famous wine cellar before each going to their respective rooms. They would meet again the following day…

Charles sat on the edge of his bed thinking of what Moon had disclosed to him during the past two days. She explained how her father, *back in China*, sent her to France because he feared the Japanese would soon invade China. She was not to return home to China unless asked to do so by her father.

She had also told him that she was married into a loveless marriage and had a young daughter who was still in China. She and her husband had lived apart for the past four years. Chinese men didn't know how to treat a woman well or consider what could be their desires. She also admitted to having never enjoyed any passion whatsoever with any man.

In the Chinese culture, once you marry a man it is forever and even if you live apart and don't care for each other, you can never marry again. There is no such thing in China as a divorce so you are married for life. Any other way would be disapproved by others and would bring disgrace to the entire family. Leaving China and her husband behind to come to France was nothing short of deliverance for her.

Moon admitted that she already cared more for him than she had ever cared about any other man before. She told him in all honesty and sincerity that he could have and take her if he wanted, but that they could never marry.

Moon was fifteen years younger than he was and yet she spoke with maturity and with such a soft and quiet voice that it inspired confidence to anyone listening. When she touched his arm or his hand, he could feel a special tenderness and gentleness such as he had never felt in all of his life.

He already cared more for this woman than any other he had ever known or been with in the past. She was by far the most appealing woman he had ever crossed paths with and he believed his destiny was to be by Moon Zhang's side…

Wednesday September 8th turned out to be a beautiful warm and sunny day. 'What a fine day to start a new life.' *thought Charles*, as he knocked on Moon's door.

"Good morning Madame," *said Charles*, as Moon opened the door.

"Good morning to you Monsieur," *replied Moon*, tenderly touching his cheek, with her soft and slender hand.

"Would you join me for breakfast at the Eiffel Tower's terrace," *said Charles*, as he gently caressed her hair.

"I would love that more than anything in the world," *she replied*, holding onto his arm as they walked down to the lobby and then out onto the street.

Once outside, he placed his arm around her pulling her in close to him as they walked towards the terrace. They shared their second breakfast together as they exchanged their inner thoughts between themselves. The more they talked the more they discovered that they liked each other. She told him that the money received from the auction was hers to keep. Her father had purposely sent those items for auction to France. This was in order to allow his daughter to establish herself and start a new life in Europe. Her father loved her and wanted the best for her.

In order to show Moon some of the interesting 'tourist' sights, they spent some very enjoyable time driving around the streets of Paris. Finally Charles drove to the outskirts of town and stopped on a hillside that offered a fantastic view of the city. Moon moved in closer to him and placed her head against his shoulder gently touching his knee with her right hand. He then told her that he wanted her to come and stay with him at his winter retreat in Tuscany.

She looked at him with tears in her eyes and joyfully accepted his invitation. Moon was now trembling as she tore open her blouse and with closed eyes whispered to him.

"Touch me Charles, please touch me,"…

He reached out and caressed her warm and tender breasts as he kissed her quivering lips for the first time. This had happened so suddenly and unexpectedly that he felt somewhat embarrassed by his behavior. Charles apologized for acting in such an un-gentlemanly way and Moon countered with her own apology for having been so bold and demanding.

Sharing no words, she held on to his arm as he drove back to the hotel. When they got back, he walked her to her room and suggested that he should return to his own room, but she gently took his hand and led him towards the bed.

They kissed and touched each other until the passion became unbearable. He slowly undressed her, picked her up in his arm and placed her on the bed.

She was crying and spasmodically shaking when he took her for the first time. She in turn gave herself in total and complete abandonment. They made passionate love to each other with a frenzy that neither of them had ever experienced before. He took her time and again and when he tired she in turn took him. They made love to each other for hours, until total exhaustion set in. It was dawn when they finally fell asleep in each others arms.

Later that afternoon they made plans for the trip to Tuscany. Moon had arranged for the museum to handle the collection of the money due her from the auction sale. She would receive payment in three days.

Charles had unfinished business to tend to in Rouen so he would pick her at the hotel the following Monday. Then, they would drive to Italy, thus allowing her to visit various European Cities along the way.

Moon walked Charles over to the waiting Bentley. They held each other close and kissed once more before he left. As the automobile pulled away he could see tears falling freely from her beautiful Asian eyes…

It was late that evening when the Bentley arrived back at the mansion in Rouen. Charles went to the library and contemplated what had to be done within the next few days.

He would arrange the same scenario with Iris and the gendarme. They would impersonate the Walkers and leave the mansion grounds in the police car and go to the small airport in town.

This time the guard would be holding a fake child wrapped in a blanket leading the Egyptians to believe, that the entire Walker family left the grounds in the police car.

Then Iris, the guard and the fake child would board the Bristol aircraft and fly the short distance to Paris. If the Egyptians followed them "*as they would most probably do'* then they would conclude that the Walkers were gone and there should be no more surveillance of the mansion by the Egyptians.

Once in Paris, Iris would live at her brother's place. Charles would give her a six months' severance pay thus allowing her time to re-establish herself in a new life.

The guard would make his way back to the police station in Rouen to resume his duties, as that would be the end of the Egyptian's siege on the mansion. No more gendarme protection would be needed.

Charles decided that once installed in Tuscany with his new found love, he would not do any further translations of the Roman soldiers' writings. He would finish translating the last three Prophecies here in Rouen, before leaving for Italy.

The care of the mansion, until the spring, would be left in the capable hands of his cook Annett and her husband John, who already cared for the grounds and looked after the horses.

The past few days proved to be exciting and tiring and it was time for rest. He fell asleep thinking of Moon Zhang, his new found love. He couldn't wait to be with her again…

The Aftermath

Several days had past and all had worked to plan. Iris and the security guards were gone and the Egyptians had quit their surveillance of the mansion. Much to Charles pleasure and relief all seemed to be back to normal here at the mansion. He would now work on translating the last three Prophecies.

Prophecy

- XI -

From the slaves of the land, and at a time of great turmoil across all lands when too many hold the secret to the Father's power, a second King will emerge. This King will reign over the strongest power of all the surrounding lands. This will be your kind's last and only chance to create a lasting peace and harmony throughout all of the lands. This newly found King will be host to a Soul from the fifth house and his burden will be plentiful.

Charles could see in this eleventh Prophecy, the possibility of another biblical reference. Mosses freeing and leading his enslaved people out of Egypt could easily be associated to that Prophecy. However once again he had to question the fact that he knew of no biblical writings having existed two thousand years ago. There was of course a strong possibility that the story of Mosses could have been circulating in those days.

Seeing that he couldn't recall from his knowledge of past history where any other person, who had been issued from slavery, had risen to be a powerful figure of any sort, Charles therefore concluded that this eleventh Prophecy must refer to a forthcoming event sometimes in the future.

Prophecy

- XII -

Many powerful hosts to Souls of the sixth house will fear this new found King and his demise will be sought after. With time, and when two legged dogs can be seen hopping about the land, multitudes of hosts to Souls of both the fifth and sixth houses will grow weary of the new found King and his removal by any means will, in utter secrecy, be contemplated.

Prophecy

- XIII -

Should this new found King fail to accomplish sought after peace and harmony across the lands, then from the Kings of surrounding lands, a final conflict will arise. These King will unleash chaos and devastation upon all living creatures of the land. The victor will be host to a Soul of the sixth house that came from the smallest of the faraway lands 360,000 cycles past. The victory will be short lived and your cycle of life will end and begin anew as it has done before since the beginning.

The last two Prophecies that had been translated made no sense at all to Charles. He had finished all of the Latin text translations that he had pledged to do. The remaining six pages that were left for translation turned out to be just as confusing as the previous ones. His friend Earl, in England, was responsible for the translation of those six paradoxical pages. Those pages could well hide a fourteenth Prophecy.

After a few well deserved brandies, he made his way to the bed room…

The Aftermath

Monday September 14, 1931. Charles wrote a last letter to his friend in England, enclosing the translations of the last three Prophecies that he had completed.

After all business with regards to taking care of the mansion had been dealt with, he was ready to leave for Paris, where Moon was waiting for him.

So after he gave his final words and instructions to the caretakers of the mansion, he made his way towards his automobile. This would be the first time that the Bentley would undertake such a long drive. He checked the extra luggage rack that the chauffeur had attached to the back of the automobile and found it suitably secured.

"Well Francois let us hope the Bentley will get us all to Italy without any problems," *said Charles*, stroking his chin.

"I am sure it will, Monsieur," *replied the chauffeur confidently.*

"Then let us leave for Paris at once." *instructed Charles.*

It was early afternoon when the Bentley arrived in front of the hotel des Saint Pères in Paris. Charles went up to Moon's room where he found her waiting for him and ready to leave.

"Ready to start our new life together my love," *said Charles*, as the couple embraced. "Yes my darling," *Moon replied*, "I have been waiting many years for this new life and I am so happy to share it with you,"

After the hotel's concierge loaded Moon's luggage onto the automobile's rear luggage rack they were on their way to the winter retreat in Tuscany. Having Moon sitting close to him and holding onto his arm gave Charles a feeling of well-being as he had never experienced before in all of his life.

TEN

The Unexpected

Oxford, England. Monday, October 12th, Earl sat in his study and reviewed the translations of the last six Prophecies that Charles had enclosed in his last two letters. He found the translation to be correct and similar to his own interpretation.

With the translations of those thirteen Prophecies finally completed, all that remained to be translated were the last six pages that contained the paradoxical text.

Charles had warned him in his letters not to disclose the Prophecies or the contents of the Roman soldier's writings to anyone else. Charles had also warned that disclosure could prove dangerous to his entire family.

Earl couldn't understand or see where there could be a danger in discussing his discovery with colleagues at Oxford University. Either way he would need some help from another university professor to properly translate those last six pages.

He already had an appointment with the University's best Roman Historian who had also mastered the Latin language. They were to meet in the university library later on in the afternoon. However he would play it safe and only bring those six pages to the meeting. For the time being, he would not disclose to colleagues what he discovered in Egypt.

It was raining that Monday afternoon when Earl arrived at the University. He made his way to the University library where he found his colleague Henry reading as usual.

"Good afternoon Henry. Ready to do some serious work with me?" *asked Earl.*

"I always do serious work and no one knows that better than you my dear colleague." *replied Henry sarcastically.*

"All kidding aside Henry, I have some old pages with Latin writings and would need your help to properly translate them into English."

"Well sit yourself down and let's see the pages you're talking about. And by the way I was lead to believe you took a year's sabbatical. How come you're back at Oxford so soon?" *inquired the historian.*

"It's a long story my friend. I will tell you about it another time. Meanwhile, here are the pages I am talking about." *said Earl,* as he laid the six pages on the table.

Henry carefully examined the writings and kept looking at the pages back and forth. When he stopped looking at them, he leaned back in his chair, and scratched his head.

"Where did you find these pages?" he asked.

"I got them at an antique shop in Cairo." answered Earl.

"What I can tell you right now is that they were written a very long time ago and that they were most probably utilized for military purposes during the Roman era." *advised Henry.*

Earl's mouth dropped open upon hearing this statement from his colleague. How on Earth could Henry, come to such an accurate assessment by simply looking at the Latin writings on those six pages, *Earl wondered.*

"There is something else quite interesting," *Henry went on.* The writings are written in a code, making a proper translation next to impossible unless the secret code is deciphered."

Henry went on and explained how he came to those conclusions. The style of the writings belonged to an educated person during the Roman era. The coded letters were used by military officers to send confidential messages between each other. By adding these two facts together it becomes obvious that the original letters were most probably written 2,000 years ago by an officer in the Roman legion. He also believed that those six letters on the table were clever forgeries being the condition of the papers. Those letters couldn't be that old.

To break the code and decipher those letters could prove to be a lengthy task in itself. First, one must find the starting word and then the order of following words must be resolved. These could be every fifth word or every seven word and can even be in a mixed order such as the third word followed by the fifth word then the seventh word etc…

Earl thanked his colleague for the information and left the University library and took a taxi home. Well he certainly didn't expect what could be involved in translating those remaining six pages. He had absolutely no clue as to how he could possibly decipher the necessary code that was utilized in those letters. If only Charles was here, *he thought*, this was right up his alley.

When he got home, he discussed the situation with his wife, Elizabeth. They both agreed to work together on deciphering the code used in the letters. Elizabeth did have a brother, living close by, who was a retired officer in the British Army. Perhaps he could also help in deciphering the code used in those last six pages written by the Roman soldier.

Seeing that both Elizabeth and her brother didn't understand Latin and if they were to help in solving the code, then, the last six pages had to be translated as written.

This would make no sense as to the meaning of the letter but it would allow others to work on deciphering the secret code.

This is certainly turning out to be a huge and complex jigsaw puzzle. If some way could be found to place those scrambled words in their proper order then one would know if those last six pages were indeed a fourteenth Prophecy.

Translation of the last six pages as written.

1…And then the of will sealed when will mankind return the have passed fate forthcomings the be to no to have first point tenth its should past come.

2…They of spare all fifth difference then those seed of and from to and time small throughout children the of be men destruction women who house come and will host slain will innocent Souls will the men the lands the panic are the will no numbers when.

3…Of chance then the come life mankind's will three of past lands destruction across for last the none the this salvation should to alter all within three will lands forthcoming across and the forthcoming rest all last only.

4…Flesh mankind care needs close from following will old to being needs not its cause his this of whence the the die to having own to and the came when without and to eat the they will given clearly own lands come their will laws be seen against left man time.

5…The fifth lowest to the will then hosts from house will all lands thousands of the and too be perish flesh eaten hosts of and by Souls massive across thousands thousands fourth houses counted their by Souls third of destructions upon to many and the second the of hosts to be house by will the begin sixth.

6…Leaving a few allow its beginning then having against mother know fury the and father's calamity was seen come upon ungrateful great of to these and whence the great three boulders size this will thrown the lands first the to of fifth sixth then a darkness land once be it in beginning but chosen to mankind new mankind turned its will the of mother the scorn as never will down the causing walls water purify undeserving from came three ships great the of mountain be against three where settled hosts Souls the and house following great the will more as was the.

Why were the last six pages written in such a confusing way when the writings on all other pages, and those in the Roman soldier's journal, were in such an orderly fashion? Earl pondered that question over and over. Could there be prophetical events so terrible that even the Roman soldier dared not put in writing. If this was the case; then for whom were they written in code for?

The more this went on, the more confusing it became. Earl now wondered if he would ever get to the bottom of this entire story written by the Roman soldier. Would he ever be able understand the true meaning of those last six pages.

He would mail a copy, of the "as written" translation, to Charles in Tuscany. This mystery was right up Charles' alley and he would probably decipher that code in a flash…

Following dinner that evening, Earl went to his study and took out the strange objects he had found in the cave. Possibly, *he wondered*, they could hold the clue to the codes of those last six pages. What did all of those dots mean? *He pondered.* Maybe they were a sort of Morse code similar to when you send out an S.O.S. on a ship… - - - … - - - … - - - spelling S.O.S. over and over again.

Elizabeth's brother would know about those things because of his military experience. Earl would have an opportunity to discuss this with him because he would be visiting the next day.

Suddenly he felt a weird tiredness overcome him and he made his way to bed where sleep instantly overtook him. His eyes started flickering again. He was having yet another one of his nightmares.

In this dream, there were seven men, each one wearing a black hood. They seemed to be the same men he saw in a previous dream, where he stood inside of a circle of hooded men. This time he was not in the dream, but instead, he seemed to be witnessing some sort of a satanic offering.

In front of the seven hooded men there were three men dressed in white. They were kneeling, with their hands tied behind their backs. All three were blindfolded and seemed to be trembling with fear. Four of the hooded men, two at both ends of the line, started chanting what seemed to be a satanic chant. The three in the middle of the line, drew knives from their belts and cold bloodedly cut off the heads of their three victims. They held up the three bleeding heads for all to see.

Earl was crying in his sleep when his wife woke him up. "Were you having another one of those horrible dreams my dear?" *she enquired.*

"Oh yes! And they get worse with every dream," *he answered*, as he turned over and surprisingly fell into a deep peaceful sleep.

Morning came and Earl awoke to a breakfast prepared by Elizabeth brought to him in bed. On the tray was a steaming hot cup of tea and lavishly buttered English.

"To what do I owe this pampering?" *asked Earl mockingly.*

"To be truthful my dear, I am starting to be worried about those nightmares that you are having," *she replied,* showing concern

"I do believe they must have something to do with the strange artifacts I found in the cave. It seems that I get tired and very sleepy every time I hold them in my hand. Once asleep I have these terrible dreams. The nightmares only started to occur immediately after that chain of events that began in Egypt," *he commented*

"Possibly you are allergic to whatever the objects are made of. For starters, why don't you bring them to the lab at the University and have them analyzed? It would be good to find out what the heck they are made of".

"That's a great idea sweetheart, and I will do that right after breakfast. What time is your brother coming over?"

"He will be joining us for dinner this evening, after which we will look into translating those coded writings," *she replied.*

It was early afternoon by the time Earl arrived at Oxford University. After speaking with a metallurgist friend of his, both men went about examining the strange artifacts. Following several tests, the properties of the strange objects could not be identified. Before leaving the lab, Earl decided to look at the dots on the artifacts under a powerful microscope.

He gasped in amazement upon seeing the dots on the objects magnified. These were not dots at all. They were miniature, circular pages that contained hundreds of strange symbols.

It was obvious to him, that these symbols were some sort of script that could certainly not have been done by a Roman soldier 2,000 years ago. They were more likely to have come from either the people who came with the three great ships thousands of years ago, or from the Soul Master himself…

On his way home in the taxi, Earl realized, that possibly, he had stumbled upon something even greater than the soldier's writings. Those six strange objects containing miniature documents, defied all logic. He knew of no existing technology that could explain the strange objects that he had discovered in Cairo.

What he had found would have had to come from both the past and the future at the same time. This idea was more than his mind could contemplate. This was a complex, dimensional labyrinth that could not be understood at that particular moment in time.

Following dinner that evening, Earl explained to his brother in law, what he had discovered about the objects. The brother in law advised that he would bring the objects to an army engineer he knew, and he was confident that they should have answers to those puzzling questions in no time flat. Earl thought that made good sense and eagerly agreed to his brother in law's suggestion.

Then, they went about the task of trying to decipher the coded message written by the Roman soldier but this to no avail. Much more time and effort would be required before solving that problem.

Following several brandies, drunk while relaxing in front of a roaring fire, the brother in law took his leave. He took with him the three objects that were to be evaluated by the army engineer.

"I must admit I was very surprised to see you allow my brother to leave with those precious artifacts of yours", *commented Elizabeth.*

"What have I got to lose?" *answered Earl.* "Those objects are not artifacts as we know them, and they certainly don't have any monetary value to me. If I could find out exactly what they are, and what they are used for, that would be enough reward for me".

"If you say so my dear, that's fine with me. Now let's have our cup of tea before going to bed", *suggested Elizabeth*, with that mischievous look in her eyes…

The next morning, as Elizabeth prepared breakfast, Earl couldn't help but notice how his wife was cheerful and peppy that morning. This was surely due to the hot and passionate love session they enjoyed the previous evening, *he thought to himself.*

"Well you certainly are in a good mood this morning my darling", *said Earl*, brandishing a proud smile.

"That I am my dear husband. You really know how to make me happy!" *she responded* blushing as she spoke.

"Tell me darling. Why did you tell my brother those strange artifacts were found at a flea market in Cairo? We both know you found them in a cave on a mountain, don't you trust him?" "Remember sweetheart, Charles advised us to keep the full discovery secret." *Earl replied in an authoritative way.*

"Your brother or anyone else must not be told what happened or what was discovered in that cave in Cairo. For the time being, we have to trust Charles' intuition on the importance of keeping this a secret between ourselves."

"I guess you are right dear. The less said the better."

Later that afternoon, as Earl was looking over the coded text to be deciphered, he was disturbed by a loud knock at the front door. It was an inspector from Scotland Yard.

"Mister Walker, I must ask you to come along with me to the local police station", *ordered the inspector.*

"What's this all about?" *Earl inquired,* showing concern.

"Just come along with me Sir", *the inspector again ordered.*

"Very well inspector. We mustn't keep Scotland Yard waiting must we," *retorted Earl sarcastically,* as he got his coat.

Elizabeth looked on with disbelief as her husband left with the inspector. What on earth is going on now? *She thought,* obviously worried by such a drastic turn of events.

As he entered the police station, Earl saw his brother-in-law sitting on a bench in what appeared to be a reception hall. The brother-in-law shrugged his shoulders lifting both hands in the air as if to say what the hell is happening here.

Earl was ushered into a room where two army men sitting in front of a table were waiting for him. These men must be from the military intelligence agency, *Earl concluded*, by the serious allure both men projected. His conclusion was right as he was sitting in front of two officers from the secret service.

"Mister Walker we need some answers from you," *said one of the men.* "Those objects you gave your brother in law. Where did you get them?"

"I bought them at a bazaar in Cairo," *answered Earl.*

"Do you have any idea of what they are made of?" *inquired the other man.*

"No idea whatsoever Sir," *answered Earl decisively.*

"There seems to be some microscopic symbols written on those three items. Do you have any idea as to which language those symbols belong to and can you translate them for us?"

"Negative, gentlemen I have no idea at all. After all, that is why I had my brother-in-law bring them to you in the first place. To try to find out what they are and what they mean."

"You have a good point there Sir and we do believe you."

The questioning continued for an hour before the military men finally resigned themselves to the fact that Earl really didn't know much about the items or what they meant.

If you remember anything that could help us understand the origin of those items or what they mean, please call me at once," *said the higher ranking officer*, as he gave Earl his card.

One of the officers got up and went to get the brother-in-law. He brought him into the interrogation room, where both men were advised that what had been discussed in the room that day was classified information. This was to be considered as top secret. They were sworn to secrecy and were obliged to sign a document to that effect. They were told not to divulge to anyone else anything at all in regards to those strange objects. The three objects were of course confiscated by the military and would never be seen again by Earl or his brother-in-law.

As Elizabeth's brother, drove Earl home, they both talked about the events of the day.

"Why such a fuss over three small pieces of metal, *uttered the brother-in-law?*" "There is more here than meets the eye", *replied Earl.* "A hell of a lot more..."

Earl thanked his brother-in-law for the ride home and was met at the door by Elizabeth who was overjoyed, and relieved to see him back. "What was that all about?" *She questioned Earl,* as she prepared a fresh pot of tea. "It's a long story sweetheart, I will tell you about in the morning. I am very tired right now and just want to get into bed and have a good night's rest.

The next morning Earl told his wife how he was questioned about where the items were found. Which one of the many road side bazaars were where the three items were found, the officers had wanted to know?

Did he know what the small symbols stood for they had asked him? All of this high level interest in three small pieces of something no one seems to be able to identify. "Mysterious indeed, *said Earl to his wife,* and rest assured we haven't heard the last of this story."

"Do you think they will go to Cairo to find out more about those objects?" *Elizabeth asked.*

"They most certainly will," *my dear,* "You can bank on that. I only hope they don't find that cave on Mokattam Mountain."

"I presume the military people don't know that Charles has three more of those strange objects?" *Elizabeth inquired.*

"No they don't my dear. Thank God, no one with the exception of you and I, knows of the existence of the other three objects in Charles' possession. Had I known about the symbols on those objects when I was in the cave, I might possibly have discovered what they were and maybe what they meant," *answered Earl,* with a bizarre look in his eyes.

"Please darling. Tell me you are not thinking of going back to Cairo," *Elizabeth stated,* obviously afraid of what the answer might be.

"No, not me my dear but it would not surprise me to see Charles leave for Cairo when he learns about the symbols. Especially if they are also on the three objects he still has. I have a strange feeling that those small sticks, *or whatever the name we give them*, may hold something much more valuable than precious stones."

"What do you mean sweetheart, by more valuable than precious stones?" *questioned Elizabeth.*

"Knowledge my dear... Knowledge! I think there is an abundance of knowledge on those sticks that could be worth more than all of the treasures on Earth," *he replied,* coyly.

"Anyway I don't like this at all," *uttered Elizabeth.* "You got quite sick the last time you went to that dammed cave and I am frightened at the very thought of you going there again."

"Can you imagine the benefits to mankind should those sticks contain information and knowledge from an advanced civilization we don't even know about here on Earth."

"That's a bit far fetched isn't it sweetheart?" *said the wife.*

"Remember my dear, that before Columbus, man believed the Earth was flat and ended at the far edge of the Ocean."

Earl went to his study to write a long letter to Charles in Tuscany. He explained how he felt that the last six pages remaining for translation were written with a complex code.

He enclosed a copy of his text translation as it was written. He also wrote down suggestions as to how the coded messages could possibly be deciphered.

He informed Charles about the microscopic script with strange symbols that he had found on the dots of the unidentifiable objects. He explained how they could only be seen using a powerful microscope. He ended the letter with a detailed account of his interrogation, by the two British secret service agents, over those unidentifiable objects found in the cave.

Earl then went outside for his morning walk and headed towards the post office to post his letter to Charles. Once that task done, he sat on a park bench where he usually smoked his first pipe of the day. As he sat there smoking his pipe, his attention was drawn to a man standing beside a tree a short distance before him.

The man was wearing a long black coat and had a strange looking hat on his head. The hat had a rather large rim and seemed to sink almost to the man's eyes. What a strange looking character, *he thought to himself.* That man seemed to be observing him from a distance. Probably someone from the secret service following me around, *Earl reasoned,* as he made his way back home.

"Did you mail that letter dear", *inquired Elizabeth*, as her husband walked in.

"Yes I did darling and would you believe the secret service people are having me followed," *he replied*, looking upwards.

"Nothing surprises me with you darling. I wonder what will happen next," *answered the wife*, as she shook her head.

The weeks went by and everywhere Earl went, he kept watch to see if he was being followed by that character in the black coat. No sign of him anywhere.

Maybe his imagination had played tricks on him, *he thought,* that was until one morning a month later, when he sat on the park bench smoking his pipe.

Low and behold! There he was standing beside the same tree watching him. Earl finished smoking his pipe while the strange man kept observing him from a distance. *Enough of this thought Earl,* as he rose from the bench and headed towards the man standing beside the tree.

Half way to the tree, the man in the black coat lifted his black gloved hand signaling Earl to stop. He froze right there on the spot as if he was paralyzed. Then the strange man moved his right hand from the right, across his body to the left and in a circular motion lifting the hand skywards and pointing towards the East. Instinctively, Earl gazed up into the Eastern sky which was the direction that was pointed to by the man. However, he saw nothing.

As he looked back toward the tree he was puzzled to find that the man in the black coat was gone. The S.O.B. is hiding behind the tree, *Earl thought*, so he ran to the tree and looked behind it, but there was no one to be seen anywhere. The strange man in the black coat had simply vanished without a trace.

When he got home, Earl went straight to the liquor cabinet and poured himself a stiff drink and gulped it down in a flash. "What has happened now my dear?" *asked his worried wife.* "It seems that the man in the black coat is not from the secret service after all," *answered Earl*, as he poured himself another drink.

"You are trembling darling. Sit down and tell me exactly what has happened," *said a curious Elizabeth*, showing obvious concern.

Earl told his wife about what he now considered to be a 'vision' that he had had in the park earlier. Elizabeth decided that, for the next few days, she would accompany her husband for his morning walks and would sit with him on the park bench. If she could see this mysterious man, then maybe they could find out who he is and what he wants from them.

Three days later, on a fine sunny morning, it happened…

"There he his dear", *cried Earl,* as he pointed to the tree a short distance from them. Elizabeth stared towards the tree in question but saw nothing but the tree. She could see no sign of the man in the black coat. "I'm sorry my dear, *she replied*, but I can't see anyone near the tree." However, Earl could still see the strange man standing there. "I must be going insane" *groaned Earl,* holding his head between his hands and covering both his eyes. He removed his hands from his face to look again and the black clothed man was no longer there. He was now trembling and losing his composure.

"That does it my dear. We are going to see a doctor right this minute," *the wife said*, seriously wondering about her husband's present state of mind. "Yes! That's a good idea," *answered Earl.* They left the park and made their way to the medical clinic to see the family doctor.

The doctor believed that Earl was suffering from some sort of delusion causing hallucinations. This could be caused by a tropical sickness he may have contacted several months ago when he was in Egypt. All should fall into place with some rest, *advised the doctor.* He prescribed a mild sedative to be taken nightly at bedtime.

From that moment on, Earl refused to leave the house for any reason whatsoever. He became a recluse, a hermit by all intense and purposes. He no longer bothered shaving.

He just sat at home with a blank look on his face. It was as if his mind had left his body leaving an empty shell behind…

Tuscany, Italy. Thursday, March 17th 1932.

Charles had finished working on deciphering the coded message written on the last six pages by the Roman soldier.

The code used would be considered primitive in modern times and when translated into English it was easy for him to break. However, in Roman times and written in Latin, the code would have been somewhat complicated and hard to decipher.

The code used a clever following pattern of continuance. To decipher the writings, you simply move the first six words of each paragraph (in order) to the end of the paragraph thus causing the seventh word to become the starting word.

Then, on a sheet of paper you place the same amount of slots as there are words in the paragraph and insert the starting word in the first slot. Then you skip six slots, insert the second word into the next slot, and so forth until all slots are filled. Once the 28 slots of the first paragraph are filled, the message appears quite clearly. The translated message in the first paragraph containing 28 words would read as follows…

1… When the first to the tenth forthcomings will have come to past and should Mankind have passed the point of no return. Then its fate will be sealed.

1st paragraph – Insert starting word then skip six slots.

2nd paragraph – Insert starting word then skip five slots.

3rd paragraph – Insert starting word then skip four slots.

4th paragraph – Insert first word then skip three slots.

5th paragraph – Insert first word then skip two slots.

6th paragraph – Insert first word then skip one slot.

When the 47 slots required for the second paragraph were filled, another troubling and confusing message appeared as follows.

2...Then the time will come when those men of small numbers will seed panic and destruction throughout all of the lands. The innocent children and women will spare no difference from the men who are host to Souls of the fifth house and they will be slain.

3... Mankind's only chance for salvation will rest within the last three forthcomings. Should the last of the three come to past, then none across all lands will alter the forthcoming destruction of life and this across all lands.

4... Following close the time will come, when the old will be left to die without care being given to their needs and Mankind having not seen clearly to its own needs will cause man to eat his own flesh and this against the laws of the lands from whence they came.

The fifth and sixth pages written in code by the Roman soldier held such devastating and horrific predictions that Charles believed that he had improperly deciphered them. Surely no such catastrophic events could possibly happen in these modern times, *he concluded.* More work would be required on his part to confirm his last two findings. Either way, for the time being, he thought it would be better to keep secret what was written on those last two pages.

He only realized that the day had passed when Moon entered the study, walked up behind him and placed her arms around him. *"Please come to bed my love"*, she whispered in her soft and seductive voice. He placed both his hands behind her to caress her firm bottom and noticed she was naked. Those last two pages can wait, *he thought*, as he carried her to the bedroom…

As they entered the bedroom, he knew by the flickering lights of the many candles she had lit, that he was in for a night of passionate love making with his Asian beauty.

"Undress darling I have a surprise for you", *she said*, as she filled a glass with some warm rice wine. As he stood naked before her, she threw the warm rice wine on him and fell to her knees and started tasting and licking the warm wine from her man's body. When she tasted his manhood, he held her head between his hands moving it back and forth increasing his desire with each movement.

"You're driving me crazy", *he cried*, as she boldly enjoyed every part of his body. "I can't take this any more", *he told her*, as his knees buckled under the mounting passion that had engulfed him.

"It's your turn to suffer now", *he shouted*, as he gently pushed her back and covered her body with the warm rice wine.

"Taste me everywhere", *she boldly commanded*, as he hungrily licked the wine off her breast and all over her soft quivering body.

"Taste this", *she said*, pushing his head between her legs. When he tasted her sweetness, she lost all control, trembling and moaning until her passion was spent.

"Get on your knees now", *he ordered.* Then, holding the sides of her lovely derrère with both hands, he pushed his way into her warmth. "Oh God I'm going to die", *she cried out,* as he slid back and forth, thrusting inside her, like a piston in a steam engine.

"Faster darling, faster", *she shouted,* as their passion mounted more with each stroke of his manhood.

Across the hall, in another room, Francois, the chauffer and his Italian girl friend were awakened by all of the yelling and screaming going on in Charles' room, and they in turn started loving each other, both shouting and screaming as if to out-shout and out-scream Charles and Moon across the hall.

Having a firm grip on her man's behind, Moon guided him back and forth, his rhythm increasing into a wild frenzy, "Oh God I'm coming again", *she screamed,* clawing at his back like a wild cat in heat. "So am I", *he cried out,* as both, exploded with the intensity of an overheated volcano during its eruption.

Charles' orgasm was so intense, that it caused him to ark his back upwards, howling like a mythical werewolf during mating. Both exhausted by their sexual outburst on the villa's hard wooden floor, they fell asleep in each other's arms…

The following morning, while they shared a romantic breakfast at a local bistro, Charles sat there admiring this Oriental beauty and couldn't help but think how lucky he was to have found her.

How could so much passion and charm, be bundled into such a small woman, *he thought to himself.* She obviously was sexually neglected all of her adult life, and he was fortunate enough to be the recipient of all that lost love and awakened passion.

The few months spent with her in Tuscany, proved to be pure bliss for both of them. She possessed him body and Soul.

When they returned to their summer villa, Francois, the chauffeur, handed Charles the daily newspaper and the mail he had picked up at the local post office.

The front page wire news mentioned that ten days ago in America, four people were killed when the police opened fire on a crowd of 3000 unemployed auto workers marching outside the Ford River Rouge plant, in Dearborn, Michigan.

The entire World is going crazy, *Charles thought*, killing people for wanting work.

On the paper's fourth page, there was a small article that caught his attention. It mentioned how Adolf Hitler obtained his German citizenship by naturalization on February 25th, thus opening the way for him to run in the 1932 election for Reichsprasident. *Was this the beginning of what Sam Bernstein had warned him about last summer in Rouen?* Charles wondered.

Amongst the mail, there was a letter from England. But this time the letter was from Elizabeth. It advised Charles of her concern about her husband's deteriorating health. She wrote how her husband had been having visions of a strange man dressed in black who appeared and vanished before him. In these visions, the strange man kept pointing skywards towards the East. She feared her husband was losing his mind.

She told of how her husband had changed over the past months and how he was not himself anymore. She asked if he could possibly cut short his stay in Tuscany and fly urgently to England. She believed that seeing his best friend, Charles again, might just be the medicine her husband needed to regain his sanity and come back to his old self…

"Is something wrong Charles?" *asked Moon*, as she noticed the worried look on her man's face after reading the letter.

"Yes my love. Something is dreadfully wrong with my friend Earl, in England," *replied Charles*, as he stroked his chin.

Charles wondered if the incidents Earl had written about in his last letter had anything to do with the apparent deterioration of his health. Could those unidentifiable objects be somehow responsible for his condition?

What do those microscopic symbols on the objects mean? Could they be linked to the strange man in the black coat? Why would the British secret service be so interested in those items? So many questions need to be answered, *he thought.*

Charles made his way to the study and examined the three strange objects that had been kept by him. He noticed that when he bent one in two, it immediately sprung back to its straight form. Even though the objects were as thin as a few layers of paper, he could not cut them, he even tried unsuccessfully with the garden shears. As fragile as they looked, these strange objects possessed incredible strength and seemed to resist normal methods of destruction.

He had no way to magnify the dots, so was unable to see the symbols that Earl had written about. The more he looked at the strange objects the more baffling they became. He could find no reason for their purpose or existence. They were just three mysterious objects that could not be identified.

He thought of the horrible dreams his friend kept having and how some of the dream descriptions seemed to coincide with the messages written on the last six pages by the Roman soldier. Perhaps that had something to do with his friend's deteriorating mental health.

But then again his friend Earl, had no idea of what those deciphered messages were, therefore that could not be the reason either. Possibly, having sent his friend to search that cave in Egypt was a mistake. Maybe, he should have gone himself, *he thought.* Was all of this his fault?

Later that evening, Charles completed the proper and final deciphering of the last two coded pages written by the Roman soldier. It confirmed what he had previously concluded.

5... Then by the hosts of Souls from the lowest house, massive destruction will begin across all of the lands. Thousand upon thousands by thousands of hosts to the fourth, fifth and sixth houses, too many to be counted, will perish and their flesh will be eaten by the hosts to Souls of the second and third houses.

After reviewing the properly deciphered message on the sixth and last page, Charles understood why the Roman soldier had written them in code. The deciphered message sent a cold shiver down his spine. The last message was nothing short of a terrible doomsday Prophecy. It could well be interpreted as a fourteenth Prophecy describing a terrible Armageddon.

The sixth page's deciphered message was so horrific, that he would keep its meaning secret. No one must ever know its content, or the final meaning of the Roman soldier's writings.

Now, there was nothing left for him to in Tuscany. The winter season was over and either way, it was time for him and Moon to return to France.

However, the health condition of his good friend Earl, back in England, called for Charles to make changes to the original plans he had previously made for returning to the Rouen mansion with his new found love.

Instead, he would have Moon Zhang return to France with Francois in the Bentley, and he would fly to England at once to be at the side of his ailing friend. Moon understood and agreed wholeheartedly with her man's decision. They would all leave for their destinations within the next few days.

ELEVEN

The Outcome

Oxford, England. Sunday, March 27th.

It was early in the evening when Charles arrived at the Walkers home in England. Elizabeth answered his knock on the front door and fell into his arms crying.

"Oh Charles, *she cried*, thank you so much for getting here so soon. Earl is not at all well and I am very concerned with his condition. I have even sent Peter to grandma's for a while."

"There, there now, *whispered Charles*, calm down and tell me what's been going on here."

"Make yourself comfortable while I make us a pot of tea and I will fill you in on what's been happening to Earl over the past months," *said Elizabeth*, while she prepared the tea.

"Where is Earl?" *asked Charles*, quite surprised at not seeing his friend greet him as usual.

"He is being kept under medication, at the hospital", *she replied*, as she begun crying again.

"Good Lord, what is the diagnosis," *Charles inquired.*

"The doctors believe that he is on the verge of insanity."

"Nonsense," *replied Charles.* He is just feeling depressed."

"When he is here at home with me, he just sits there with a blank look on his face and doesn't speak a word".

"I will go to visit him first thing in the morning", *advised Charles.* "His place is here with you and not at the hospital".

"I agree and I do want him home. I am sure that seeing you again will make him feel much better. Come now – You must be tired. Let me show you to the guest room, *said Elizabeth*, we can talk more about this in the morning."

The following morning, Charles took a taxi to visit his friend Earl at the local hospital. When he got to his friends room, he found him sitting in bed with that blank look on his face. Obviously the same blank look Elizabeth had told him about the previous evening, *he thought to himself.* Charles greeted his friend but to his disappointment there was no reply from Earl. He just sat there and said nothing.

Charles was learned in the mysterious art of hypnosis and post hypnotic suggestion. He decided that he would attempt to bring his friend back to reality by using a technique that had been taught him. He believed that his friend Earl had conditioned himself into believing he was crazy thus closing the door on himself and to reality. The trick now would be to reverse that conditioning.

One short hour later, the post hypnotic reversal process worked and his good friend Earl was talking again. There was no need for medicine here as the problem was psychological.

They talked for two hours and the blank look on Earl's face had vanished. He was asking how young Peter was and wanted to go home to his wife Elizabeth. He was on his way back to reality where he belonged. Sanity had returned!

After having Earl released from the hospital, Charles hailed a taxi and the old friends headed back to Earl's place talking and reminiscing of the good times shared in the past.

When they got back to the house, Earl opened the door and walked in. "Honey I'm home," *he called.* Elizabeth couldn't believe her ears when she heard her husband's voice.

She ran to him, excitedly, throwing herself into his arms unable to keep back the tears that were flowing profusely from her eyes. "I can't believe the change," *she said*, while staring at Charles.

"Everything is going to be fine now," *said Charles*, as he placed his arm around the shoulders of his best friend.

Charles explained what had happened to Earl and how the process was reversed. He also explained how to prevent this phenomenon from reoccurring in the future. The three old friends talked together late into the night until it was time to get some sleep.

The next morning, during breakfast the old friends talked again. "This reversal process you used on Earl yesterday, *asked Elizabeth*, from whom did you learn such knowledge." "The Rose Croix teaches these principles to practitioners that attain a high position in the organization," *he explained.*

Charles went on to further explain that this secret science will one day be of common use amongst the medical profession. For the time being the techniques are restricted to a limited few that seek knowledge pertaining to the occult.

"What is beneficial to one person can prove disastrous to another."

"When the science you are working with relates to the mind, then you can imagine what the consequences could be if the science is improperly applied. In this present time, much of the surgery performed on the human brain is strictly experimental."

"And even the medicines prescribed by doctors for some mental disorders or breakdowns, are often prescribed without any idea, by the doctors, of what the usage of those particular drugs will do to the patient's brain."

"In plain words, you can destroy a brain by simply loading it with improper drugs. Sounds silly of course, but it's true."

"A good example of what I am saying is the state of an opium smoker's mind, when he indulges in that practice. His mind goes haywire from the drug's effect and he hallucinates."

"This is why my dear Earl, that there will be no more medicine for you from this day on. Instead you must concentrate on sharing your deepest thoughts with your wife instead of keeping them to your self, thus causing your mind to overload. A free and open mind is a healthy mind."

"What I want to do with you, for the next few days, is go over everything that happened to you since you entered the cave in Egypt. I believe that by reviewing those details, we might find the answers to a lot of the questions we have been asking ourselves."

Later that afternoon, they begun going over every page of Earl's journal that referred to his examination of the three walls in the cave. From what he read and from Earl's comments, Charles deducted that the wall with the cross lined circle could be the culprit to his friends horrible dreams, and that possibly the wall with the circle could have something to do with both the mysterious man in the black coat and the six strange objects, that were found in the cave's floor cavity.

Charles would use regressed hypnotic suggestion to try and see if Earl had missed anything important when he examined that particular wall.

"Earl I want you to close your eyes and breathe deeply," *instructed Charles.* "Now, as I count backwards from ten to one. I want you to see in your inner mind, the crossed lined circle as if you were standing there before it in the cave."

Elizabeth watched in amazement as her husband's head slumped down on his chest and he began answering Charles' questions in what seemed to be an exaggerated slow rhythm.

Under this regressed hypnotic state, Earl could describe with accuracy, what he saw on the wall several months ago. This time however, under the influence of a hypnotic trance, the numbers and pictures that had previously flashed before him at incredible speed were now going by much slower. He could now visualize in detail what the individual pictures were.

As suspected by Charles, the nightmares his friend kept having were simply detailed accounts of the pictures that his sub-conscious mind had picked up while viewing the strange projection in the mirror like circle on the wall.

These detailed accounts of the pictures would have been missed by his conscious mind due to the excitement that took hold of him during that particular discovery.

When reviewing his first examination of the wall with the crossed lined circle, Earl was able to give a more accurate description of the recessed slot that was below the circle. This time, he was able to describe the slot as being a possible slotted hole leading into the wall.

Charles concluded from the testimony of his friend under hypnosis, that the recessed slot cavity was a receptacle for the six strange articles found in the cave's cavity. The identical dimensions of both the slot and the object confirmed his theory.

He was now convinced that if one of the strange objects were to be inserted into the slotted hole, something would happen with the mysterious crossed lined circle.

Enough had been accomplished for the day. It was time to bring Earl out of his hypnotic trance.

"Earl, I want you to breathe deeply and listen to my voice. As I count from one to ten you will begin awakening more and more with each number counted. When I reach ten you will be fully awake and feeling well rested. You will remember each and every detail you spoke off during your hypnotic sleep."

Elizabeth was mesmerized by what had just occurred and at seeing her husband hypnotized by Charles.

When Earl woke up, he remembered everything that he had said under the hypnotic trance. Both he and Charles were jubilant of the results of the post hypnotic experience. A lot was learned that day to clarify the mystery surrounding the discovery that was made in Cairo last July.

Following a late dinner that evening, all retired to their rooms for some well deserved rest. Charles rested in his bed thinking of the events of the day. One thing he knew for sure was that it was his destiny to go Cairo and visit the cave to see if indeed, the three sticks he possessed would slip into the recessed slot below the crossed lined circle.

The following morning, during breakfast, all discussed what had been happening since the Walkers return to England. Charles believed that it would only be a matter of time before the British secret service discover to the cave in Cairo.

They showed too much interest in those three objects they seized. They must know something about them that we don't know, *reasoned Charles.*

The unknown technology needed to inscribe microscopic symbols on the dots of the objects would certainly be of great interest to the military.

"I think I should fly to Cairo at once and visit the cave," *said Charles*, frowning as he spoke. "I don't know, *replied Earl*, maybe we should leave sleeping dogs lie."

Earl knew his friend better than anyone else. He knew full well that Charles had already made up his mind to visit the cave in Cairo. Nothing on Earth would stop him from going there now.

"Yesterday, when we looked over the Roman soldier's journal, I noticed some deterioration in the structure of those old documents," *advised Charles*. "I also noticed that," *remarked Earl*, "maybe old age is catching up on them."

They examined the old documents again and realized that their condition was indeed deteriorating at an alarming pace.

"We must do something to protect them," *said Earl*. "As an archeologist, I can't let such an important and historical find disintegrate. It would be a crime against humanity."

"I fully agree and understand what you mean," *replied Charles*, "and we do have our friend Luigi at the Vatican you know."

"You mean the Cardinal that visited our booth at the Parish auction?" implied Earl. "Exactly!" answered Charles.

Later in the afternoon, Earl underwent another hypnotic therapy with Charles. This time, they reviewed Earls' sightings of the strange man in black. Once Earl was out of the hypnotic trance, Charles explained his assessment of the sightings and what he thought they meant.

"The Rose-Croix believe that spirits, or entities as we may call them, are amongst us in every day life. We can't see them but sometimes we get messages from them. Most of the time, these messages are interpreted as premonitions by people."

"But the Rose-Croix believes that they are in fact messages from one subconscious mind to another. What it breaks down to is communications between Souls.

First of all, one must not fear such sightings. Secondly, one must not try to approach the entity that is sighted but should invite the entity itself to approach. You cannot go to a spirit. The spirit must come to you. Invite it and it will come.

"You see Earl, when you placed your head through the encircle triangles and saw the other side, you most probably awakened your senses to a degree where you are more capable of communicating with unseen entities. The man in the black coat was a messenger telling you to seek answers in the East."

"Something important was missed by you when you were examining the cave on Mokattam Mountain, *claimed Charles*. For some unknown reason, that entity you visualized wants the missing information brought to light."

"I guess you will be leaving for Egypt shortly," *uttered Earl.*

"You guessed right, *replied Charles*, the sooner the better."

After one week at the walkers, Charles' work was done. Earl was back to his old self and everyone was happy. The psychological therapy applied to Earl by Charles, had worked wonders.

Only two tasks pre-occupied Charles for the time being.

First of all, the deteriorating artifacts written by the Roman soldier had to be delivered at once to the Vatican.

Charles knew that only the Vatican experts could assure the preservation of those priceless treasures.

Secondly, he had to find out for himself if the strange objects did indeed fit into the recessed slot under the crossed line drawing and what would happen if they were inserted into the slot.

Later that evening, Earl and Charles, carefully wrapped up the 2000 year old codex and other documents that were written in Latin by the Roman soldier so far back in time.

These would be turned over to the Vatican for safe keeping. Before retiring for the evening, the old friends shared a bottle of fine brandy in front of the fireplace.

The very thought of his friend leaving for Cairo, brought a sadness to Earl's heart. When, will they meet again, *he thought to himself*, and under what circumstances.

"Tell me Charles, will you try to talk with Saadi when you are in Cairo?' *inquired Earl.* "Of course I will. I am sure he will have a lot to tell me," *replied Charles.*

"I will also visit the merchant at the road side market. He would be the one to know if anyone else had been inquiring about the cave since you left Cairo," *said Charles.*

"This merchant at the road side market, who is he?" *asked Elizabeth.* "He is the man who told Charles about the cave in the first place. The road side market was where Charles got the talisman, which in turn led to the discovery," *answered Earl.*

A lot had been accomplished in the past few days and the mental energy used up by both men had taken its toll. They were both exhausted and it was time for some well deserved rest. The following day would be a busy one for Charles.

Charles was fast asleep in his room when he had a dream. In the dream, he saw himself being chased by men dressed in black. Kill him, they were screaming, as they chased him through the darkened streets of Cairo. He woke up reflecting on the dream. How one's mind can play tricks, *he thought*, then slumbered back into a peaceful and undisturbed sleep.

The next morning, following a hasty breakfast, Charles bid Earl and Elizabeth farewell. Then, he took a taxi and headed for Oxford's local airfield. Once there he chartered a plane for his trip to Rome and Cairo. The plane would leave at once…

The Vatican, Friday, April 1st, 1932

How ironic all of this was turning out to be, *Charles thought to himself.* Here he was on April fools day, sitting in the Vatican's reception hall, waiting for a Cardinal to see him.

A Bishop came towards him. It was the same Bishop he had met in Paris during the auction. "Monsignor Capotosti will see you now. Please follow me," *said the Bishop.* He then led Charles through a labyrinth of richly decorated corridors.

When Charles entered the reception room, the sight of the masters' paintings lining the walls left him speechless. "I had a feeling that we would meet again," *said the Cardinal*, as he stood and extended his hand to Charles.

Charles kissed the Cardinals ring then placed the package containing the artifacts on the rich mahogany desk. "It doesn't appear to contain the sword that I was interested in. Does it?" *said the cardinal*, as he opened the package. "No your Eminence; it contains much more than a sword," *replied Charles.*

Both men talked for two hours during which Charles told the Cardinal the complete story of how those priceless artifacts were discovered and how they needed special care that only the Vatican experts could provide in order to preserve them.

The Cardinal advised that the right decision had been taken and that the Roman soldier's writings would be preserved and kept safe, here in the Vatican where they belonged.

Charles refused the kind offer made by the Cardinal to dine with him that evening, explaining that he had urgent matters to tend to and that he must leave Rome at once.

"The Bishop will drive you to Portonaccio's air field, where your aircraft is waiting." "Thank you Eminence," *replied Charles.* He then followed the Bishop to a waiting automobile.

Cairo, Sunday April 3rd.

Charles woke up in a room he had taken in a dingy hotel earlier that morning. He glanced at his pocket watch. It was noon and he had only slept for four hours. He was disgusted at the condition of the room he had rented, but he wanted to keep a low profile during his stay in Cairo.

He walked over to a nearby clothing shop and bought some clothing that he would wear and allow him to mix, inconspicuously in with the local population. The less people would pay attention to him, the better he would feel.

He returned to the hotel and changed into his new clothing and then made his way to the roadside market hoping to see the merchant who sold him the talisman several years ago. Sure enough, there he was still there peddling his goods.

If you wanted to know anything about what was going on in town, this was the man with whom to speak. He knew everything about everyone in Cairo. As Charles approached him, the merchant didn't recognize him dressed in local apparel. But once the head scarf was removed, the merchant remembered him well. He also remembered Earl and inquired about his whereabouts.

The merchant told Charles that a lot of action had taken place since Earl had left Cairo. Soon after Earl left, Egyptian men came searching the cave on the mountain. Rumors have it that all they found buried in the cave's floor were wooden crates containing excavation tools. They said the Englishman found a treasure in the cave and took it away from Egypt.

Well that explains the Egyptian at the auction and the men that were watching the mansion in Rouen, *thought Charles.* He inquired about Saadi and was horrified, when told that he was dead. The merchant told Charles, that they found him in an alleyway with his throat slit from ear to ear.

This was not good news and things were not turning out to be what he had expected, *thought Charles.* He decided that he needed some bodyguards and needed them fast. He was with the right man at the right time. This merchant could supply all the protection that Charles needed. Two armed bodyguards would be at Charles' hotel within the hour.

Charles returned to his hotel room and waited. It didn't take much time before two men knocked on his room's door. It was the bodyguards. These two look like they would kill you for a bottle of rum. Each brandishing a pistol in their belts they were the meanest looking men he had ever laid eyes on. All they were interested in was money and protecting him well, Charles assured them that they would be well paid.

Charles felt safe again. They spoke French as could most of the habitants from this old French colony, so conversing was no problem.

They followed him around and stuck to him like a shadow following you on a sunny day. He went to eat at a restaurant and they sat with him throughout the meal. When he retired for the night, they slept on the floor in front of the door to his room. The next morning all three left for Mokattam Mountain. Charles only took with him his note book, a lantern and the three objects that could not be identified.

When they got to the cave's entrance, the two bodyguards advised they would not enter that ghost cave. As fierce and mean as they projected to be, the bodyguards were afraid of folklore and, scared of ghost stories, *Charles couldn't believe his ears.*

A strange feeling overtook him as he entered the cave. It was the same weird feeling that he had experienced many years before when he had first entered this mysterious cave. He set the lantern in front of the crossed lines drawing and took the unidentifiable objects from his pocket. Sure enough they were the same diameter as the recessed slot below the crossed line drawing.

He took in a deep breath and inserted one of the three sticks into the slot. Within seconds, before his bewildered eyes, the encircled drawing turned into a mirror like image of clear blue water. This was exactly what Earl had described in his journal, *thought Charles.* Then there appeared in the center of the circle, a back dot the size of thumb nail which grew outwards to reveal a circular white page containing strange symbols. He was unable to identify those symbols, so he carefully copied them in his note book as best he could.

This procedure with the first stick, took a good hour to complete, this because the pages would change to another every few minutes. He then inserted the second stick into the slot. This caused the same mirror image scenario as for the first stick, but this time, when the black dot developed into a circular page, it contained close knit groups of letters and numbers, and they were in English. The letters and numbers were in a set sequence and appeared to be mathematical formulas or equations of a sort. It took close to two hours before he had finished carefully, copying all of those equations into his note book.

"Is everything O.K. in there monsieur," *hollered one of the bodyguards.* "Yes everything is fine," *Charles shouted back.*

Then it was the turn of the third and final stick to be inserted in the slot. Once again the Circle drawing turned into a blue mirror image. This time the scenario was different.

Images were moving by at an approximate rate of one every five minutes. These images appeared to be detailed blueprints of God knows what. Charles couldn't make heads or tails of these blueprints and copying them was next to impossible. A camera would be needed for such a complicated task. But he did manage to sketch at least three of the blueprint images in his note book. He didn't know what these images represented, but one thing for sure, they were of gigantic proportions.

Charles had passed a solid four hours in the cave and hunger had set in. He decided they should all go and eat at a small café situated at the bottom of the mountain. After lunch he would return to the cave and complete his mission. He left the lantern on the cave floor and walked down the mountain with the two bodyguards following close behind.

Three quarters of the way down the mountain they ran into a contingent of six men on their way up to the top. Two of the men were wearing military uniforms and as they passed by, *Charles noticed*, they were speaking to each other in perfect English. Possibly the British secret service, *he thought*, as he and the bodyguards continued down the mountain.

As he sat on the terrace of the small café, he noticed a truck, a short distance away, where men dressed in military uniforms, were unloading some equipment. This could only be an English army intelligence unit, *Charles thought.*

He decided there and then that his plan to return to the cave had to be abandoned. Too much was happening, too fast at the cave's site. He feared that his security could be in danger if he remained in Cairo any longer.

He returned to the hotel and gathered his belongings, and made his way to the road side market to talk with the merchant one last time before leaving Egypt. He gave the merchant his address in Rouen and asked him to write advising anything he could find out about what the British were doing in Cairo.

Using the merchant's old truck, the bodyguards drove Charles to his chartered plane which was ready and waiting at the local airfield. He paid the bodyguards with gold pieces, thanked them for their services and boarded the twin engine Lancaster aircraft.

"Are the tanks full of petrol," *Charles asked the pilot.* "Of course monsieur," *was the reply.* "Then let's get out of here."

As the plane taxied towards the take off strip, Charles noticed a huge four engine plane sitting on the tarmac. On its side, in bold letters, were the words R.A.F. 247. He had beaten the British secret service to the cave by only one day.

Had it been reversed, *he thought*, maybe he would have never discovered what the sticks were for. He may never have experienced the wonders that he had witnessed when he had inserted the sticks into the slot nested below the encircled, crossed lines drawing that was on the cave's wall…

"Where are we off to this time?" *asked the co-pilot.*

"Paris, France, *replied Charles*, it's time for me to go home."

Charles sat in the plane pondering upon what had happened earlier that day in the mountain's cave. The mirror like image that appeared when he inserted the sticks into the recessed slot in the cave's wall could be compared to an advanced and futuristic cinema. The cross lined circle would be the viewing screen, the recessed slot would be the projector and the sticks would be the film. One thing he knew for sure is that there was no technology to his knowledge that came close to this.

Whatever this thing was or wherever it came from was certainly not a fabrication by anyone from our period of time. This was so advanced it defied logic. The phenomenon he had witnessed had to be from the three great ships mentioned by the Soul Master. There was no other explanation possible. The whole story as written by the Roman soldier had to be true…

The flight to France would be a long one and Charles had plenty of time for reflection. He used the time to review the notes inscribed in his note book. The close knitted letters and numbers, *such as E=mc2,* that he had previously recorded in the cave, must be either mathematical or scientific formulas. They surely meant something of importance. The strange symbols on the other hand, didn't resemble any modern or ancient language and didn't seem to have any continuity.

The three sketches of the blueprint drawings were mind boggling. He had no idea of what they could possibly be. When he got to France, he would have engineers look at these notes. Then maybe they would be able to see some logic that could be derived from what presently seemed so illogical to him. He had not slept much during the past few days and the monotonous humming of the plane's two engines got the best of him. He slowly drifted into a deep sleep.

Paris, Tuesday April 5th 1932.

"Wake up monsieur. We have landed in Paris," *advised the co-pilot,* as he shook Charles' shoulder. "So soon," *answered Charles drowsily*, having slept through the entire flight.

He shook hands with the pilot and co-pilot, descended from the aircraft and hailed himself a taxi. "Where to monsieur," *asked the driver.* "Take me to l'Hotel du Cadran," *instructed Charles.*

Later that afternoon, he sat on a terrace waiting for a friend to join him. This friend was an engineer and possibly he could provide some answers to the notes he had taken in the cave.

"Bonjour Charles," *said the engineer*, when he arrived at the table. "Bonjour Jean, thank you for coming," *replied Charles.*

He had the engineer look over the notes in his book. Jean confirmed what Charles had suspected. The closely knitted letters and numbers separated by an equal sign were indeed formulas. They could be mathematical, chemical or scientific formulas. However the meaning of the formulas as written could not be explained by the engineer.

Jean also had no idea of what the sketches meant but agreed that they would be of colossal proportions. After a quick lunch, they shook hands and Jean left the café leaving Charles as bewildered as ever.

Charles just sat there looking at the notes in his book and wondered if he would ever get to the bottom of the mystery. It was a beautiful sunny day, perfect for a walk around the Champ de Mars. He walked for an hour then returned to the hotel and made arrangements to have someone drive him to Rouen the next morning. That evening, following dinner, he went to bed early as he would be up at the crack of dawn for the long drive ahead to his mansion in Rouen.

Morning came and following a hasty breakfast, he was on his way to be with Moon Zhang, his one and only love. Joseph the driver, who insisted on being called Joe for short, was a rather pleasant chap and quite the comedian. The conversation exchanged between them made the drive seem much shorter.

"Have you heard the one about the man who swallowed his glass eye," *said the driver.* "No I haven't," *replied Charles.* "Well this drunk was eating a bowl of soup, when his friend slapped him on the back causing his glass eye to pop out and fall in the bowl. The drunk didn't notice, kept eating the soup and swallowed his glass eye. Needless to say, he had some terrible stomach cramps for weeks caused by severe constipation, so he went to see a proctologist.

The doctor told him to undress, bend over and rest his chest on the table. Then the doctor took a look up his behind to see if there was any obstruction causing the constipation.

The doctor suddenly stumbled backwards, let out a horrid scream, fainted and fell on the floor.

When the nurse revived him, she asked what had happened. For 20 years I've been staring at ass holes, *replied the doctor.* Today, for the first time, I saw one staring back at me."

Charles laughed so hard that tears ran down his cheeks. That was by far, the funniest joke he had ever heard. He must remember to tell Earl that one, *he thought to himself.*

Halfway to Rouen, they stopped at a road side café for some lunch. As they talked at the café, Charles asked the driver if he had family living in Paris. All of a sudden Joe fell silent and his eyes filled with tears. Charles asked if he has said something wrong. "No monsieur, it's just that what you said brings back sad memories. You see back in 1918, most of my family died during the Spanish Flu epidemic."

"I lost both of my parents and five siblings. Apart from myself, I only have my younger brother left alive and I almost lost him too. I was lucky and living in the country at that time with my wife and five children. It seemed that those living away from the city were less prone to get that terrible sickness. When everyone died and only my brother was left, I went and took him from the city and brought him to live with me and my family in the country."

"Having him living in our home was a great danger for my family, so we kept him locked in a room and passed him food and water through a window. He lived alone in that room without seeing anyone for five long months. Slowly his strength returned and he finally healed."

"The day he left the confinement room, to be with what was left of his family, he weighed less than 30 kilos. He was skin and bones but thank God he had survived. Had he been left alone in Paris, he would surely have died like all the others."

As they continued on to Rouen, Charles could feel the pain that had been endured by Joe during the past twelve years and understood why the comedian part of the driver had gone.

It was early evening when they arrived at the mansion. At first the driver wouldn't accept Charles' invitation to spend the night, but under Charles' insistence, the driver finally gave in and agreed to stay until morning…

Having heard the car pull up, Francois came out to greet Charles. "Welcome home monsieur." "It's good to be home," *answered Charles.* "This is Joe who drove me here from Paris. Please take care of him and make sure he is comfortable. He will be staying the evening with us here in Rouen."

"Very good monsieur," *replied Francois.*

Moon Zhang was descending the stairwell as Charles walked into the mansion's main entrance. She ran to him and kissed him passionately. "I am so happy to have you here with me," *she said*, as she held him with both arms around his neck.

"Not half as happy as I am my beautiful darling," *answered Charles,* holding her firmly by the waist. "So tell me sweetheart. How do you like your new home?" *he asked her*, as they walked towards the fireplace. "It's beautiful here at the mansion and I love it even more with you here beside me," *she replied.*

Later, in the master bedroom, Charles relaxed and enjoyed a cognac while Moon went about preparing him a hot bath.

"Your bath is ready my love. Get in and I will massage your shoulders and back for you." *Said Moon,*

Charles undressed and got into the warm water. The sight of her naked man stepping into the bath excited Moon and in a flash; she was naked and sitting on top of him in the bath.

They made wild love as best they could under the circumstances, paying no attention to the water that was spilling all over the master bedroom floor.

They got out of the bath, dried each other off, got into Charles' comfortable bed, and continued loving each other until exhaustion finally set in. Moon was the first to fall asleep in her man's arms. 'Its good to be home,' *thought Charles,* as he slowly drifted off into a deep and peaceful sleep.

One week later, Sunday April 10th, Charles woke up and realized that life for him would never be the same again. The experience of viewing the images on the cave wall had changed his perception of life as he knew it.

Life and its meaning would be altered in his mind forever. He now understood that all he had been taught and believed in all of his life was false. The world around him was nothing but an illusion as perceived by most of Mankind.

Moon had already noticed and mentioned how much he had changed since they left Tuscany. All he could think of was the images he had seen in the crossed circle and all his energy was spent on trying to understand what it all meant. The more he tried to understand the more confusing it became. He felt like a schoolchild who couldn't understand his lessons.

None of the lodge elders he confided in were able to help him. He felt as helpless as a lost child. Slowly, day by day then month by month he became more and more of a recluse. Old friends that were once close were now keeping their distance. He had become a hermit living in his own shell.

Apart from Moon who loved him regardless of his state of mind and Francois his loyal chauffeur and confident, Charles had no more friends close by.

He had begun writing his memoirs as if he were an old man trying to tell a story knowing full well that none would believe him. The months turned into years. Still he found no answers to the many questions he kept asking himself time and again. Every day he read the Scrolls and Prophecies written by the Roman soldier. Eventually his mind unconditionally accepted the fact that the Soul Master existed 2,000 years ago and would keep on existing for as long as Mankind exists. As far as he was concerned, the entire story as written by the Roman soldier was true.

Everything Sam Bernstein had predicted came to pass. The British went off the gold standard. Japan invaded China. Hitler took power in Germany.

Europe was in turmoil and its people were starving. Poverty rose to an alarming rate across the World. History was repeating itself as it had done countless of times before in recorded history.

Charles started believing that the past, the present and the future were all happening simultaneously on Earth, but in different dimensions, with each dimension being invisible to the other. He started giving conferences at Rose-Croix lodges in France, Italy and England, where he explained his theories on invisible interfaced dimensions where past, present and future coexisted at the same time here on Earth. Some believed his theories to be somewhat avant-garde while others discarded them as pure lunacy.

By the end of November 1939, Hitler's Germany and the Russians had both invaded Poland. Charles knew that it would only be a short mater of time before the Nazi war machine would invade and occupies France and that the World would be heading towards World War II.

The Outcome

Two years previously, Moon's estranged husband had fled China and migrated to Canada to work for the railway. Moon's only daughter Mini was now in Canada living with her father.

Concerned with Moon Zhang's safety, Charles decided to send her to Canada to be with her daughter and out of harms way. Moon agreed to leave France and join her daughter in Canada. Before leaving, she told Charles that her heart would always be with him in France, but that her place, during these troubled times, was with her daughter. "I will pray for you every day" she told him as he helped her board the boat for her voyage across the Ocean. He would never see her again…

The following 6 years were pure hell for all of Europe. The Germans had the biggest war machine that the World had ever seen. Their army launched attacks on all of Europe and Countries fell one after the other to the Nazi invaders.

June 3rd 1940, The Germans bombed Paris then on July 10th 1940 the Battle of Britain began. There was no longer any doubt in anyone's mind, Hitler, was aiming for World domination and he was approaching his goals at an alarming rate.

In England, Elizabeth, fluent in the German language, worked as a translator for British intelligence. She was stunned at discovering that both the English and Germans were using the technique of shrinking down a full page into a dot, and inserting it in secret messages. It would appear, *she thought*, that the Germans would have also known about the cave in Cairo.

With the money he had made by selling the gems found in Egypt, Earl built a manufacturing plant that produced bombs for the allied forces.

In France, Charles played up to the Gestapo. With his flamboyant allure and lavish receptions at his Rouen mansion, he was able to get in close with a German General and high ranking officers of the Gestapo, enabling him to get priceless information for the French resistance and the allied forces.

Charles also acted as liaison between a secret financier, *'code named Manny'*, and the French resistance in Normandy. This secret financier would funnel a lot of money to the French resistance, in order to help finance disruptive operations against the occupying Nazi forces. No one in the resistance knew who this financier was with the exception of Charles, who had befriended him at his Rouen mansion in 1931. This friend and secret financier was a lodge brother from a Rose-Croix chapter in America.

At times during these conflicts, Charles believed that it was the beginning of Armageddon as predicted on the Scrolls found in Egypt. Stability would only return in Europe after the surrender of Germany on May 8th 1945.

Several months later, following the end of the war, the old friends would find each other again. Earl, Elizabeth and Peter came to France and joined Charles at his mansion. They stayed there for months reminiscing about the good times spent together in the past and trying to forget the horrors they had all witnessed during the past seven years.

One day Charles got a letter from Moon in Canada. In it she wrote that she would never forget him nor the wonderful moments shared together. He never heard from her again…

TWELVE

The Understanding

Twenty years later…

July 14, 1966 - Montreal, Canada

It was a muggy rainy morning when Paul Drake opened his mail box to find a card from the local post office. It advised that a package had arrived and he would have to pick it up at the post office. The package was a large cardboard box to big for regular delivery by the postman. He often ordered magic apparatus from suppliers in the United States and believed that one of his orders had arrived. However this was from Oxford, England. "Well, well," *he thought to himself,* this had to be from Peter Walker. Could it be copies of the story Peter had related to him in Senneterre a few years ago.

When at home he opened the box and he couldn't believe how many papers it contained. Good Lord, *he thought*, there must be hundreds of pages in here.

He wondered why Peter would have gone to all the trouble of copying hundreds of pages to send them to a stranger who lived so far away? The answer was in a short letter from Peter. In it Peter explained that when he had showed his mother Elizabeth, the promotional photo of Drake, she had immediately started to cry.

She claimed the photo had an uncanny resemblance to a young Charles Bouthillier, who had been her husband's dear friend.

Earl, having heard Elizabeth sobs, came into the den wondering what was wrong. When Peter showed his father the photo, he became furious accusing Peter of playing a cruel joke on them. After some explaining, both the mother and father accepted that it was indeed a photo of a performer Paul Drake, a magician with a mind reading act that their son had met at an Air Force base in Canada in 1964.

Charles Boutillier had passed away at his Rouen mansion during a celebration party on France's National holiday. Both Elizabeth and Earl saw seeing this photograph as a message from the beyond. They insisted that everything relating to the Scrolls' discovery should be copied and sent to Paul Drake in Montreal.

Peter explained in his letter, that he had access to a Gestetner copying machine at the air force base. However usage for personal purposes was limited to just a few copies a day. So it had taken close to two years to copy all of the documents in question. Hence, this explained why there had been such a long delay before sending the package to him.

Drake sat at the kitchen table staring at all the papers in the box. He thought to himself that it would take ages to read it all. He made himself a ham sandwich, some French fries and while he ate, he settled down to read. It was late afternoon when he had begun. The stories he was reading were so incredible and intriguing that he lost all notion of time. He simply couldn't stop reading those bizarre tales. It was only when he ran out of cigarettes that he realized it was close to midnight.

He had read for a solid seven hours without stopping. Finally, he placed everything back in the box, and reflected on what had been revealed to him. Rubbish, *he thought to himself*, did Walker think I would believe such a story? He glanced around his small two room apartment. After opening the hide-a-bed sofa he lie-down and promptly fell asleep to the sound of his black and white television.

The following morning, he looked at the box of papers from Walker, and he picked it up from the kitchen table and placed it on the top shelf in the cloth-room. There it would sit virtually undisturbed for a good year. Every now and then he would fleetingly think about some of the stories that lay in that box. However at that time he never placed much store to most of the stories contained in the box or what they represented.

There was however one part of the revelation that intrigued him. It was the method described in Earl Walker's journal for playing roulette. Drake was a bit of a gambler and enjoyed to play blackjack and poker. There were no legal casinos in Canada and no legal 'blind pigs' where you could find roulette tables.

Three days a week Drake would meet his buddy Jacques in front of the Chez-Paris strip club situated on Stanley, a side street in downtown Montreal. Four floors above the strip club, there was Judo academy operated by Master Marc Lalonde. In the evening, there were Karate classes given by Tran Quan Ba, a certified black belt instructor from Vietnam. Jacques and Drake were devoted students in this martial art.

Jacques' father owned a club, called the Bistro, which was situated next to the Forum, a large sports arena, situated on St Catherine, Street, the bustling main thoroughfare, in Montreal.

Jacques worked there as a waiter and Drake could be found there every Friday and Saturday evening. Once the club was officially closed to the public at three a.m. a friendly poker game got underway, and the club then became an illegal 'blind pig'. Some of the players were officers from the R.C.M.P detachment situated a short distance away. Once the club was closed to the public and the card game got underway, the club became an illegal blind pig. These unlawful activities, *of course*, were unknown to Jacque's father, the owner of the Bistro.

Those were great times. The sexual revolution in America had begun. Meeting girls after hours in a 'blind pig' was the thing to do in those days. Both Jacques and Drake made out with many of the fine ladies that gathered after hours at the popular Bistro.

During that year, Jacques and Drake discussed Boutillier's roulette system. Las Vegas was only a five day drive away, where gambling was legal. If they could make a fortune with this roulette method of play, it could well be worth the trip.

They bought a miniature roulette game from Eaton's Department Store to test the system. This resulted in an adventure in its own way. For six months they practiced with this miniature roulette using Bouthillier's system. Much to their surprise, they discovered that it worked rather well. They were up 25,000 dollars on paper. That was all they needed to know. They were convinced they would be able to make a fortune in Las Vegas and a plan was set in motion.

Drake bought an Oldsmobile on finance. Once the finance loan was approved, he quit his job. Jacques borrowed 1,000 American dollars from his father and quit working at the Bistro. Nothing could stop the two adventurers now. They were on their way to glory, fame and fortune.

At that time, they also belonged to a private club in Montreal called the New Breed. When the staff at the club heard of the plans for Las Vegas, two of the pretty hostesses from the club wanted to accompany Drake and Jacques to Las Vegas.

Drake was a hot blooded ladies man. He wanted to bring the girls along. Jacques said that there were many action seeking girls in Vegas. Bringing two Montreal girls with them to Vegas was like bringing sandwiches to an all you can eat buffet. Jacques purchased a money belt at Eaton's. With the ten one hundred American dollar bills stuffed safely in the belt, their 3,000 mile journey to Las Vegas begun.

All they talked about, excitingly, during the long drive was the dream they both had of fame and fortune. They took turns driving and one would sleep while the other drove.

Along the way they only stopped for two reasons, bathroom breaks and food from A&W papa-burgers. After three days of driving, when they saw a sign that read Las Vegas 100 miles ahead. They yelled and cheered. They would soon be at their planned destination.

After another three hours of driving later, they saw another sign Las Vegas 100 miles ahead. "What the hell is this," *shouted Drake*. "The last sign must have read 200 miles ahead and we misread it," *was Jacques reply*. "Yes of course that's what happened," *said Drake*, agreeing with his buddy. They drove another three hours and there was another sign again, Las Vegas 100 miles ahead…?

That was too much for them. They stopped the car, got out and walked over the median to have a closer look. Under the (100 miles ahead) written on the billboard; *in small print,* it said *'to the next sign'*.

Both laughed out loud until their ribs ached. They had just experienced the Las Vegas Magic.

It would be seven signs later and one and a half more days of driving before they finally arrived in Las Vegas.

The thrill of standing on Vegas' Freemont, Boulevard was worth the long drive on its own. Jacques took out his camera and had a passerby take pictures of both of them standing together in front of the Freemont Casino hotel.

On a side street next to the Freemont Casino they found a small hotel where the rate for a large room was 25 dollars a week. After they checked in, they took a short walk along Freemont, Boulevard.

The Golden Nugget Casino sat on the next corner. Next to the Golden Nugget was the Lucky Casino and next to that the Pioneer. There were Casinos all over the place. This was certainly a gambler's paradise.

When they walked into the Golden Nugget they were flabbergasted at the sight of all the gamblers. Games were being played that neither of them knew had existed. It had been a long journey getting to Vegas and both elected to get some decent rest before playing. They would start playing roulette the next day.

In their room they saw a sign on the wall. It was the gambler's prayer. *"Now I lay me down to slumber I pray the Lord I hit my numbers. If I should die before I wake bet five chips on number eight"…* What an incredible city this was! The feeling of being there at that precise moment in time, to them was so exciting and beyond description. For the first time in a week, they slept soundly in their comfortable beds. That first Vegas sleep lasted a good 12 hours.

The next afternoon they walked into a 24 hour diner for their first Las Vegas breakfast. Before ordering, Drake noticed that there were two burgers listed on the menu. A loser burger priced at 50 cents and a winner burger at 5 dollars.

"What's the difference between the loser burger and the winner burger," *Drake asked the waitress.* "None" *replied the waitress*, "if you're a loser you pay 50 cents for your burger, if you're a winner it's 5 dollars."

Everything about this town was a surprise. Nothing closed. Everything stayed open 24 hours a day, 7 days a week. There were so many lights on the gambling strips, that in the evening you couldn't tell if it was night or day. There are no calendars or clocks anywhere. After a few days in Vegas you lost all notions of time and aren't even aware of what day it was.

This was Las Vegas. The city, that never sleeps. Well this was it. The big moment had arrived. It was time for them to start playing. Time to win all that money they had been dreaming of for months.

They decided to play for the first time at the tables in the Freemont Casino hotel. Jacques would hold the money and Drake would do the gambling. Drake sat down at the roulette table, bought 100 dollars worth of chips and was to place his first bet. *When, an unexpected disaster struck.*

Drake suddenly picked up his 100 dollars of chips and stormed to the cashier's cage with Jacques following behind wondering what the hell was wrong. "Why didn't you make any bets?" *inquired Jacques.* "Didn't you notice the wheel," *answered Drake.* "Yeah so what's wrong?" *asked Jacques.*

"That roulette wheel has an extra double zero on it.

The fucking numbers are not laid out the same way as the wheel we had practiced on," *replied Drake angrily.* "Oh shit," *cried out Jacques.* "No! Not shit" *exclaimed Drake*, "we're in deep, deep shit."

After some inquiring about the different number configuration on the wheel, they learned, to their dismay, that in Vegas, they used American roulette wheels. Not one of the European wheels, with only one zero, could be found in any Las Vegas casino.

Back to the hotel room they went to try and work out a system that would work with the American wheels.

On the Freemont strip you could place bets for as little as 25 cents. So for their first week of gambling in Las Vegas, they experimented with several methods they had conjured up. Eventually they found a system were they were able to make an easy 25 dollars a day.

This consisted of playing the green. That was the single zero and the double zero which could be bet using only one single 25 cent chip. These two numbers were placed evenly apart, facing each other on the wheel and paid 18 to 1.

This system allowed for a long progression of bets where one win would generate a gain of several units. With a bankroll of 1000 dollars, *they concluded*, this simple method of play was failure proof.

The system worked rather well for the next two weeks but the gains made with such a small starting bet left a lot to be desired. They would never get rich playing the system starting with a one 25 cent bet. One day the stake bet rose to five dollars before the zero won. It paid out 90 dollars for 5 dollars and produced a profit of 15 dollars.

During those two weeks they played the tables for 4 hours a day. Extra time left, *after playing*, was spent sightseeing and visiting the high roller strip on the other side of town. There you could find Casinos such as the Thunderbird where the elite of Las Vegas played. The minimum table stakes required at these casinos was 5 dollars making it out of reach for them. They however were thrilled when they managed to get their pictures taken with Frank Sinatra and Dean Martin at the Thunderbird casino. That, in itself, was worth the trip to Drake seeing that Dean Martin was his favorite celebrity.

Jacques suggested they should increase the starting bet to 50 cents instead of 25 cents. Maybe even a dollar which would double or quadruple their winnings.

Drake didn't agree. Using as an argument, the time the stake had risen to a 5 dollar bet. Had we started that session with a 1 dollar bet, *Drake explained*, the final bet would have been 20 dollars instead of 5. This could prove disastrous should a long progression take form before either the zero or double zero won.

But Jacques insisted they should start playing with a bet of at least 50 cents. As Jacques had been designated the money manager and Drake, *the player*, he had no option but to agree.

So the day came when they felt brave and decided to play a session with the 50 cents starting bet. Every gambling session that they had played so far had been at either the Golden Nugget or the Freemont casino. The Freemont casino was Drake's favorite.

Today would be a special day, so they decided to try their luck at the Lucky Casino. There was only one roulette table at that casino. One man was playing alone against the croupier.

When Drake bought some chips and started playing, the other player left the table. Drake was now the sole player at the table and the spins were going by rapidly. Then it happened. That feared and long progression without a win materialized.

After a considerable time playing without a win, they were down 800 dollars and a sense of panic had over taken Jacques.

"Give me the rest of the money," *ordered Drake.* "No. We have to quit now before we go broke," *was Jacques' pathetic reply.*

"We can't quit now," *pleaded Drake.* "I'm sorry but it is no," *replied Jacques*, shaking his head.

"I guess maybe you're right," *mumbled Drake*, as he stood up from the table.

"Thank you sir," *said the table croupier*, voicing an air of sadness at seeing the two young men lose all their money.

In Vegas the wheel never stops turning. Even when no one is playing, the croupier will still spin the wheel. The other player who had left when Drake sat at the table suddenly returned and started playing. He was a bloody 'shill' paid by the casino to keep the action alive at the table. Drake and Jacques watched on, counting how many rolls were going by.

They wanted to see if the zeros showed up. It did exactly 8 spins later. Had Drake continued playing they would have won all their money back plus a cool profit of 25 dollars.

Drake walked, dejectedly, out of the casino and went back to their hotel room. Jacques followed close behind. He looked like a scared dog, following his master. He knew Drake would be furious at his decision for stopping the play. Drake was right, *thought Jacques*, but it was too late now. He should have held strong, continuing the play until the end.

To Jacques surprise, Drake wasn't angry but quite calm considering the disaster that had just taken place at the Lucky casino. Jacques handed Drake the remaining 200 dollars and told him to do his best at trying to win back their losses.

No mater what they tried, nothing worked anymore. By the end of the following week they were broke and 3,000 miles from home. They had a measly 30 dollars left and would be without a room in two days. They tried to get jobs at the casino as 'shills', but were informed that they needed a Gaming Commission Permit to work at any casino in Las Vegas. There was no way they could find work in Vegas. They were in big trouble and they both knew it.

In Las Vegas they found out that you could sell a pint of blood for 10 dollars. Doing that gave them a total of 50 dollars. Added to that, Jacques pawned his camera for an additional 20 dollars. With their kitty now at 70 dollars, they had enough money to get to the Canadian embassy in San Francisco. Once at the embassy, they were able to borrow a total of 100 dollars for the two of them.

Luckily, this was enough to get them to Vancouver, Canada, where they could apply for Unemployment Insurance.

It was two days later when they crossed the Grandville, bridge in Vancouver. They had just made it with only 25 dollars left to survive.

Right across the bridge there was a hotel for bums, drug addicts and alcoholics. However, the rooms were only 5 dollars a week. Each floor had one bath that was shared by all.

The hotel desk clerk was a ruff and tumble looking guy. The kind of guy you don't mess with. He looked the boys over and gave them a key to a room on the fifth floor.

While Drake filled in the papers for the room, Jacques went to the car to collect their luggage and brought it inside.

After paying the 5 dollars for the week's rent, they placed the clothes and luggage in the old elevator which clanked its way up to the fifth floor. This elevator was a real relic. It had one of those half-circular arms you used to control if it went up or down or to stop. There were no floor numbers on any panel. When the elevator went by a floor you could see the floor's number through a window set in the door for that purpose. Jacques drove the elevator and stopped it a good foot above the floor level. They got out and headed towards their room.

"Mother of Jesus," *said Jacques*, when he saw the seedy room. It was terrible. It had one old double bed, a flimsy commode and two battered wooden chairs. There wasn't a cupboard to hang the clothes, just a few hooks on the wall for that purpose. They hung the suits on the hooks and both sat on the edge of the bed staring at each other. "Hell can't be worse than this," *said Drake*, holding his head between his hands. "I want my mother," *said Jacques*, pretending he was about to cry. They both laughed out loud. All of a sudden the situation was funny.

"Let's laugh today," *said Drake*, there will be plenty of time for crying tomorrow. "Well it can't get much worse," *said Drake*. "We have had all the bad luck one needs in a lifetime."

"There is something else you won't be happy with," *said Jacques*. "Oh, I don't like the sound of your voice," *said Drake*, lifting his eyebrows as he spoke. "I forgot to take the film out of the bloody camera, before pawning it," *said Jacques*, closing both eyes as he spoke. Drake was ready to jump on him and tear his head off when; there was a knock on the door.

"Who the hell can that be," *whispered Drake*, as he looked at Jacques. Drake walked over and opened the door. It was the hotel clerk. "Boys, I'd like to talk with you," *said the clerk*, "come down to the office and join me for a beer." "Fine, we'll be down in five minutes," *answered Drake.*

"What the hell does he want?" *inquired Jacques.* "Let's go downstairs and find out," *said Drake.* This time Drake drove the elevator. "I'll show you how to drive this thing properly," *he said.* However he went right past the ground floor and ended up in the basement. They eventually made it back to the first floor and the hotel's Reception Office.

"Come on in boys." *shouted the clerk*. "Help yourselves to a beer from the fridge." "Thanks a bundle," *said Drake*, scrutinizing the office as he spoke. On a desk there was a photo of the clerk with a woman and child. "A beautiful woman, your wife?" *complemented Drake.* "Yes; she sure is a looker," *relied the clerk.* There were two worn sofas facing each other in the office. As the clerk sat on one sofa, he invited the boys to sit on the other.

"Something doesn't fit here boys" *said the clerk*. "Are you guys on the lam?" "Hell no" *answered Drake*, "We're just down on our luck these days." "We lost all our money in Las Vegas," *interjected Jacques*, "were just broke and 3,000 miles away from home."

Drake told the clerk the entire story. He explained that he and Jacques were buddies from a Karate school in Montreal and how they developed a system for winning at roulette.

"Figured you didn't belong here," *said the clerk*. "Go back to your room, and bring all your stuff down here," *he ordered.* "Are you throwing us out," *inquired Drake.* "Of course not" *replied the clerk*, "I'm just giving you boys a better room, that's all".

When they brought their luggage and clothes down to the office desk, the clerk showed them to their new room.

It wasn't a room. It was a small suite, with a bedroom, living room and a kitchenette. It even had an old television set, but didn't have any bathroom only a sink for washing.

"Boys, I own this hotel," *said the clerk*. "And this suite is for my hotel manager and I don't have one these days."

"The suite is lovely sir," *said Drake*. "But we can't afford anything more than 5 dollars a week for a room."

"You boys don't get it do you?" *said the owner*. "You both need a job and I need some help around this place."

So the boys were hired as night managers for the hotel. Their duties consisted of driving the elevator and seeing as to it that there were no disturbances on the premises after 10 O'clock in the evening.

It seemed that in Vancouver, every second person was a bootlegger. Their new boss was no exception. The boss had a secret room hidden in the hotel's basement filled with moonshine. One of their duties as night caretakers was to supply booze to anyone who wanted some. The price was 3 dollars a bottle and the boys could keep 50 cents commission for each sale. They had become the official bouncers and bootleggers for the Granville hotel.

Later on, the hotel boss told them a story of how he almost froze to death in a boxcar many years ago. It had happened during a harsh Manitoba winter. When the railway police found the half dozen homeless people freezing in a boxcar, they brought them to a hospital. The boss explained that as he was thawing out in the hospital, the pain was unbearable.

He promised himself that if he survived that ordeal, he would fund 1,000 beds where the homeless could sleep and keep warm during the winter. He now owned 5 cheap hotels and 1,000 rooms with beds for the homeless, those down on their luck and the destitute. He had kept his promise and became a successful entrepreneur.

Drake and Jacques had great respect for their employer and respectfully referred to him as the "The Boss". Weeks went by, which turned into Months. The boss liked the boys and treated them as if they were his own sons.

One day he invited them to his house to watch a close circuit fight on television. There, they met the boss' wife and young daughter. Following a superb dinner they watched, on the television, a young aspiring boxer by the name of Cassius Clay *(Muhammad Ali)* beat the hell of a Swedish boxer. Ali went on to become heavyweight champion of the world.

Later that evening when Drake was on his watch at the hotel, he reflected on his life, and how fate sometimes intervenes in one's daily life without one realizing it. When his luck had run out in Vegas, he cursed the day he had met Peter Walker. Now he realized that receiving those documents from Walker, had lead to the great adventure he was experiencing in Vancouver.

Had it not been from these turn of events in his life, caused by his encounter with Walker, he may have never seen and understood the hardships suffered by so many unfortunate people. Often they found themselves in circumstances, which were no fault their own.

One day during his watch, he found a young woman lying naked and unconscious on the hotel's fourth floor. She had obviously over-dosed.

So he carried her to her room and called for an ambulance. He was saddened when the next day he found out that she had died in the hospital early that morning.

Another time, as he sat in his hotel living room, he heard a loud thump from outside. A fight had broken out between some drunks on the third floor and one of the men had thrown an Indian girl out of a window. She was lying on a ledge, facing his window, and by the way she was positioned it seemed obvious that she had a broken back. Drake had never seen so much misery and hardship inflicted on his fellow man. He would never look at life in the same way again.

Lady luck comes and goes without warning and you must seize the occasion when she appears, and assuredly she will many times throughout one's lifetime.

Another two months went by and they had accumulated enough money to get them back home to Montreal. Then one evening, they decided, on the spur of the moment, to leave during the night as unexpectedly as the day they had arrived at the hotel.

Drake wrote a letter to the Boss thanking him for his kindness and advising of their decision to return home. In the envelope, Drake placed the key to the liquor cache in the basement, and all the money that was due to the Boss from the sale of booze.

One week later they were thankful to be back home in Montreal. The Las Vegas adventure was over.

Upon his arrival, Drake's mother advised him, that his grand father had passed away while he was away. Drake had been close to both his grand father and grand mother. This greatly affected him.

From that moment on, his outlook on life, and priorities changed forever. He no longer was that carefree young man that had left for Las Vegas, six short months ago.

Months passed, followed by years. Drake and Jacques lost track of each other as both went on their separate ways.

Then one day, Drake met the woman that would become the mother of his two children. He quit the entertainment world and became a hard working family man. He became involved in industrial diamonds as a technical sales engineer. Five years later he built his own house and started his own company importing and distributing industrial diamonds. After two years in business his company employed ten people. Business was booming and the middle class was getting richer with each passing day. Then there came, inflation. Interest rates rose and many investors pulled their money from the market and deposited it in the banks contributing to the cause of a collapse of the booming economy.

This was the early seventies. Credit had been easy to obtain and pushed onto many poor unsuspecting victims. An unprecedented number of people had bought homes and we're deeply indebted.

The International Money Fund (IMF) decided to pull the plug. They let the interest rates rise to 20%. Home owners' mortgage payments doubled, causing many people to lose their homes. The bankruptcy rate skyrocketed. Banks were picking up houses by default and selling them to the rich that had a lot of cash available. Drake's company had been selling industrial tools to clients on a 30 days credit basis. These clients started going under and Drake saw his money going down the drain. He could do nothing about it. He had also become a victim of the IMF *(The International Money Fund).*

He was forced to close his company and went work for a large German company specializing in premium industrial cutting tools. He was one of the lucky ones who survived the bloodbath caused by the inflated interest rates. He managed to keep his home and being named Regional Sales Manager for the German company, he was able to provide a comfortable life style for his family. This position with the German company allowed him to travel across Europe. Lady luck had smiled on him again and what could have been a disaster, turned out to be a blessing in disguise.

Drake had always been a sort of a pack rat. He never threw anything away. He still had a wooden totem pole his uncle Raymond had made for him forty years earlier.

He still had the papers sent to him from England. Every now and then, he would re-read through the papers that Peter Walker had sent him. Each time and the more he would read what that Roman soldier had written, the more Drake began understanding what those old writings meant.

Then, on October 9th 1993, a special event happened that would change Drake's life forever. The Quebec Government opened its first, *European styled*, gambling casino in Montreal.

There had been talk of this Casino opening in Montreal since 1989. Drake's wife had told him, that if they opened a casino in Montreal, she feared that it would cause the breakdown of their marriage. She knew of her husband's weakness for gambling and of his adventure in Vegas twenty five years before.

The Casino opened to record crowds, on a cold and crisp Saturday morning. You couldn't drive close to the place by car. You had to park several kilometers away and take shuttle buses to get into this new casino.

Drake sat in one of the buses as it drove over the small bridge leading to the casino. Looking out of a right side window, he could see the casino getting closer and closer. From that short distance, *thought Drake*, the five storey casino resembled a demon towering over the Earth.

Once inside he stared in awe at the sight of the quantity of slots and tables situated on every floor. This casino was understandably ranked as one of the 10 biggest casinos in the World. Men had to wear jackets and women wore dresses. No jeans were allowed in this casino. It was unquestionably a classy place to go to, and it catered to the middle and upper class of Montreal. As this was in French Quebec, the casino was naturally of European style, the same as the French casinos of Monte Carlo.

There were so many people in the casino during the opening day that one had trouble walking around the place. The first floor had only slot machines. There must have been a few thousand of those for sure. The second and third floor had many gambling tables. At least a hundred and fifty blackjack tables and a few dozen roulette tables. Drake walked around taking this all in. He had waited a long time to have a casino situated close by. This was like a dream come true for him.

He walked over to look at the roulette tables and got the surprise of his life. He realized that the tables were of the European style and only had one zero. The same as mentioned in Walker's papers.

The system to beat the roulette table as described by Charles Bouthillier, in his letter to Earl Walker, could be utilized on this type of roulette tables.

Unlike the American roulette table, with the zero and double zero, the European wheel having only one zero cuts the casino's percentage in half giving the player a better advantage. This odds difference is huge, and favors the player big time.

Drake was euphoric at the thought of making money with a system for beating the roulette tables in casinos. He was excited when he left the casino and returned home. Once there, he went into his office and enthusiastically re-read the method for playing that was described by Bouthillier in the letters that he still had from Walker in England.

He remembered the disaster he had lived through in Las Vegas many years ago, and could not afford to make such a mistake again. He decided that he would visit the Montreal casino during the next few weeks but that there would be no gambling, only record taking.

Each table had an electronic display that showed the numbers that won during the last 15 spins. He would note the numbers that won on 100 consecutive wheel spins on six tables at a time. By recording the spins on six tables located close to each other, Drake could acquire the information data he required to check the safety of Bouthillier's system when played with real money.

The casino was overcrowded on week ends so the recording of numbers would be done Monday through Friday from 6 p.m. in the evening until the 100 spins results were finished. By the end of two weeks of recording spins, he had accumulated the results for 60 sessions of 100 wheel spins for a total of 6,000 spins on the European wheels in the Montreal casino.

Now came the hard part. He would have to play all these games on paper to evaluate the results had he bet real money.

Playing the games on paper had to be done in his spare time as Drake had to earn a living in the meantime. It took months before he had completed the task he had set out to do. When the results were tabulated, he discovered that the system did indeed work and that he had possibly stumbled upon the goose that laid the golden egg.

Had he played the 60 games recorded on paper, he would have won 48 of them. Bouthillier's roulette system was winner 8 out of ten times at bat. For 6,000 spins of the wheel, he would have pocketed a cool 15,000 units. This meant he could win an average of 85 units for every hour played at a table.

A casino works on a method called the grind. This means, that with an odd advantage of as little as 1%, when a gambler bets the same dollar 100 times and loses 1% with each bet, then; in less than 100 bets he goes broke and the casino has all of the gambler's money.

Bouthillier's system used a reversed process whereby the player grinds a small amount from the casino with each spin. This system was not a lazy gambler's game. It was hard work that needed ample concentration and a decent mathematical mind. There were no quick winnings here. There were also no large gains in a short period of time at the table. One session of play at a table lasted a good 3 hours. The player had to work hard and long hours to make a living gambling, but the tax-free money won, made it worthwhile.

Drake had established that his pay for playing roulette would be 85 units per hour. Now, the casino had $1, $5, $10 and $25 dollar tables. So with the necessary capital required to play he could earn $85, $425, or $850 dollars per hour.

The 25 dollar table would require too much capital stake to play, so that table would be disregarded. He had discovered that the best time to play was Monday through Thursday between the hours of 4 p.m. and 10 p.m. Weekends were out of the question as there were too many players, thus making table selection difficult.

Remembering the lesson he had learned in Las Vegas, *when he went broke,* he decided to try the 1 dollar tables for a month or two. This would confirm the winning projection results, when he had played the 60 games on paper.

Drake played the 1 dollar roulette at the Montreal casino for a period of four months, and these are the results of the games played. During the 4 months of playing at a 1 dollar table, he had played exactly 135 games. This represented slightly over 400 hours of hard work at the roulette tables.

His clear, tax-free earnings, for the 400 hours amounted to $36,800 dollars… An astounding - 92 dollars per hour. Not bad at all for working 3 hours a day. 4 days a week with no boss to report to. Drake now had enough playing capital to work the 5 dollar tables which would earn him a cool 460 dollars per hour. More than enough for any man's wants.

The most beautiful part of all this, was that he could do it anytime he wanted. It was like going to a money fountain, and turning on the tap. The dollars were always there waiting to be taken. The grind from the tables was so gradual and small that the casino never knew what was going on.

By the end of a full year of playing the 5 dollar tables, Drake had earned the respect of other players and was referred to, *by other players*, as the roulette Master.

Life can't get better than this. *He thought to himself.*

The Understanding

In due course Drake stopped working and considered himself retired. He owed all of this good life to Charles Bouthillier, a Frenchman from the past that he had never met.

This fast living and high rolling had its costs. *Just as his wife had predicted*, the casino and the gambling, ruined his marriage. In a strange way he started feeling that Charles Bouthillier had possessed his Soul. Or was it the Devil…

All at once he had become a playboy, *just like Bouthillier*. He drove fancy cars and held lavish parties at his pent-house. Women were drawn to him as if by a magnetic force. He had friends everywhere and all were so happy to see him and be seen with him. Oh but, he learned quickly, that money only brings you false friends. Upon realizing this, he became a recluse, keeping alone and distancing himself from everyone.

He was financially very successful but at what cost. With time he realized that family was the most important thing in the world, but it was too late. The damage was done, and there would be no repairing it. He had made his bed and would have to lay in it.

With time, one thing became clear and clearer to him. There was more to life than money and the meager existence he had created for himself. With plenty of time on his hands, he decided to seriously look at the copies of the papers that were written a long time ago by a Roman soldier. Fate had brought him to where he was, and surely there was a reason for what had happened to his life.

As he started studying the translated Latin writings, and by checking up information and facts on the internet, he also became convinced that the Soul Master did indeed exist. The entire story had to be true and it had to be told to anyone who would listen…

THIRTEEN

The Conclusion

There were so many questions without answers. '*Drake pondered on this*' as he stood on his penthouse patio overlooking Montreal's Mount Royal.

Months had gone by and during this time he had scrutinized the copies he had received from Peter Walker. Having eventually checked all the details he had found them to be accurate.

a) The records of times and dates of events had coincided.

b) Names of people mentioned were real.

c) Places referred to in the story matched.

d) The majority of the Passages and Prophecies on the scrolls corroborated.

All of this led Drake to truly believe that the story was in fact a detailed account of events that had taken place in 1931.

Incredulity had set in as facts emerged that left Drake realizing that there were many similarities between Charles Bouthillier and himself. It had become clear that many of Bouthillier's beliefs and the arts that he had practiced coincide with many of his own.

One of the strangest coincidences linking the two men together was that Drake was born on the same day as France's national holiday, which in turn coincided with the day Charles Bouthillier was deemed to have died.

Drake had never believed in reincarnation but this idea of his now came into question. At times, during the past few months, he had had dreams that were so lifelike and detailed that he would wake up wondering if it really was a dream, or had he somehow found himself in another time or dimension?

During those dreams he found himself walking on the streets of what appeared to be Paris. Upon investigation of the names of the streets and sights he remembered seeing in those dreams, it was confirmed that it was truly Paris he had been walking around. And yet he had never visited Paris so he had never walked on its streets!

It is a known fact that when the Dalai Lama dies, High Priests immediately seek out a new born baby that they believe to be the reincarnation of the deceased Daily Lama.

Was he, Drake, the reincarnation of Charles Bouthillier?

Montreal with its French language and its European atmosphere made it unique on the North American continent, and was a beautiful city to live in. The view from this 18th floor was uninterrupted and simply breathtaking.

Weather permitting He would have his morning coffee on the patio as he read his morning paper.

That particular day an article buried on page 5 caught Drake's attention. It reported a bizarre incident that had taken place the previous day.

"A man sitting peacefully at his kitchen table was enjoying a cup of coffee as he read his morning paper.

He had been working too much overtime and had been feeling exhausted so he had decided to take the day off."

"Two kilometers away, at a rock quarry, an alarm went off announcing that blasting would occur in three minutes, warning all to take cover. Drill holes had been strategically placed in a huge slab of stone and been filled with explosives ready to be ignited. The quarry superintendent gave the signal and the blast was set off."

"One small rock, the size of a baseball, flew trough the air, crashed trough the window two kilometers away, hitting the man, peacefully drinking his coffee , in the head killing him instantly."

The irony of this story is that the man killed by that rock, worked at the very quarry where the stone that killed him came from. Had he not taken the day off, would he still be alive? Of course, no one will ever know the answer for sure.

Now, what are we to think of such an event? Was this fate or just being at the wrong place at the wrong time?

Drake recalled another weird story of fate and destiny. In that particular story, a pregnant woman and her husband were on their way to her sister's wedding in a neighboring state. On the way to the airport she suddenly had severe stomach cramps that were increasing at an alarming rate causing concern. The husband instructed the taxi driver to change course and head for the hospital. They made it just in time as she gave birth to a baby boy, born six weeks premature.

The small plane that they had been booked on to go to the sister's weeding crashed on that flight, killing all 14 people aboard. The lucky couple's lives had been spared by the baby's premature arrival.

The newborn baby had to remain at the hospital in an incubator for at least two weeks. Three days later, the mother was given her release from the hospital. On their way home from the hospital, their taxi was hit by a truck, killing both of them along with the driver. The couple didn't escape their destiny but the newborn child lived to fulfill his.

Stories like these are too numerous to tell, but we all at one time or another experience strange events in our lives that at times defy all logic. Most of the time, we don't even realize that they happened, but they do, more often than we can imagine.

For some strange and unknown reason, our 'Souls' at times seem to intervene to change the course of events in our lives. Possibly such interventions may occur not to change the course of events, but instead; to assure that the destined events do take place.

Going back to what the Roman soldier wrote; the Soul Master makes it clear that certain events continue to occur over and over again in Mankind's history. It's as if we are repeatedly given chances to do what is right and expected of us in this World.

However, Mankind, repeatedly, continues destroying nearly everything it has, itself, created beforehand.

Mankind systematically pollutes the Earth and the atmosphere that we need to survive. Mankind has littered the World and its Oceans with garbage, and is now in the process of littering 'space' around the Earth

Unfortunately for all of us, what is happening in the 21st Century has happened many times before in our un-recollected history.

The Conclusion

One must remember that, if we were to build this day, a gigantic concrete building supported with the best inter-twined steel beams. In ten or fifteen thousand years, only dust would remain of this seemingly un-destructible structure.

As an example; if we look at the inexplicable and complex construction of the Great Pyramids of Egypt, the construction of these Wonders of the World still defy explanation or logic even in these modern times of advanced technology.

The Pyramids' huge blocks, were cut out of limestone and were cut perfectly square and rectangular to tolerances within one thousand of an inch. A task, that still as to this day, can't be duplicated even with our modern technology and best engineers. Could it be that these limestone blocks were not man made?

Not to mention the puzzling questions as to where exactly do the blocks come from? How were they delivered to the sites on which they stand? No one really knows the answers and all our historians and engineers can do is to continue to guess and try to phantom as to the way it was done.

No cement of any sort can be found between the huge blocks, that at times weighed many tons; and yet they have been sitting undisturbed for unknown thousands of years. One cannot even slide a sheet of paper between those blocks of stone because of how tightly they are seated upon each other. Built by Egyptians to serve as tombs? Of course not!

They were most probably built by an Ancient advanced but forgotten civilization, in order to let those that followed know that they were once here on Earth. Maybe they were even built by the legendary and lost Atlantis civilization? Who knows! We've just not figured it out as of yet.

In a nut shell, nothing fabricated by Mankind itself, can exist for any extended periods of time. Only folk tales passed on by generation to generation survive the test of time.

When we read Biblical accounts of events that ostensibly took place thousands of years ago, chances are that these events did indeed take place. However because they are recounted and retold over and over again; then, it is easily concluded by anyone, that the facts have been distorted, and can no longer be considered as being totally accurate. But there is a distinct possibility that the main theme of the events must be accepted as factual, and as having indeed occurred.

For example; we have only to look at the Biblical reference to Noah's Arc. We are presently at a point in time where that scenario might well re-produce itself.

With climate change brought on by Mankind's disrespect of the environment, we presently face a situation where the Polar Caps are melting at an alarming rate. And, it's already too late for Mankind to correct the damage and depletion it has done to the ozone layers, causing the temperature of our planet's atmosphere to warm up to a point beyond repair.

One doesn't have to be a rocket scientist to see that it's a question of time before the great rains fall upon us and that the Earth will be covered with water. Continents will disappear and all of the strong and mighty Countries will waste away to oblivion and become history. Armageddon will be upon Mankind as it has done before and this maybe countless of times during the Universe's existence.

This time, our Governments will build great ships capable of supporting life for its occupants for extremely long periods of time.

Species of each animal will be placed upon these ships along with seeds to assure the growth of the necessary food to support life on these ships for undetermined periods of time.

Humans that would be spared from the coming doomsday scenario would be selected by our good Governments. Precise qualities will of course be required in order to preserve our so important heritage for future generations.

These qualities will be measured by health, intelligence, reproduction capacities and persons deemed necessary, for the survival of the species, such as Doctors, Engineers, Scientist, scholars and so forth.

Of course, Country leaders and military personnel would have to be considered as essential for preserving the much needed law and order in the new World order that would follow. This even though there would no longer be Countries.

From these great leaders who decided the fate of the survivors, future Kings and Lords would of course be designated in future generations. Unfortunately the poor and the old would be left to tend for themselves. With luck, some would find high grounds and survive, but their survival would be short lived.

However, before these terrible events take place, the World as we know it to be, will have already ceased to exist.

When Mankind realizes what is coming, then; unbelievable chaos will strike Mankind to the likes of what has never been seen before. The fittest will survive and the weakest will perish. Man will turn on Man and there will no longer be a civilized order across the World. All of this as clearly stated in the Soul Master Scrolls' 45 passages and its first 10 Prophecies.

The second Prophecy has been fulfilling itself since the beginning of documented history until the present time.

But one must accept that it was predominant in the 20th Century and is more than ever in the present 21st Century.

Never since recorded history has the World population been so unreasonably disproportioned in respect to the peoples personal wealth. As the establishment get's richer with each passing day, so do the people get poorer.

We presently have a scenario where less than one percent of the people, own more than ninety-five percent of the total wealth of the World. As if that isn't enough, the rich are still trying to extract even more from the poor. These rich vultures are none other than the evil hosts of the Souls of the sixth house as described in passages 24, 25, 36 and 37 written on the Scrolls.

Our politicians, the IMF, financial institutions and our good Governments are all part of this evil and destructive force that will bring Armageddon upon our heads. It is just a question of time, *and a short one at that*, before the poor revolt and turn against these hypocrites who make believe they act in the best interest of the collectivity. It need not be mentioned that those who dare turn against the establishment will be slaughtered without pity for they are the poor host to Souls of the fifth house, this; as mentioned in the 2nd Prophecy.

The fourth Prophecy could have been thought to have passed with the coming of television. But it now becomes obvious that the true time of its fulfillment, was with the coming of the internet and web cams. So the warning of *"the end is coming and for all to flee"* must be interpreted as referring to the present time. The beginning of Century 21…

The fifth Prophecy *(the father's power)* can without a doubt be interpreted as the discovery of nuclear fusion.

And the sixth Prophecy, as the horrid destruction caused by the deployment of the Atomic bombs over Japan.

Part of that sixth Prophecy also refers to *"soon after man will venture and stand far away on a new found land"*. This can be none other than man landing on the moon introducing *"a new era of a different kind"*

Just reading the eight Prophecy is enough to understand that it is upon us at this very period of time in Century 21.

The ninth Prophecy, although it seemed ridiculous ten years ago, now hits home. *"The big powers of the World will fall helpless to small numbers of men."* We can now clearly understand such a Prophecy. These small numbers of men are none other then terrorist cells implanted in different regions of the World. The big powers are helpless against this unseen enemy.

Since as far as we can recall, wars have always been fought between large powerful armies, facing each other, with the strongest winning most of the times.

However, now in modern times, small numbers of men can spread unheard of terror at will, while our great leaders watch helplessly as their mighty armies cannot stop these increasingly effective terrorists from striking their selected targets, at will.

Where strength once stood with a military power, it would now seem to stand with the determination of small groups of men wearing no uniforms. One could call these terrorist, *"The invisible enemy"*.

One of these invisible enemies might well be worth a thousand men if you consider the destruction they can cause.

Only one thousand of these silent warriors equal's an army of 1,000,000 men.

The World is changing drastically and so is warfare. The next 'World war' will be one of Religion and it could prove to be the bloodiest Mankind has ever witnessed. When you can't see who your enemy is or where he is situated, you are in great danger.

If this enemy believing that he is a messenger from his God feels that every non-believer *(in his particular God and Religion)* should be put to death, then; you don't have much of a chance of surviving against him. When a fanatic decides to put you down, chances are that he will succeed. If a person is willing to pay with his life in order to take yours how do you stop him?

How can our leaders protect us from such fervent, fanatics? A simple way would have been to keep our borders closed to immigration. But as we all now know, it's too late for such preventive action as these invisible enemies have already implanted themselves in all major Countries of the World.

We are already surrounded by fanatical lunatics who are none other than human time bombs; strategically placed amongst us, waiting for the orders to rid the World of infidels.

The invisible enemy we now are forced to deal with may well be our pleasant and quiet next door neighbor. There is no way to positively identify this enemy or even to understand how his sick mind reasons.

These Religious warriors have been brain washed since childhood to hate and kill all who are different and who don't embrace the lunacy which with they have been indoctrinated.

The only way the civilized World can rid itself of these barbaric foes would be to destroy them before they can strike.

They have no principle of justice. They hide amongst their own, many of whom are not in agreement with the philosophy preached by their deranged spiritual guides. So to destroy them, would mean destroying the innocents along with the evil ones. This in turn, would turn the civilized World into the same barbaric lunatics that they so fear.

There is no way to solve this problem. Mankind has set up its own destruction. Now it's just a mater of time for the inevitable to takes place and there will be no stopping it.

So, we must ask ourselves! When will these Prophesied events take place? By understanding *the 10th Prophecy* there is very little doubt as to how and when they will happen. Things are happening right now. And their full implantation is approaching its completion.

The 10th Prophecy, which coincides with the **Bible's REVELATION 13,** clearly states ***"13:16 - And it puts under compulsion all persons, the small and the greats, and the rich and the poor, and the free and the slaves, that they should give these a mark in their right hand or upon their forehead, 17: And that nobody might be able to buy or to sell except a person having the mark, the name of the wild beast or the number of its name. 18: Here is where wisdom comes in: Let the one that has intelligence calculate the number of the wild beast, for it is a man's number; and its number is six hundred and sixty-six".***

The IMF along with the Governments and the financial institutions started the systematic marking of people with the mark of the wild beast in the middle seventies with the introduction of the now famous banking debit cards.

These debit cards, *the innocent lambs were told,* would save the bank account holders money by reducing the handling charges for the banks. You could pay your bills with the card and so forth meaning you didn't have to write checks thus realizing savings of time and money.

Many reasons were given to justify the many benefits of using the new plastic debit cards, and within the short period of time following its introduction, everyone one got hooked on using the 'plastic.'

The innocent victims *(the host to Souls of the fifth house)* soon learned the true reason of those debits cards. Banks started laying-off their workers and bank tellers. Personal services to customers were slowly replaced by automated bank machines.

Then the true insidious plot for plundering more of the hard earned cash from people slowly came to light. Charges were introduced for each usage of the debit cards.

The innocent lambs had carefully and unknowingly been led to slaughter. The marking of people with the number of the wild beast had begun.

The banks that were earning millions of dollars in profits before implementing the debit card system are now earning billions of dollars in profits resulting in billions of dollars taken out of the economy. Being the banks don't invest that money back into the economic structures of the system, this slowly drains the monetary value of the Country and its people.

Slowly and without realization the middle class is systematically getting poorer each day as the financial institutions and major businesses get richer. It would seem that some unseen powers are systematically ensuring that the majority of the World's population is reduced to poverty.

The Conclusion

With the implantation of a universal *'bar code' for all products sold, the 'mark of the wild beast' is utilized for any transaction between consumer and merchant. The proverbial saying that *"none can buy or sell without the mark of the wild Beast or its number"* brings us to the terrible conclusion that *"the end is near and for all to flee"*.

The irony of these 'bar codes' is that they are invisibly identified with the number of the wild beast which is 666.

Pick any product from your shelf and take a close look at the bar code inscribed on it. You will see two thin lines close together which represent the number six. These two lines stick out past all other lines and appear at the beginning, the center and the end of the bar code, thus; marking each and every product with the secret and hidden number of the Wild Beast.

***The bar code that is showing on the left can be found on the lower right side of the back cover of this book. Without this bar code and number, a person cannot buy or sell this book on line, or at any retail book store anywhere in the World. Every product manufactured today or sold anywhere in the World must have one of these bar codes.**

These three, *two lined*, numbers serve no purpose, except to mark the product with the hidden number of the Beast 666

We are now at a time where the Establishment, *or big brother,* can trace what someone bought, where they bought it and at what time they bought it. When you use your debit card or credit card to buy gasoline for your car or to rent a room, the same principle applies. 'They' know where you go and almost everything that you do, and the time you did it at.

Now, you can't even rent a room without a credit card. They won't even accept cash anymore. They tell you this is to prevent fraud and theft, but in reality it's the control of people.

Soon they will try to have the people insert a micro-chip in their hand to replace debit cards and credit cards. This, *the lambs will be told*, will make one's life simpler and will reduce fraudulent usage of your number.

No more need to worry about bringing our plastic with you. One simply passes his hand over the scanner and the money, or credits, will be taken from your bank account.

Eventually, laws will be legislated by Governments, whereby; all newborns will have one micro chip injected under the skin on their head, and another micro chip injected into the infant's right hand thus marking the person with a number for life. Following this, money will be replaced by credits.

These micro chips will also act as a location device by which satellites will be able to tract and locate the marked person anywhere on Earth. This of course, *the lambs will be told,* to assist the police in locating missing or kidnapped children.

But let us not be fooled. The real reason will be, the total and complete control over every living being on Earth, by the hosts of the Souls of the sixth house.

At this very moment in time, the military powers are contemplating the implantation of tracking chips in the head of soldiers in order to track their positions by satellites and to enable the rescue of soldiers captured by the enemy.

We must accept that what is Prophesied in The Soul Master Scrolls' 10th Prophecy, and the Bible's REVELATION 13:, has come to pass at this present time, and that it is nearing its completion at an alarming pace.

The conclusion

It seems that Mankind will still have one chance to save itself from the path it is presently embarked on which could cause the obvious destruction of the existing system.

This last chance depends on the 11th Prophecy in which a savior is prophesied to emerge from the slaves and free the World of its perilous position.

This new King as described in the 11th Prophecy must appear soon and he must accomplish his destiny without the 12th and 13th Prophecies fulfilling themselves or Mankind will face the terrible Armageddon as described in the last six pages written by that Roman soldier 2,000 years ago.

So horrible and terrifying are the events prophesied on those last six pages, that Charles Bouthillier didn't disclose the complete deciphered message preferring to keep the details a secret. He however left clues with which it would enable the full message to be properly translated, deciphered and understood.

After placing all of the mixed words of those last six pages into their designated slots, Drake found the following message which appears to be a hidden 14th Prophecy describing the end of the World as we know it.

The prophesied message on the last six pages written by the Roman soldier, explains the events leading to the final and complete destruction of the civilized World.

When Drake saw the final message and its horrible conclusion, his only consolation was that there was a good chance he would not be around to see the end when it came, as the hands marking time on his clock of life had full circled many thousands of times, and his days were surely counted.

The hidden Fourteenth Prophecy

14:15- When the first to the tenth forthcomings will have come to past and should Mankind have passed the point of no return then its fate will be sealed.

16; Then the time will come when those men of small numbers will seed panic and destruction throughout all of the lands. The innocent children and women will spare no difference from the men who are host to the Souls of the fifth house and they will be slain.

17; Mankind's only chance for salvation will rest within the last three forthcomings. Should the last of the three come to past, then none across all lands will alter the forthcoming destruction of life and this across all lands.

18; Following close, the time will come, when the old will be left to die without care being given to their needs, and mankind having not seen clearly to its own needs, will cause man to eat his own flesh and this against the laws of the lands from whence they came.

19; Then by the host of Souls from the lowest house, massive destruction will begin across all of the lands. Thousands upon thousands by thousands of hosts to the fourth, fifth and sixth houses, too many to be counted will perish and their flesh will be eaten by the hosts to Souls of the second and third house.

20; Then Mankind having turned against its mother will know the fury of the mother and the father's scorn. Calamity as was never seen will come down upon the ungrateful causing great walls of water to purify these undeserving, and from whence came the three great ships, three great boulders the size of this mountain, will be thrown against the three lands where first settled the hosts to Souls of the fifth and sixth houses. Then following a great darkness, the land will once more be as it was in the beginning, leaving but a chosen few to allow Mankind its new beginning.

Drake understood exactly what the hidden 14th Prophecy meant. In the new warfare to come, *(16)*, no exceptions will be accorded to women and children, and they will be slaughtered along with the men and this in all Countries. Attacks will be made on schools and sporting events etc…

The ones being slaughtered will not be the military people, *as in conventional wars,* but, it will be civilians being murdered, thus causing great fear and terror for the people, when they see that the authorities are helpless to stop the attacks on the innocent.

Then; should the Prophesied 2nd King appear *(17)***,** and should he fail to establish the sought after peace and stability in the World, then chaos and revolts will overtake people all over the World.

Governments will have no choice but to increase spending to the point where no money will be left to care for the elderly. *(18)* The old will be left to die and food supplies will diminish causing humans to consume humans in order to prevent starvation.

Following this *(19)*, germs which are hosts to Souls of the lowest house, will kill off billions of people from every corner of the Earth. Needless to say the birds and insects, who are hosts to the Souls of the second and the third house, will pick the flesh from the bones of the dead.

The last passage in the hidden Prophecy *(20)* is by far the most terrifying message left by the Roman soldier. Drake understood its meaning and he shuddered at the very thought of what was in store for his fellow man. The mother and the father's scorn referred to in the last passage of the hidden 14th Prophecy is none other than the Earth and the Sun using nature's power to purify the World.

The last passage has to mean, another great flood and another great epidemic similar to the one that struck mankind in the early twentieth Century. But that epidemic, the Spanish Flu, only killed an estimated 100 million people. The next one will be a massive epidemic that will kill billions of people.

This will solve the problem caused by the over population of Earth. With close to seven billion people now alive on Earth, the scientific World already knows that mother Earth won't be able to sustain so many more humans.

So nature will do what it must to save itself.

The last passage of the hidden Prophecy warns that three boulders the size of mountains will strike the Earth leaving it in a great darkness.

The American space agency "NASA" has already been placed on the alert and instructed to seek and find any potential Asteroids that could be heading towards a collision course with our beloved Earth. They have located several killer Asteroids that have a good chance of crashing into the Earth.

NASA presently knows of one, 900-foot diameter killer Asteroid, with a 1 in 40,000 chance of hitting the Earth in 2036 or 2037. This Asteroid even has a name. It's called Apophis. And they are also watching a smaller one that is only 430 feet in diameter which has a 1 in 3,000 chance of hitting us.

Not too long ago, a large Asteroid passed between the Earth and the Sun, and our scientists didn't see it coming until it passed before our bewildered Astronomers' eyes. These events happen more often than we know and there is nothing we can do to prevent these incidents from occurring. Life threatening objects in the sky are getting closer and closer without our being able to stop them.

Now, if a killer Asteroid with a diameter of 1,000 feet were to collide with Earth, the impact could completely destroy a small Country, a major state or province wherever it crashed. But if the killer Asteroid has a diameter of 10,000 feet or more, then; the destruction would be worldwide and catastrophic.

This clearly concurs with what was written 2000 years ago by the Roman soldier. The Armageddon described in the last passage of the hidden Prophecy would certainly take place, as described, if one of the killer Asteroids was to hit the Earth. The last hidden Prophecy mentions 3 Asteroids the size of small mountains.

Our Governments have knowledge of many things that they keep hidden from the population. Governments have already built huge underground facilities that can withstand direct hits of megaton bombs or small Asteroids. In these underground facilities, among other items, are stored seeds of every living plant life on Earth. *Why these underground facilities?*

These underground facilities are built into solid rock, thousands of feet underground and are waterproof as well as shock proof.

If and when our Government were to find out of a coming disaster that could kill billions of people, *and with them being unable to intervene, or prevent,* then; it would serve no practical purpose to warn its citizens of the coming calamity. This would cause futile panic and lawlessness amongst the frightened population.

It is no longer a question of will Armageddon happen? The question now becomes. When will it happen?

By taking into account what was written by the Roman soldier, the nightmares that Earl Walker had had, in 1931, and Bouthillier's memoirs, Drake came to a frightening conclusion.

With further evaluation, of current World events, Drake believed that, *unless the eleventh Prophecy comes to pass producing a second King to save Mankind from its own destruction,* the beginning of the end of the World, *as we know it to be,* will start taking place in the year 2025 with total Armageddon by 2040.

Drake also believed that Mankind is presently at a period in time where it is facing its last chance to attempt to do what is right and expected of it. He also questioned himself as to the purpose of Mankind?

But in essence, the entire existence of Mankind on Earth is not even equal to the blink of an eye in time, when you compared it to the age of our infinite and endless Universe.

Man thinks that he is so big and powerful. Yet compared to the Universe, he is smaller and less significant than the smallest of the billions of invisible cells that make up his body.

Drake believed that Man is but a miniaturized replica of the Cosmos itself. Just like the leaf of a maple tree bears a resemblance to the tree from which it came, so does man, regardless of his size resemble the Universe of which he is a living part of.

If one was to take a grain of salt from a salt shaker and crush it into a million pieces, the smallest piece of crushed salt from that single grain would still be bigger, in essence, to our entire solar system when compared to the Universe.

Our scientists keep improving the capacity and distance of the perception of the Hubble telescope in space in hopes of comprehending the big bang, the beginning of the Universe and possibly where it ends. Their feeble attempts are futile. For some unknown reason, man refuses to accept that the Universe has no end nor does it have a beginning...

We presently live, in that could be considered to be, the fourth dimension. A dimension measured by height, width, depth and time. But as surely as there is a fourth dimension, there could possibly be a fifth or sixth dimension occurring at the same time as ours, but unseen and unknown to us.

When we gaze at the Stars at night, we can see some that are millions of light years away. As we see them, they exist in our time and dimension. But some may have died millions of years ago and no longer exist in their own time and dimension.

This has to mean, that no events or existence in the Universe ever ceases to exist. They simply move from one dimension *'or time'* to another. Without exception, our human existence here on Earth, must follow the same universal pattern. Souls, *from every house,* must therefore have the same eternal life as every other entity in the universe of which we are an intricate and living part of.

When any living thing dies, it simply moves on *(by the way of its Soul)* to another dimension or time somewhere else in the ever living Cosmos.

The Universe is what it is, and it will always be! This vast and never ending Universe which we are part of resembles a gigantic and well oiled clock with intricate parts assuring its perfect and orderly movement. It has so many Celestial bodies and countless Galaxies circling each other in perfect unison that such a perfect clock cannot exist or function without the care of the Master Architect who built it.

Drake at times wondered if we were not simply an experiment under a microscope or maybe just a scene of a play being acted out for the benefit of an unknown observer.

Mankind to this day still has no idea as to what the big picture is or to what their karma is here on Earth.

And yet, just as they have done during the past 2,000 recordable years, the hosts to Souls of the sixth house keep plundering and robbing the poor innocent hosts to the Souls of the fourth and fifth houses.

They willfully and maliciously keep on destroying the very mother which gave them life and which supplies them with the food and water that they need to survive.

If this senseless systematic plundering and destruction of the environment and its people does not stop, and stop soon, then; may the Master Architect who created and oversees our magnificent Universe, have mercy on all of the poor hosts to the Souls of the fourth and fifth houses here on Earth.

For; as it is written in the last passage of the hidden 14th Prophecy. ***Mankind having turned against its mother will know the fury of the mother and the father's scorn.***

Gérard Desjardins, the author, is a steadfast believer in the disputed theory whereby the Soul governs each and every event that takes place in the past, present and future existence of every person on Earth.

He is also a bitter opponent of Government policies which undermine the personal wealth and freedom that each person is entitled to as a citizen of the World.

He opposes how the people of the World are treated as slaves of the state. His self improvement courses and conferences, titled; 'Citizen of the World not the State' has helped many in staving off the greedy State.

Other books by the author:

The Soul Master Saga © 1998

The Soul Master Prophecies © 2000

Citizen of the World not the State © 2002

Grey Diamond Books

www.greydiamondventures.com

www.soulmasterscrolls.com

www.ingramcontent.com/pod-product-compliance
Lightning Source LLC
LaVergne TN
LVHW020703110826
845149LV00012B/2098